Contents

CATRINA BELL

A Frenemy in Need

MERRY MISCHIEF
a Winter Bliss Romance

Book Cover Illustration by H. Holden @beholden8

Book Cover Design by Catrina Bell

Chapter Headers by Trisha Monroe @infinitetrishaart

Illustrations by Serval @subtleserval, Victor @koijix, Daniel Toro @dan-notc_art, Lianne Peterson @fantasyspritestudio, Lucy @riolint_art

Editing by Reed Editorial Services

ISBN 979-8-9911305-1-6

First edition 2024

To my two Bs,

Barb, the smelliest Snow White with the biggest heart
&
Selina, writing love to make the Muses blush and Mother proud

Chapter One
Rex

April 1st

"**F**uck yeah, cheese dip!"

From the back seat, I pop open the Tupperware slowly so no one will hear. Oh shit, better than dip, it's a full charcuterie spread, complete with a warming plate for the baked brie. Fancy! I grab a flaxseed cracker and aim for the jelly topping. It sinks straight into the good stuff. *Ooooh, blackberry*. When the creamy, salty, sweet combo hits my tongue, I groan like a porn star.

"Rex!" Noelle gasps and claws at my arm from the front seat. "That's for the party."

"But . . . cheese." I pout, snatching another couple pieces as we tussle over the container.

"Give it back," my brother, Rom, booms from the driver's seat. His eyes find mine in the rearview mirror, blazing blood red and black. Ugh. He's so protective of his new human girlfriend.

With a sigh, I pop a piece of pepperjack in my mouth and hand it over, trying and failing to get comfortable in the back seat. I choose manspreading in the middle of the SUV's back bench, but my knees still dig into the sides of their seats and my horns only have a couple inches clearance up top, making me want to slouch. Thus, my need for emotional support cheese.

"Sorry, Noelle," I grouse with the big apologetic eyes that always work on my mom. A reluctant smile stretches across her face. Bingo! My brother's girl is a softie and can't stay annoyed at me for more than 2.5 seconds.

"Here we are," Rom says as we pass under the tall, curving sign of a ranch on the outskirts of town.

Wild Hearts.

I hunch down further and peer out the front window. The local volcano smokes in the distance. Pretty fucking cool. Snowcapped, gray-blue mountains stretch around the infamous Teapot Lake ahead of us. There's a great view of the steaming hot waterfall that stays warm year-round too.

I'd never admit it to my brother, but it's kind of nice being back in Winter Bliss.

"My friend owns the place." Noelle's eyes light up over the sign. "It's amazing! She's rebranding the ranch to Wild Hearts Retreat because she's going to build some luxury cabins for tourists. I just love the new name. So cute!"

"More like corny as fuck," I mutter under my breath.

Noelle turns and blinks at me in shock. Oops, she wasn't supposed to hear that.

"Keep the joy killing to a minimum, please. And no bad behavior tonight," my brother drones from the front. "This is an engagement party. Classy."

"Engaged on April Fool's Day?" I laugh. "That's a choice. *Definitely* not doomed from day one."

Noelle is still silently just staring at me, blinking like she's on the fritz. It's kinda funny seeing her glitch out in real time. "Are all your brothers so . . . so . . .?"

She's too nice for her own good, probably struggling to not say the mean thing she's thinking about me. Growing up with a house of brothers, I can take it. I grab a piece of sharp cheddar that fell out of the container onto the floorboard, pop it in my mouth, and lean back, folding my hands behind my head.

"So . . .?" I try to get her to finish her sentence, dare her to make me seem like anything other than what I am—a mean-spirited, dim-witted oaf. The loser in the family. She must know it already. It's been a couple days since I showed up on their doorstep to help. Help? More like my family got sick of me and wanted me out of their hair.

"So awkward?" my brother asks.

"Asshole." I punch him in the shoulder. Not that he's wrong.

"No," she says.

"Grumpy?" Rom tries to fill in the blank. "Dangerous? Foolhardy?"

Noelle looks at him like he's serious for a beat. Shit, maybe he is. We . . . well, we do tick a few of those boxes.

She shakes her head and looks back at me. Her eyebrows furrow and pitch down. Oh crap, she's looking at me like a lost puppy. "Are they all so hopeless?"

Ouch.

Rom chuckles. "Every one, goddess."

Ewww with the pet names. Talk about corny.

"Cheese gives me hope." I dive forward and snatch the container. "Cheese is life."

"Rex!" Noelle shouts.

When she pulls at my mustache, I stiff-arm her and then flip my hand to tickle her ribs, managing to grab a hunk of parmesan—not ideal—and a single crumbly cracker before the car veers to the side of the road, screeching to a halt.

Rom rotates in his seat. He's a year younger than me but was always so tough and had his shit together in a way that kind of intimidated me. Normally the easygoing one among my brothers, I know that firestorm look, the smoke trickling out of his nose and the slight downturn to his head. Like he wants to gouge my eyes out with his jagged broken horn.

He's had it. He's about to fuck me up.

"Give. It. Back." Each word is low and slow and accompanied by hand-wrenching me by the horn like an errant child.

"Ouch," I grumble and shrug free, scratching the side of his headrest with the tip of a horn. *Whoops.* He doesn't need to see that. I resecure the lid and hand it back. "Fine, four-eyes."

"Jackass."

"Fuckface."

My brother sighs and shakes his head. He picks up his girlfriend's hand and kisses her knuckles before interlacing their fingers and getting the car back on the dirt road.

"I think you'll like my friend's ranch, Rex!" Noelle says brightly, prettying up the disheveled contents of the Tupperware, all annoyance at me already forgotten. "One of the moneymakers is the Christmas tree farm. But her real heart is in rescuing animals—a mix of pets, livestock, and wildlife." What makes her think I like animals, I have no idea. I mean, they're better than people, but that's a low bar. "The fireflies are my favorite though," she continues, staring at Rom like he's made out of angel dust and cookie dough ice cream. "They fly around the property every sunset. It's so romantic."

Remembering the rainbow-hued fireflies of Winter Bliss does bring a smile to my face all the same. They're unique to the area and, according to an old wives' tale, a sign of good luck. A rare happy memory in the midst of an otherwise shitty high school experience surfaces—the time I built a habitat for the shiny little buggers in shop class.

I hear a giggle and look up. Noelle is watching me in the rearview mirror with a soft smile on her face. "Told you he likes animals." She wiggles in her seat. "I just know he'll have fun tonight. I caught him teary-eyed over *Where the Red Fern Grows* yesterday."

"What monster doesn't cry at that book?" I ask.

Rom parks in a gravel lot surrounded by trees. "I thought you hated reading."

"Sometimes I like to remind myself how depressing it is." I pop open the door and squeeze out of the back seat. The two of them rush ahead, but I stretch my arms overhead with a deep inhale, soaking in the scenery.

As properties go, Wild Hearts is pretty sweet.

An old ranch-style house sits back a little ways from the lakefront. It's got some modern upgrades judging by the solar panels, generator, and a detached garage that looks newer. There's also a couple of plots cleared out on a hill to the left. That must be where the rental cabins are going. Nice setup.

The *smell* is the best part though. I take a deep breath and hold it, closing my eyes and imagining paradise as a mix of dark pine trees, sulfur from the nearby hot springs, and a distant smoke. This place is catnip for demons. It hits all the right notes.

No wonder our ancestors who founded Winter Bliss never left. While the lava pits, active volcano, forest fires, and dangerous wildlife may be a caution to some, for us, they're selling points.

Demons love a little chaos.

Before I know it, I've wandered closer to the barn, two stories surrounded by a maze of ramshackle, fenced-in paddocks. The doors are closed, but I see horses and goats out in one pasture. It brings to mind all the summers I spent at my uncle's ranch while my brothers went to fancy, enrichment camps. It was the first time I really felt different from them. Not good enough.

Even still, those months working outdoors are some of my happiest memories.

"Hey, girl," I laugh as a big dark mare snuffles right up on my face. I pet down the softest part of her nose. My heart rate slows and a calm washes over me, like my body knows it needs to be chill as fuck to keep her at ease.

Fuck, I miss being around horses, especially Umbrans. This one's got thick horns circling her ears and is around twenty hands tall. I scratch up her nose to the raised skin over her protected third eye. It doesn't open often, only in times of stress, when they need to regulate their temperature.

My uncle worked this same type of horse on his ranch. Demons love them because, like us, they came from volcanoes, and we domesticated the first ones. Rather than red like demonkind, Umbran horses evolved in shades of gray, a color that blends in with rocky mountain terrain. This old girl is dark, nearly sleet blue in the early evening sunlight.

I click my fingers and a flame ignites along with delicate sparks, almost like snowflakes. Umbrans eat demon fire like snacks.

Something jostles my shoulder.

"Oh, we've got another hungry one, huh?" I laugh at the light-gray girl.

Judging by her smaller horns, she's younger, but a lot about the two of them strikes me as similar. They must be a local variant of Umbran, if the longer hair around their feet are an indication. Built for colder weather.

"Mama and baby, I'm guessing?"

They blink at me, licking up sparks from both my hands. Like demons, their eyes glow, but if they want to stay hidden, they use translucent under-eyelids and smoke from their nose to mask themselves from predators.

These two aren't hiding anything from me, which is a good sign. They're happy enough to snatch up a treat and nudge me for pets.

My chest feels light. When an animal trusts you implicitly, on instinct alone, there's nothing quite like it. Who needs money or success or any of that shit when you can stand outside in the sunshine with a wild soul and just be?

Some black-nosed goats in an adjoining paddock start bleating like I stole their food. They like fire too, but I don't have time for those little shit starters. Most people think that particular breed is the likely origin of some of the tales surrounding a devilish, three-eyed, goat-man figure in human folklore.

I get it. All goats are kind of evil, in a cute way. These more than most.

Instrumental music starts up from a speaker near the house, reminding me I'm here to hang out with people. Bummer. I find a group of humans, demons, fae, and orcs gathered on a big flagstone patio nestled in a grove of trees. A few party tables and wooden folding chairs are set up under layers of string lights, lending the whole place a, dare I say, charming glow. There's an outdoor kitchen and a small herb or flower garden by the looks of it.

I spot Noelle leaving the table of appetizers and rub my hands together. Perfect timing. Just before I can snatch some of that pesto burrata I spied, my brother appears out of nowhere and bats my hand away, stepping between me and my prize.

That cheese is mine by rights now. I growl. A battle to the death it is.

"What did the electrician say about the south Boise site?" he asks.

Work? Are you fucking kidding me?

"Cheese," I grunt.

"One plate." He points at me and steps aside.

I grumble while I load my plate, letting the orgasmic creamy goodness of the first bite wash away my hangry rage.

"The electrician?" he repeats.

I chew and glare at him. The electrician said the work to up the wattage in the rental unit we want is more than we budgeted, which will mean my brother has to renegotiate the lease with the property owner. But it's Friday evening, and he doesn't need to be thinking about that all weekend. He's spending time with his girl on some staycation getaway, and I'm not about to let him drag himself back into work mode. Once Rom clicks his out-of-office, he's good at disconnecting, but until then, he can be a bit of a ballbuster.

"It's five fuckin' thirty. Why are we talking shop?" I sneer and pop a pepperoni in my mouth. "This is supposed to be a party celebrating love or some shit."

"The electrician needs to finish before the painters, which I have on retainer for two weeks from now."

"We sling caffeine to the weary masses, bro. We're not saving the world." Perkatory is our family's business, a chain of coffeeshops we are slowly but surely expanding nationwide. Pretty cool, I guess. I'm not really in leadership, too much of a mess to be trusted beyond odd jobs. But I try to pull my weight.

"If I need to hire someone cheaper," he continues. "I can make some calls now and—"

"That's my job." My chest heats in anger. I can't do much, but if there's one thing I'm half decent at, it's working with contractors and tradesmen. I cross my arms and lean my head forward, letting him know I'll lock horns if he wants to tussle.

"Right," he says. "Of course."

I know what he's thinking, why he wants to just do it himself. I'm the weak link in the family, sent away because I'm probably annoying our oldest brother too much. Though, to be fair, the type A, CEO bosshole deserves it. Generally, I'm not too upset about being here. After Rom announced he was staying in Winter Bliss because he met the love of his life, the fam decided to turn lemons into lemonade and double the investment to expand Perkatory in the western market ahead of schedule, starting with two locations between here and Boise by the end of the year.

And of all the siblings, they sent *me* to help. Me, the brother who not only never made it to college, but only finished my GED under duress because the trade school I wanted to pick up classes in wouldn't accept me otherwise.

I don't usually fight with Rom either, but if he's implying I can't handle haggling with an electrician, that stings. I thought a few months here would be a nice break from constantly disappointing my family back home. Rom may be half decent in negotiation but he doesn't know shit about wiring in buildings constructed before the 1930s. The electrician is more liable to up the price if he catches wind that my little brother has no technical knowledge.

"Sorry," he sighs and squeezes the back of his neck. I must have made the silence awkward, standing here glowering at him, up in my feelings. Rom reaches out and grabs my shoulder which turns into a friendly pat on the neck. "I've just been managing the expansion on my own for the last few months. Got used to having no support. But I need it. I'm glad you're here, brother."

Oh, shit. He's *glad* I'm here? He *needs* me? My throat tightens in surprise. Our family doesn't really talk about emotional shit. Is this new empathetic Rom because of his always-smiling, watery-eyed girlfriend?

Yikes.

"Business schmizzness. It's nothing big. We'll chat on Monday." I slap his chest with the back of my hand.

Back to cheese, much safer territory. I pop a mozzarella ball in my mouth and it practically melts on my tongue. That's the good stuff.

My phone dings with a calendar notification—*Site 2 contract review with Logistics Coordinator.* I scoff. Logistics Coordinator. I do the random tasks no one else in my family has time for. The easy shit I can't screw up. I look over at my overachieving younger brother in his nice suit and horn-rimmed glasses and can't help but flick his nose. "Such a nerd."

"My nerd," Noelle croons and slides along his side. His hand skims down her back, then up her arm, finding its way to the back of her neck. She arches against him.

I roll my eyes and make a puking sound in my throat. It's adorable or whatever, but they can miss me with the PDA. Still, it's kind of sweet. If anyone deserves a happy ending it's my reclusive, bookish brother. Here I thought we'd be bachelors for life together. Him because of crippling insecurity. Me because everything I touch turns to disaster.

Being tall and built like an ox only gets you so far with the ladies. I'm not the happily ever after sort. Oh well.

"Ahh, she's here." Noelle pats Rom's chest several times before rushing off. "I need to find Randy."

"Who?" I ask.

On the Dark Mother's sacred panties, I don't get how that woman knows everyone in town. At least Mom has a Rolodex. Not only does Noelle know everyone's name, but who their family is, their home address, and favorite book tropes, whatever that means.

"The guy proposing tonight. It's a surprise, I guess." Rom finally tucks his phone away. He snatches a glass of bubbly from the table and grabs a long pretzel stick, waving it to point out the party tables and nicely dressed guests. "Remember?"

"Right." I snap off half his pretzel and chew on it. "What kind of guy needs to surprise a woman into getting married? Sounds like a red flag." But what do I know? Though now it makes sense why the cheese is top tier. Wedding money.

"Fair point, well made," Rom mutters, eyes tracking Noelle. "But no joy killing. You're on your best behavior tonight."

"Sure, sure." While my brother's distracted, I fill a fresh plate with more cheese and a few palate cleanser fruits. As expected, he drifts away within seconds. The lovestruck demon can't seem to be more than five feet away from his girl at any given moment.

"Oh wow, Noelle brought the fancy cheese!" Someone with a husky, feminine voice slides right beside me. "My favorite! Blackberry baked brie. Cheese is life."

A woman after my own heart. I cut a look sideways and all I see is dark curly hair. Her forearm brushes mine, and goosebumps prickle from the contact. She smells nice too, like grass and wildflowers.

I straighten my mustache and pass a hand down my shirt, making sure it's tucked in. Thank the Blessed Darkness my brother insisted I wear a button-up. This pearl snap cowboy number is all I got, so it has to do.

I turn to get a better look at my fellow cheese lover.

Her eyes find mine, and the sight of her hits me like a ton of bricks. My chest heats. Tendrils of fire snake up my throat and I shake my head to fight the heady instinct of desire. *No fucking way.* She should be long gone.

But who could forget those dark eyes? *Sharp*, I always thought. Like a fox. Even as a teenager, when she looked at me it was like an arrow to the heart, like she could see straight through me.

"Fuck me," comes out on a shaky exhale. *There's no way she's still in this town.*

"Hmm?" She finishes chewing.

Shit. Not my best line. My eyes dart around, but nothing comes to mind. What I know about her is limited to the nerdy girl paired with me on a group project fifteen years ago. But we do have one thing in common right now.

"Cheese." I thrust the untouched plate of food toward her.

She chuckles and takes it from me, gingerly picking up a cube of muenster and popping it in her mouth. Full red lips close around it as she cocks her head at me. The tight black curls framing her face bounce hypnotically. Her hair is even prettier than I remembered, probably because she usually wore it back due to our strict private school dress code.

Even though she's laughing at my expense—for acting like a fucking imbecile—my chest warms at the stupid fact I gave her food and she's eating it. She moves back to the baked brie and her eyelids flutter closed.

I think it's a fae thing—trapping a damsel by tricking her into eating your food—but I send a prayer down to Mother Darkness that there might be some crossover. Because I'm gonna need a shitload more than one-word answers and party food to impress the smartest girl I ever knew.

Fuck me. I want to say it this time—beg if I have to—in a completely different context. But ladies don't usually take too well to my bluntness. Flirt, asshole! I gulp, take a deep breath, and clear my throat.

"Hey, Birdie Lynn."

It was a nickname only I called her, and she must recognize it. She looks me up and down, smile fading as her jaw drops. My chest heaves, trying to take in air. She was pretty at sixteen, but beyond beautiful now. Full-figured, full hair, and full of life.

"Rex?" Her voice pitches up before she recovers with a mean little smile. "Didn't recognize you with that fuzzy caterpillar on your face."

I grin like the cat that got the cream. If she's being mean, she remembers me just fine. We were always half friendly, half hateful to each other. It was our way of flirting. I think. Let's test the theory.

"Still as sweet as a two-by-four to the face, huh?" I twirl the end of my facial hair to make it curl and wink. "The ladies never complain about the sensation of an old-fashioned pornstache."

"Pig," she snorts, eyes twinkling. "Haven't changed one bit, I see. How are you?"

"Cleaner than you." I pick a piece of straw out of her hair, curious. An image fills my mind, followed by a deranged bolt of jealousy. "Rolling around in the haystacks with somebody?"

"No." She huffs and pulls up her phone, checking her reflection in the camera. Even back in school, she was always perfectly put together. Prim and proper. The only time she wasn't was when she'd pop off at me. I took it as a compliment, naturally.

"Still pretty as ever," I say, quieter, realizing I need to stop with the teasing and try a different approach.

"You're making my hair a mess, you little goober." Her voice goes soft as she lifts a hand to her neck. It's then I see the fucking bird cuddled up right behind her ear, one violet eye blinking at me. Their dark-green feathers are dead giveaway.

"A horny wood owl?" I snicker. "You know those things are deadly, right?"

"They're just a baby." She glares at me. "And the species name is *Lampros Ascalaphus*."

"*Lampros Ascalaphus*," I repeat in a mocking tone. "Also known as the fae death owl or, more locally, the horny wood owl."

"They may have been used by fae royalty to hunt and poison prey, but it's just their nature. They're really no threat to people." The backs of her fingers brush against the little bugger's emerald-colored feathers. It figures that a tough, smart girl like Birdie would have a deadly bird as a pet. Kinda cool, actually.

"Fun fact: *Lampros Ascalaphus* feathers are green to blend in with the upper pine forests of North America, but molt to white every winter to camouflage with the snow." She smiles softly at the bird.

"As nerdy as ever." I steal a cube of her cheese and shudder when the owls cocks its head at a sharp angle. Before it can poison me, she smacks my hand away. A hot thrill shoots through me. "And as fiery as ever."

"No one would describe me like that." She sniffs and straightens her necklace chain. Goddess forbid the clasp be visible or she be messy in any way.

"That's a shame," I say. And it is. In school, she was the spitfire that never let me get away with slacking off or flirting too much.

Her gaze narrows.

Oh, but I loved when she got mad at me. Could never predict what she'd say next. But I'm not trying to actually piss her off. It's a dance. Time to hit her with a safer topic—nostalgia.

"Did you get an A in shop class after all?" My family moved away before final grades were posted.

"Yeah." She pauses, watching me carefully. "It was a really great project."

I wonder if she's thinking about that last day of class too, when we got caught in the rain and everything changed between us. For a minute, at least.

I could keep pressing the flirtation, but I need to tread carefully. A girl like Birdie is smart enough to know I'm still bad news.

"Valedictorian, then?" I ask. While I was two years behind my peers, she was a year ahead and working toward graduating early. She was headed to an East Coast Ivy League college to follow in her dad's footsteps.

"Salutatorian." Her jaw ticks on a swallow like she's not proud of being the second fucking smartest person at Infernus Academy. Right here in Winter Bliss, it's the most elite private business school out on this side of the country, almost exclusively demons too, except for a select few like Birdie. My parents spent all their meager extra money ensuring all my brothers and I went there, not that I ever made good on it for them.

"That's badass." I nod. "Life's been good to you, then? Surprised you're here and not busting heads on Wall Street with your dad." He was a guest lecturer in the honors program, a retired trust fund manager for old money families.

"Oh, I was for a while. It wasn't a good fit. I moved back a couple years ago and bought my stepmom's land to help rescue animals like this." She scratches the neck of the little owl in her hair.

"That doesn't surprise me one bit, Birdie Lynn," I say, a little quieter so when I lean forward to steal a slice of strawberry, neither she or the bird gets spooked. She doesn't even slap my hand this time, just watches me put it in my mouth in a way that gives me a jolt of confidence. Something pings in the back of my head—an alarm—something I'm forgetting, but I bat it away. I'm making progress here. She's letting me get closer. "You always had a soft heart for animals. Brutes, even."

Her expression shifts to surprise and she leans away slightly. Hmm, I pushed too hard.

"What brings you back to Winter Bliss?" she asks, more guarded.

"That dork." I try to lighten the mood, thumbing to where Rom stands behind Noelle. They're both whispering to each other and staring at the sunset.

"Rom's your brother. I almost forgot." A hint of her smile is back as she looks at them. Okay, this is salvageable if I can keep the conversation going.

"Yeah, I'm helping him out with Perkatory for a while. Found this sweet bed-and-breakfast in town. It's got a weird looking oval roof, so they call it The Deviled Egg. I may or may not have been swayed by it being named after my favorite party food. Turns out, they make a mean continental breakfast with cheesy eggs and don't mind when I raid the communal fridge. Great snacks." My nervous laugh is higher pitched than normal, and even though I realize I'm rambling, I can't seem to stop. "They also have this free family dinner every week—

"On Thursday nights." Birdie's full-on grinning, and my heart squeezes. Score!

I always liked her smile. Her teeth were a little too big for her mouth but in a cute way. Some prick at school made fun of her for it once, but I roughed him up between classes. He was lucky my brother pulled me off when he did. Anyone who thinks Birdie doesn't have the prettiest fucking smile is an asshole. A dumb asshole.

"My moms own the place," she says. "And the cheesy eggs are *menemen*, a Turkish omelet dish with garlic, veggies, and *beyaz peynir*. Best breakfast you'll ever have."

"Wait, your moms?" I must have misheard. Miss Eda is a cute white-haired human, but her wife is a hardass de-moness. How is that—

"Yeah, doofus. Orla is my stepmom."

"Whoa."

What are the chances? Also, it makes me realize how little I know her. All we shared was one high school semester together, a class where the only way to get her attention was pulling her ponytail or kicking the backs of her shoes. She fully hated me by the time we were paired up for the final project. I won her over all the same. Kind of. I think. But that was fifteen years ago. Birdie's still smiling though, eyes twinkling in the ambient light. Looking at her is like a drug. I feel like I could float away.

"Are you high?" she laughs.

"On life? Always." I grin back. Good recovery!

"*Pfft*. Dork." But her smile doesn't fade. It makes me bold. I lean down, close enough to be eye level with her, only to see hers widen in surprise.

"Be mean to me, Birdie. I like it," I say. It's time to push. "What're you up to after this engagement party?" No time like the present to make good on some teenage fantasies. I keep the second part to myself for now.

Birdie sucks in a sharp breath, but not the sexy kind. The shocked kind. Uh, were we not flirting just now?

"Engagement?" she glances around with a tense laugh. "I think you're at the wrong party."

The alarm bells in my slow-ass brain start blaring again just as a gangly human guy comes up behind her. He's wearing a black felt cowboy hat that has never seen a hard day's work in its life. *Poser.* But when he sets his hands on Birdie's full hips and chin on her head, I see red. My mood darkens, like a band of discordant bass guitars thrumming in my body at the same time.

Who the fuck is this cock-blocking son of a bitch?

Wait.

She owns land here. A wildlife refuge. *This* place is hers. Birdie is Noelle's friend that's about to get surprise proposed to.

She looks back at the weasley, dime-store cowboy who he kisses her on the fucking cheek, all while still holding the plate of cheese I gave her. I silently beg that evil little owl to gouge his eye out.

Instead, he turns her around by the shoulders and drops to one knee.

"Fuck me," I whisper under my breath.

It's April Fool's after all, and there's no surprise who the biggest one turned out to be.

Chapter Two
Birdie

Did I drop a piece of cheese? That's the only thing I can imagine when Randy gets down on one knee.

Then, he looks up. Pasted-on smile. Wide eyes. He takes a deep breath and reaches inside his jacket pocket.

I connect the dots, and my stomach drops.

Oh, God.

A matching smile cranks out of me like a drawbridge on an ancient wheel.

I know what this is, even though his muffled words barely reach my static-filled brain.

Tonight was supposed to be an open house for the rebranded Wild Hearts Retreat. A way to try and get the word out about the cabins we'll have up and running for the holiday season.

I'm a little . . . lost. It's been such a whirlwind getting a new entrance sign commissioned and figuring out the right mix of catering and potluck to make sure everyone was fed while keeping it under a tight budget. I've also been tracking the growth of the Christmas tree crop for this winter and the first stages of the cabin construction.

Mine and Randy's relationship has been an afterthought lately.

This wasn't supposed to be—

"Aylin *Birdie* Badem, will you marry me?"

My smile tightens. I've tried to remind him that the second syllable of my given name sounds like *linn* not *leen*, but he always says it wrong. It irks me to no end. The way he said it is so awkward. Not right. All for show. Birdie isn't even my middle name. It's just what I've been called since I can remember.

I take a quick sip of air so I can get the next word out. The expected answer. I glance around at all the smiling faces.

"Yes." The word comes out rushed, like the aftermath of a punch to the gut, leaving me before I even mean to say it.

He stands up, and we hug. I squeeze him tight, angling to one side to keep my little owl out of striking distance. He's not a big fan of Randy.

A mile a minute, information processes in my mind. I was not expecting a surprise proposal. I don't like surprises. He should know that, right? But the proposal is also not out of the blue, so I can't really fault him for it. We've talked about marriage more over the past few months as we worked on the cabins and rebrand concept. But I thought it was more hypothetical. Like, hey, even when we get married, let's keep our businesses separate. The plan was that I would contract his travel agency to book the rentals, while the property remains mine.

His voice tickles my ear, soft and serious. "I kind of marketed Wild Hearts Retreat at the Chamber of Commerce meeting as a husband and wife thing. It'll help with marketing. Figured we should get a jump on it and do this before the cabins open. Shoot for a fall wedding. Something small. Is October enough time to plan?"

It's business. Okay, that makes sense. Randy's sensible. I've always liked that about him. And October is plenty of time to sort a little ceremony out. The winter holidays are high season for the Christmas tree farm and tourists. Best to get a simple wedding out of the way if it'll help him book the cabins and cash in on all the investments I'm about to make in construction.

A wedding. I'm getting married.

He pulls back and searches my face. "Make sense?"

I swallow and nod. "Mhmm."

It does, doesn't it? He's a good guy.

Randy slides a ring on my finger as I remember how my lungs work, taking in several deep breaths. The center stone sparkles. Diamond, probably. Classic. Nice, I guess. The way the stone sticks out, I probably can't wear it too much doing ranch chores. And I'd always kind of pictured having something vibrant, maybe a ruby. It's just . . . not my favorite.

What is wrong with me? I already had my quarter-life crisis moving back here to live out my dream rescuing animals instead of working in soul-sucking finance. I'm thirty-one. What am I waiting for?

With the ring on, Randy exhales too. Sweat beads on his brow. He's as nervous as me. Maybe this isn't the most romantic possible moment, but that's not really who we are together. We're practical to a fault. He's trying here. I use a paper napkin to dab at his face and we both laugh.

We've always worked well together. I should be happy.

Randy is a catch, my first serious boyfriend since moving back to Winter Bliss. He ticks all the boxes—showers regularly, treats me well, and has a good relationship with his family. When I see my future, my ranch, there's so much I know I can't do alone.

And he's a small-town guy with ambition. Not only does he own the only travel agency in town, he's also started investing in real estate lately, flipping houses for short term rentals. Building these luxury cabins on the ranch is our first big project together. The rebrand to Wild Hearts Retreat was his idea. For us!

What's not to love?

And yet the idea of marriage makes me cringe. But I'm the firstborn daughter of divorced parents in an immigrant family. Powering through life with grit and courtesy smiles is my autopilot.

The hugs and congratulations begin.

A lot of people are here, all of my local friends and some of my family. I'm kind of gutted my dad and brothers aren't here, but my mom and stepmom made it. Everyone who asks about the animals I'm fostering gives me a small reprieve from talking about the proposal I was not prepared for and the cabin construction I don't even want to think about yet.

And then there's Rex, frowning at his brother on the outskirts of the crowd. I was *not* expecting him in a million years or the confused teenage feelings that flared to life when he started teasing me. That guy was the bane of my existence in shop class until, well, until he wasn't. Until I saw the softer side of him.

But that's ancient history.

The party starts up in earnest, like a living organism around me. The appetizers and barbecue are a hit. My favorite is definitely the crispy cheese pastries Mom made. One friend even brought some primo home-brewed liquor. Everyone pulled together to make the retreat's open house—err, proposal—a success.

The night blurs together, and once sunset turns to dusk, the guests are mostly gone.

"Gotta head back, babe," Randy kisses my cheek from behind as I start folding up the chairs.

"Oh." I turn. His collar is hiked up on one side, so I go up on my toes to fix it. He's so tall and handsome in a not-too-much way. My ring sparkles in the soft ambient lighting. We're really engaged. "You can't stay?"

Randy only stays over at my place one or two nights a week and our love life is perfunctory, but I would have thought tonight of all nights we'd get more alone time.

"There's a sunrise yoga and mimosas thing at the Emberlight Resort I sold to a corporate group," he says. The early morning tractors on the road from here to town always slow him down. "I need to make sure it goes off without a hitch. Could be a big contract if they make it an annual retreat."

"Of course." I nod, a sense of relief leaving my body on my next exhale. Without Randy, I can clean up and do a last animal check-in without feeling guilty. How did they do with all the guests at the ranch tonight? Did the noise or strangers bother any of them? These are all things I'm frankly dreading when I imagine cabin rentals with rich guests actually coming to fruition.

"We're doing it." He smiles.

"Wild Hearts," I say.

"No, us."

Oh, right. We're getting married. I smile back. He gives me another peck, familiar and light. This is going to work.

We'll just do a small wedding, something low stress. We've got to keep our eyes on the prize.

This is right.

Randy looks at me funny and squeezes my waist. "Of course it is, babe."

My face heats. I didn't mean to say that out loud.

When he walks off, it's just my moms left. They're the best and help me clean up. While Mom deals with the leftovers and Orla packs the tables and chairs away, I check the garage to make sure the ferrets, rabbits, and prairie dog are all good.

I also tuck my little owl friend into their cage. Birds are notoriously hard to sex, so I have no clue if they're a he or she, and I'm doing my very best not to name them. It's common knowledge that once an animal has a name, they're a pet. But this horny wood owl is getting released back into the wild if I do my job right. I smirk at the name. While *Lampros Ascalaphus* can reproduce asexually in some environment conditions, they tend to prefer the tried-and-true method. I want to give this little owl every opportunity to return to nature, even if that's only three treetops down from my house. Close but out of the nest would be ideal. Having a fae death owl as a pet is not an extra responsibility I need in my life right now.

I gather three dozen eggs from the chicken coops on my way back to the patio, where my mom is sweeping up.

Everything is back in its place.

"Thanks, Mom." I hand her the eggs, which she sets on the edge of the wrought iron table.

With both hands, she holds my face, slowly brushing the curls behind my ears. I had my hair loose all night, and with all the hugs, let alone my little feathered companion, I'm sure it's a huge mess now. Her thumbs sweep along my cheeks.

It's how she used to say goodnight to me as a young child, a familiar gesture that always made me feel so cherished. The older I got, the more distant we became. I latched onto my dad instead. It's only after she married Orla that we grew close again, slowly over time.

Sometimes though, her tenderness can almost feel like too much.

"What a big night, *minik kuşum*," she says.

Ach. I wasn't expecting that. Since I can remember, she's always called me that nickname. In Turkish it means *little bird*. As a baby, she said I used to sit and watch the scarlet finches out the back window for hours. Early on, my love for animals was obvious. I feel the surprising, telltale heat of tears behind my eyes measure my breaths to hold back the emotion.

"You're happy?" she asks.

My lips pinch as I nod, like all of my racing worries and thoughts will tumble out if I don't. But she doesn't need that, not tonight. I'm a big girl now with land and animals and responsibilities and a boyfriend—err, fiancé. She searches my face but finally nods.

My stepmom's car tires crunch through the gravel nearby, and she hops out.

"All good?" She surveys the patio, looking for more ways to help, but they left the place spotless.

"All good." I give my mom a quick squeeze and step away to hug my stepmom as well. She's a tough old demoness, but she's been nothing but wonderful to me since coming into my life as a teenager. "Thanks for everything."

"Your *baba* would have been here if he'd known," Mom says, and I cringe a little but wave her off. My dad won't be happy that he wasn't consulted.

Our relationship has been getting better. He was disappointed when I left New York to move home, but he still has my brothers following his footsteps in finance. And if he thinks he can get stubborn about not giving me permission to get engaged, we'll have a little chat. Respectfully. He's got some old-fashioned ideas, but my dad's a good guy at heart. I would have wanted him to be here just because.

"It's fine. I'll call him in the morning. It's not a big deal."

My mom shares a quick look with Orla, then nods and picks up the eggs. "Talk soon, yeah?"

"Every day." I wave as they pack into their car, and watch their little hatchback drive off until I see them leave the ranch entrance up the hill. I trigger the entry gate to close behind them.

With the last guests gone, I let loose a little, wagging my arms at my sides and groaning to the sky like some dying dinosaur.

"Gaaaaarrrghhhh."

Finally, I can breathe. Rolling my head around both shoulders, I refocus on my last task of the night—the barn animals.

I hop in my Jeep and head out, since it's a good quarter mile of snaking dirt road.

My horses, Gigi and Mimi, are munching on some hay in their stalls, their lavender tails flicking side to side. I was assigned the mother-daughter pair from a local judge after they shut down some shady racetrack. They're a special demonic breed and so highly prized for racing that he didn't trust anyone else who came forward to adopt.

My ranch becoming an animal refuge just kind of . . . happened. The goats came with the property. They love eating evergreens, so naturally are a good fit for a Christmas tree farm. But the rest of the animals I've picked up by the most random of chances.

I peek in on my little herd of Blacknose Cythraul goats. They're cuddled up in their lean-to, but notice one particular lady missing: my perpetually pregnant mama goat. Like the horses, this breed is local to the Winter Bliss area and closely associated with demons. With three eyes, black fur, wicked sharp horns, and both genders growing long beards, they're really something to behold.

"Now where did your mama get to?" I open the double front doors and peer around. They're unlocked, which is strange. Maybe I left it that way after the walk-through tour I gave a few people earlier.

"You in here, missy?" I call out, loud enough that my voice echoes off the rafters.

I hear rustling from the makeshift bathroom, a front stall I enclosed to install a toilet, big aluminum sink, and faucet with shower along the wall. On this side of the ranch, it's the only bathroom, but it's also the best place to bathe the animals who I need to prep for adoption handoffs.

"Shhh," a deep voice rumbles alongside the telltale bleat of my missing nanny goat. "Ouch. You little asshole."

I burst in and grab the first thing I see, a long scrub brush, and whack the intruder over their formidably sized back. In a flash of reason, I realize this may have been a bad idea. I'm alone on my ranch with no weapon to defend myself. Because guests were over tonight, the shotgun I keep in here to ward off predators is locked in my safe instead.

I clutch the scrub brush to my chest, but before I have the chance to flee, my mama goat rams into their backside, knocking them sideways.

She rears back two little steps before launching to head-butt him.

Funnily enough, the intruder has horns too.

"Rex?"

The demon blast-from-my-past grunts as the goat makes contact and they both twist. In a flurry of flames and smoke, they tussle on the ground, their horns becoming more and more entangled as they twist together.

"Gentle! Gumdrop's pregnant!" I jump into the fray, fire be damned.

With a last couple jerks of their heads before realizing they're well and truly stuck together, they both pause at my touch. The scent of mildly burnt hair and clothes hangs around us. Her furry chest and his arm are both warm to the touch, like they could burst into flames again at a moment's notice.

"Take it easy." I look between them.

Rex is baring his teeth at her. When he lets out a low growl, she bucks forward again, the tips of her horns coming perilously close to the big demon's eyeballs.

He grips both of her horns to forcibly hold her back and sneers at me. "A little help, before my eyes are gouged out of my skull?"

I whistle a short demon ditty.

"Bahhhh," Gumdrop bleats and freezes, blinking at me like the soul of innocence. I learned the cue from my stepmom who used to care for the herd before I bought the land from her.

When Rex attempts the same tune, she snorts two curling rings of smoke and lunges forward again.

"Hey, cut it out." I smack his forearm. "There, there." I pet down her neck and scratch back up to the top of her head, where I try to work out the best way to untangle them. Her horns are spiraled with ends pointing forward, while his arc wider before curling out. I'm slide her left horn out easily as it was only partially looped, but the other one is really stuck.

"Slide toward the wall." I shove at Rex's chest. He tries but can't quite figure it out. I won't be able to get them free unless he moves just so.

"Oh, fuck it." I grab his mop of hair at the top and yank his head to achieve the desired angle.

He gasps and stares at me. Rather than be angry, his eyes swirl golden-white as he blinks up dreamily. Gumdrop slides free, stomping back a few paces and looking between me and Rex with the blank expression goats have just before they're about to do something completely insane.

"No." I put a hand up and stop the forward momentum of her lunge. "Bed."

She waggles her head and snorts, but there's no smoke coming out now. She's calmer. After a few more blinks, she trots out the door, hooves clacking on the tile.

I wait, because I know that ornery nanny too well. When she's on the hard-packed dirt floor of the barn, she turns back around and pauses. Before she gets another wild idea in her head, I point left.

"Bed."

Then I grab the scrub brush and use the end to slam the door closed. Even with all the alpha-woman energy I can muster, that old girl only listens half the time.

I drop the brush and spin on Rex, moving back to a standing position over him. He's still rubbing that spot at the top of his head I yanked him around by with a dopey smile on his face.

"Explain yourself."

Rex Perchaz is not my friend. He's a stranger. Sort of. At least, he's a stranger to my ranch after hours. And the hulking demon is probably twice my size. Those should all be caution signs to take it easy on him, but with adrenaline pumping through my system and some older memory of the way things worked between us, I feel oddly in control.

"I-I-I" he stammers. "Uhhh."

I pinch the bridge of my nose. "Why are you here?"

"I'm drunk." He shrugs. "I don't know how it happened. I mean, I was drinking."

"There's your answer." I glower at him.

"Ugh, obviously. But the punch made me lightheaded after just two glasses. Then on the third glass of the thick stuff—"

"That wasn't punch! That was straight hooch." Randy's friend, Greg, bartends at Under the Volcano, a local tiki bar, and brews his own stuff on the side. He brought a bottle tonight for the potluck, but clearly Rex didn't know what he was getting into. "You had three cups of liquor. One shot is plenty. My God."

He blinks at me and nods, eyes glassy. "One shot is plenty." He breathes a little faster, his complexion growing more purple than red by the second.

"Oh, no. Over the toilet. Now." I race forward and position his head over the bowl, pulling back his unkempt wavy hair from his brow.

"You have such soft han—" he starts, and then retches. I have to breathe through my mouth and look away. His whole body convulses into the movement, and it makes me realize, again, not only how massive this demon is, but how strong. His back muscles alone are huge and thick. He's got the build of those guys who throw giant logs across a football field and pull buses with their teeth.

As the spitting and heavy breathing calms down, I pat his back. Before I can say anything, he chuckles darkly.

"I'm such"—every couple words he knocks his forehead against the back of the toilet—"a fucking loser."

My heart pangs, but only for a second. I'm a take action kind of girl.

"Up." I stand and motion for him to do the same.

He struggles to his feet and rubs his temples.

"Feel any better?" I ask.

His gaze trails over me, from my face to my messy hair and down to my fancy dress and shoes. I'd think he's checking me out, but it's more like he's cataloging me to memory with the saddest expression on his face.

He shakes his head and looks away. "Worse."

"Welp, time to clean up. Wash your face and rinse out your mouth. There may be some mouthwash in the medicine cabinet." It's mostly animal medicine and first aid supplies, but I like to keep travel-sized toiletries in here when I think about it. "I'll drive you back to my mom's B&B."

He groans. "Your mom. *Shit.* She's going to be so disappointed in me. And Orla's going to cook up my liver for breakfast."

"At least it'll be well marinated." I smirk. My stepmom always does love to soak her roasts in the closest alcoholic drink overnight. "Though the meat may be a little tougher than she likes."

He snorts and glances at me in the mirror.

"Also, I know the alarm code for the back entry." I put my hands on my hips. "We can get you in with minimal fanfare."

"Why are you being nice to me? I just puked all over your bathroom and fucked up your lovey-dovey proposal after hitting on you over a cheese plate."

He hit on me? I was so shocked to see him again it didn't really register. The back and forth barbs we threw at each other were so natural, like a muscle memory from adolescence. But he always kind of flirted with me in school too.

It was just his way to get a rise out of me. Rex was never a serious guy. Case in point.

"Fuuuuuuck." He groans and braces down on an elbow against the sink, turning on the faucet to splash his face and swish water in his mouth. "That fuckstick is still around here somewhere. You know what? Have Ryan drive me back. I'll face the music with your moms. I deserve it."

"Excuse you, his name is Randy." And fuckstick? That's new. "Besides, he can't drive you back. He went home. It's just me here."

Rex's bleary eyes find mine in the mirror, narrowing. "That doesn't make sense."

I don't like that his moment of clarity lands like a dart in the bullseye. "He just got you to agree to marry him. Y'all should be tucked away near a fireplace, cuddling with hot chocolate or whatever romantic people do."

Instead, my fiancé is in town, and I'm wrestling a pregnant goat off an intruder. I wave him off with a messy sound. "He's got business to take care of. He's a responsible adult with a very sensible head on his shoulders."

Rex blinks, the look of confusion still on his face.

"Clean up. I'll meet you out front." I look back, just before I close the door to find him still watching me, like he's trying to figure something out but it's not connecting. "And don't worry about the bathroom. I hose off animals in here all the time. It's seen a lot worse than the bad end of Greg's hooch."

"You need help with any of the late-night chores? It's the least I could do."

"So you can body slam my pregnant animals into submission? I'll pass."

He smirks as I shut the door between us.

A few minutes later, he emerges, shirtless.

"Sorry." He grimaces. "I had to throw the shirt away. Didn't want to stink up your car."

He folds himself into my Jeep, hair and skin dappled with moisture. I almost wonder if he took a full shower with how clean and soapy he smells.

"Why did Rom leave you here?" I ask as we pull out of the main gate and I wait for it to close behind me. He and Noelle were all smiles as they said goodbye, not a care in the world. I can't believe they'd forget about him.

"I lied." Rex gulps down one of the water bottles on my floorboard and grabs a stick of gum from the console. "I texted him that I'd hitched a ride back with your mom."

"Why?"

"Rom is so fucking happy." He huffs. "With his girlfriend and Winter Bliss and even the idea of having me here in town. He said he was glad I was here. Me! And even after he warned me not to fuck up tonight, big surprise, I fucked up and drank that sludge like a complete dumbass. I figured I'd sleep it off in the barn and walk back to town in the morning."

"It's four miles to town."

"Like I said." He thumbs to himself. "Complete dumb-ass."

Who was trying not to let down his brother. I get it. Not letting people down has pretty much been my de facto state since birth.

He melts into the seat and turns his head in my direction. His stubble-covered jaw works to chew the gum. I can only see him in my periphery and try not to let on how weird it feels that he's just staring at me.

"You sure you wanna do this?"

"It's no problem. I like driving." It's peaceful, especially at night. Hands at ten and two. I've got everything under control. The whole world is before me, and I'm the one in charge.

"No. That?" His head nods toward the ranch.

"Build the cabins? Of course." I take a breath and launch into the well-developed pitch Randy delivered over half a dozen times tonight. "The vacation rental market has a burgeoning new niche—luxury accommodations with a wildlife experience. There's this place in Texas where you can swim with otters and have breakfast with giraffes. *Wild Hearts Retreat* can fill this need for the community."

"Your animals do seem cool as shit."

"Right? They are!" I smile. The fact he says that even after tussling with my nanny goat means he gets it. "And based on Randy's market research, with even two cabins over the high seasons, I can cover the construction cost within a couple years." The numbers for what high-end travelers will pay are staggering to me.

"Is the ranch not profitable? My uncle runs cattle. I know it can be hit or miss based on the season."

"He does? Wow." I glance over briefly, and my face heats at the broad, rolling flesh of his shirtless chest. I clear my throat and refocus on driving. "I don't have any cows. Yet, at least. My place is kind of a mishmash of income streams—Christmas tree farm, ranch tours, petting zoo, and I take donations for the rescue portion. It's doing fine, actually. The Christmas tree farm is still developing. It'll start paying off more each year as I'm letting a lot of them continue maturing before they're cut. So I keep the lights on between the current income and my financial investments. But my dream . . ."

Oh, God. I'm rambling. Why am I telling him all this?

"Is what?" he asks, and his tone is clear, like he really wants to know.

I readjust my grip on the steering wheel, and give voice to the thing I haven't even really plotted out yet. A pipe dream, really. "When the cabins are in low season, once I can afford the loss, my dream is to promote community education about wildlife and connect with academic re-searchers. I want to offer lodging or a base of operations, so the rare species unique to Winter Bliss can be studied from the ranch. It's lakefront with easy access to the volcano by water. Not-so-fun fact: The Gosta fireflies were almost exterminated five years ago because of a single crop duster dropping pesticides. There are so many more species in and around this one volcano than most people realize. And if they can be appreciated and studied, they can be protected."

Wow. That's it. Have I ever actually articulated the daydreams swirling in my head so clearly? Since I was a kid, I've loved animals. If I'd really known myself in college and had the courage to not blindly pursue what my dad wanted, I'd have studied animal biology of some kind.

"You've always been so passionate." Rex's deep voice washes over me, above the sound of the ambient radio and the wind whooshing by. When we pause at the first stop sign in town, I turn to him, still a little stunned.

Passionate? No one would describe me that way. I'm a hard worker. I'm a peacemaker. I'm goal-oriented and realistic.

"When I asked if you're sure you wanna do this, I meant"—he pauses—"get married."

I roll my eyes and get back to driving.

"Friends ask these kinds of things." He pokes my side.

"Stop it. Ugh." I swat his stupid, hairy, shirtless chest. His skin is overly warm, like the embodiment of a heated blanket. "You puked in my barn and got in a fight with my goat. We're not friends."

"We were," he says softly.

"Were we? I don't recall." Okay, I'm playing dumb. We were . . . something. Junior year was a weird time in my life. I was so focused on grades and graduating early that meeting Rex threw me for a loop. "I mean, we weren't enemies."

"Frenemies, then." His tone tells me he's smiling even if I can't look over. I don't think that's really what we were either, but maybe there just isn't a word for it. "And you didn't answer the question. I'm tipsy, but I can focus on what's important."

He says it as though I'm important. To him. A guy I shared one class with fifteen years ago who waltzes back into my life in a cloud of alcohol and chaos. His fingers trace the stitching on my car's seat, and the proximity makes me feel like I'm missing something.

"What question?"

"Are you sure you wanna get married?"

I sigh. All night I smiled and nodded my way through every conversation, but I can't deny that it felt good to unload a little bit. And surprisingly, Rex is a good listener. Maybe it's the alcohol dulling his senses.

"Randy is the best option by a mile. Especially in this town. As much as I love it, Winter Bliss doesn't exactly have a bustling singles scene."

Rex's mouth curls in a sneer I can barely see because of that overly thick mustache, but his sharp canines flash in the streetlight. The sight makes me shiver. Before he can say anything else, I park with a sudden jolt.

"We're here." Two doors down from The Deviled Egg in the back alley. "This neighbor doesn't have a security system, so stay close to the wall here and we'll scoot over so we don't trigger Mom's motion lights. I'll punch in the code, and if you're quiet going up the left side of the stairs, you won't wake them."

He follows, whispering behind me. "Never would have guessed Miss Birdie Lynn was the kind of girl who snuck boys into her house."

"Never?" I stop at the back door and cock an eyebrow at him. Truth is, I learned this trick when my moms were recovering from the flu and I didn't want to wake them up while dropping off groceries. But Rex can think I evolved into some mysterious cool girl with lots of boyfriends after he left.

"Nah." His voice is so low and quiet, I lean closer to hear it. "You were the good girl who made me think bad things."

Oh no. The goosebumps lighting up my arms are *not* a good girl reaction. Danger zone. Not good at all. This is his drunken nostalgia talking. And for me, it's been a long day. I'm way too tired to investigate the weird reactions and trains of thought this disaster of a demon is triggering in me. It's a fluke. A one-off.

I've had a strange night, and he's had a lot to drink.

He gives me an exaggerated wink and finger guns.

"Joker." I shove his shoulder. That mustache is not a good look and he's just as annoying as ever. Still, I can't ignore the little jolts of electricity I feel being around him again. What on earth is Rex Perchaz doing back in my life?

No. He's not in my life. He's in town for a few months. And okay, he's staying at my mom's place and I'll probably see him every Thursday because I don't miss my mom and Orla's home-cooked food. But *ahhh*. Maybe he'll forget all about this. Greg's hooch is the stuff of legends.

I punch in the code to the back door and step back, sending up a prayer to the gods and pantheons of every people group. *Let Rex forget about tonight.*

"Thanks for the ride." He passes by so close, I can feel the heat of his skin.

"A frenemy in need"—I click the side of my mouth and shoot finger guns back—"is a frenemy indeed."

After kicking off his shoes near the door, instead of closing it, he cocks his head and leans against the wooden frame, both forearms high on either side. The pose makes his already ginormous chest expand like he's got bat wings for back muscles. Barefoot, shirtless, in only jeans.

Honestly, it's kind of obscene.

"You know what I just remembered?" he asks.

"Hmm?"

"You never did answer that question, Birdie Lynn."

Chapter Three
Rex

15 years ago

There's something about this girl.

I'm just closing my locker door when she speed walks past the end of the hall.

It's gotta be that she's a human. Infernus Academy is serious and uppity and like 99-percent demons. They really only care about teaching us business skills. Humans don't usually go for that. But this girl's dad is some fancy big-city finance guy. He lectures here sometimes. I guess that's how she got in.

Birdie is her name. Cute, right? She kind of looks like one too, in a cool way. Her nose is long and straight, almost hawkish.

She's also the smartest person in school, tied for valedictorian and on track to graduate a year early. End of next semester or so I hear. Not that I ask. Too often.

I mean, I see her around from time to time. Hard not to. A brown face in a sea of red. Plus, she's pretty. I'm not blind. But she doesn't mess with demons, with anyone really. I don't think she has any friends besides her younger brothers.

The next bell won't be for a couple of minutes, but I fight the stupid urge to see where she went. I have to jog to another class to drop off my brother's notebook he left in my bag by accident. By the time I get back to the end of the hall, she's gone.

Crazy thing is, this Birdie girl and I are the same age, sixteen. But she's a grade ahead in the honors program and I'm two behind. Let's just say, the Special Education support is lacking at Infernus Academy and they didn't catch my dyslexia until I was already floundering.

My brothers make the grades. They'll achieve our parents' dream of running a successful corporation one day. I'm just sort of . . . here.

I don't really mind being the big idiot in a class with kids younger than me. Unlike the pretty human girl, I do have friends besides my brothers. Two actually. Who needs more than that? We're misfits but we don't take shit from anybody.

Today is the first day of fall semester's Manufacturing Handmade Goods. I trudge into the fancy name for shop class and see *her*.

My heart races. She's front and center in the first row, knees tucked together with a white satin ribbon in her hair. And Sneaky Simon is parked up behind her. Fuck that. He's a flirt to his core. I pick him up by the collar and shove him back, then claim the seat instead. My big, awkward body struggles to get comfortable in this metal cage they call a desk, and even though I'm jostling her chair, she doesn't turn around.

I've never been this close to her. When I lean in and inhale, it's just like I expected. She even smells pretty. Girl shampoo and spearmint gum.

She straightens and half turns, but pauses before I can see her face. Her shoulders rise, breathing a little faster. My demon sensibilities perk up. She's hiding *something*. We can only really sense heightened emotions in others, and she's giving off nothing. Totally locked down. Probably learned it from going to school with my kind for so long. But I could swear she wants to turn around.

If she'd just talk to me, I could figure out what it is about this girl that's got me so curious.

As the days drag on, the first thing I learn is that she's not as perfect as she looks. She's a total nerd, collects these dorky animal magazines. They peek out of her backpack. Oh, and she's really bad at shop class. Hilariously so.

She'd never even held a hammer in her life before our first project to build a six-inch box using a variety of techniques. After stubbing her thumb, she superglued two fingers together. I don't think my laughing at her gained me many brownie points.

No matter what I do, how much better my daily projects are than the rest of these losers, she never looks my way. And for some stupid reason, it's all I want. Impressing her isn't working. But one thing I'm really good at? Being annoying as fuck.

I start tapping my foot against the side of her chair leg. *Tap. Tap. Tap.* For minutes and minutes.

It bothers me that she's always so still and quiet. No fun and games. How every answer she gives the teacher is textbook. Something about it doesn't sit right with me.

So I tap the hard sole of my leather boot on her chair leg, real quiet but consistent. My brothers would have put me in a headlock and thrown my shoe across the room within the first two minutes. Not Birdie.

This girl has nerves of steel.

Until finally, she cracks.

Just before the end of class, right when the teacher steps out to the hallway, Miss Prim-and-Proper exhales a little huff, turns around, and glares at me.

"Stop it."

My foot drops and I widen my stance to lean in a little.

Man, oh man. It's the first time I've seen her eyes up close. Black lashes that curl up like a doll around her wide-set eyes. I know the color—brown—but hers is something better. A new version, I decide. A color that only exists for her. Two black ringlets fall out of her updo and over half of her face. When she blows them off with a quick exhale, not breaking eye contact, it's like seeing a real-time chink in her armor.

She doesn't say anything else, just glares at me. I'm no stranger to an old-fashioned staring content. And even though I'm happy as a pig in shit that she's finally paying attention to me, I want to keep pushing her buttons.

"See something you like?" I cock my head to the side.

Her eyes flare. The bell rings. And in a flurry of girl-scented air, she whips her bag over her shoulder and leaves the room.

I'm a goner.

That one moment—finally seeing up close all the fire she keeps restrained behind a sharp steel trap—it's the only thing my longtime curiosity needs to become a full-blown obsession.

Underneath all the *yes sirs* and *no ma'ams* is another girl, full of secrets.

And I want to see them all.

June, Present Day

"It'll get done," I growl at my brother through the phone, keeping my voice down since I know Thursday dinner at the inn is about to start and everyone's already gathered just downstairs. "I'm doing the drywall myself." He has the balls to sigh at that. What the fuck? He should take it as good news. I'll do a better job than the flake who backed out on me anyway, and I'd rather just get it done than waste more time finding someone new.

I've been back in Winter Bliss for two months now, and the Perkatory renovations have started spiraling into chaos. It's manageable, though. I think.

"Rex, come on," Rom says. "You've already got a lot on your plate."

"And I'll take care of all of it." I try not to hear his comment in a backhanded way, try not to believe he wants to limit my work because he thinks I'll fuck everything up. I may be a hot mess, emotionally and otherwise, but when the rubber meets the road, I get shit done for the family.

"We'll talk tomorrow," he sighs.

With that, I hang up and pause at the window in the stairwell. My forehead taps against the glass a few times, then I rock my head side to side, just to feel my horns hitting the solid wood of the framing. Since I was a kid, physical ticks like that helped me calm down, ground me in reality and my surroundings, rather than the chaos of my mind.

I'm not a thinker; I'm a doer. Tasks and projects are my bread and butter. A log that needs chopping. Quick concrete and water. Furniture to be assembled (with a cursory glance at the instructions). While the rest of my family are pros at boardroom negotiations and pulling together presentations on how to run a business where other people do the work, that's just not how I'm wired.

With that last call out of the way, I pocket my phone and straighten my shirt. The innkeepers don't need some sweaty elephant stinking up their dining room for The Deviled Egg's weekly family dinner, which all the bed-and-breakfast guests are invited to. I took a quick shower and put on my best button-up to make a good impression, even threw on a double spritz of cologne.

Ah, who am I kidding? I'm making the extra effort because Birdie will be there. Since I've been lodging here, she hasn't missed a family dinner yet. And some weeks, it's my only glimpse of her, since she mostly stays busy out at her place.

Rounding the dining room entrance, I pause when I catch sight of her. For a moment, I lose my breath. Her curly hair is piled high in a big bun and I think she's wearing a little makeup. Her dress is checkered, the kind of pattern you'd see on a picnic blanket or something but in cotton candy rainbow colors. The poofy short sleeves remind me of what an old-fashioned school teacher might wear.

Damn, she's cute.

Like she can hear my thoughts, her gaze shifts to me before straightening and facing her mom again. "Randy's been such a help with the planning." Birdie smiles and turns to the side. Only then do I register that her boyfriend is right beside her.

Fiancé. Fuck.

She's really doing it. She's getting married. And I've got a front row seat.

I grit my teeth and shuffle in, trying to be inconspicuous as I plop down in the only available spot, smack dab in the middle.

At least I can drown my sorrows in kebabs. I reach for one and my knee jostles the table. A bowl of gravy and the flower centerpiece almost topple over in the process. All seven guests grow quiet, some reaching for their glasses, like the table would shake itself upside down. Come on. It was just a little wiggle.

"Sorry," I mumble and give the married couple down the hall from me and Birdie's mom, Miss Eda, a sheepish smile. "Food looks great."

Birdie's fiancé clears his throat so she turns back to him instead. "We settled on a venue just today."

"Lovely!" her mom says.

What does Birdie see in this guy? Sure, he runs his own successful business. And yeah, maybe he smells nice, but almost too nice, like four spritzes of cologne instead of a respectable two. And okay, he can charm old ladies with a slick compliment and polite conversation. Is that what wet dreams are made of?

He just isn't right for her. Anyone can see that.

Can't they?

I glance at Orla, Birdie's stepmom, seated at one end of the long table, but the old demoness isn't even watching them. She's got a soft smile for Miss Eda. Ugh, she's no help. I move down the line to Old Ethel, her sister, at least ten years her senior.

I give a start when I realize she's watching me, sucking on her vape. The old bat always made me nervous as shit as a kid. I couldn't believe straightlaced Rom used to steal candy from her store. I wouldn't dare. She sees *everything*.

With a wordless smirk, she passes me the plate of kebabs. I sigh and give my first skewer a long, loving look before taking a bite. Grilled meat never let me down.

"That inn has such a pretty garden and ballroom," Miss Eda says.

"Wait, what?" I ask, mouth full of half-chewed lamb. Birdie loves her ranch. She should get married there, obviously. I swallow before asking, "Where?"

Birdie glances over like she forgot I was here. Probably did. Ever since that first night she drove my drunk, flirting ass home, she's done her best to ignore me.

"We're getting married at the Hellfyre Inn," she says, complete with a courtesy smile.

"What an inspiring venue for marriage," I mutter, hearing a low chuckle from Old Ethel.

Birdie's eyes narrow. If she's glaring at me, she's not ignoring me. I call it a win. Now it's time to ask the obvious question, surely on everyone's mind.

"Why not the ranch?"

"Retreat," Birdie corrects.

"Tuh-may-to, tuh-mah-to. That's really just the new glossy spin on it. You've got a tree farm and a ton of animals. Ranch is more correct."

Randy's smile is frozen on his face. The creases around his mouth don't match his eyes. I flick my tongue out to lick my lips, but really I'm tasting the air. There it is—a hint of smoke and sour milk. He hates me. It's something a demon just knows. Well, buddy, the feeling is mutual. And while Birdie may bite back at me, I never sense anything like that from her. She's a fresh flame and marshmallows. Even if she'd never admit it, she likes me. The nose knows.

Randy turns back to Miss Eda. "Centrally located in town is easier all around considering the logistics of visitors and such."

"In and out." The smile Birdie aims at her mom is wooden. She's trying to hide behind it, and it makes me itch. "It'll be done before we know it."

I raise an eyebrow and lift my water glass, in a mock toast. "Weird way of looking at your wedding day."

Birdie exhales, a cute almost snort, and cuts a murderous gaze my way.

I keep eye contact, determined not to look away first, and the longer she glares at me, the warmer my chest grows. Excited to have her signature intensity trained only on me. Her brows pinch tight, and she knows we're in a staring contest now. But I know Birdie, and she's a stubborn thing. So I pop a roasted potato in my mouth and suck on my finger, delighting in the half second her eyes fall to my lips before turning to her mom again, admitting defeat.

"We're keeping it small. Family and close friends only. Maybe fifty people, give or take."

My jaw rocks side to side, the soft innards of potato the only thing stopping my teeth from grinding together.

The translation of that statement is clear as day. I've got no chance of an invite.

Chapter Four
Rex

August, Two Months Later

Fuck, it's hot out there. I kick off my shoes and sigh at the air-conditioning in The Deviled Egg. I just took a shower, but one trip down the block to check in with my brother at Perkatory, and sweat is already beading between my horns.

I've got to hydrate or die-drate. It's almost time for Thursday night dinner, but a snack never killed anybody. As I head into the kitchen, I find Miss Eda bustling around, prepping savory smelling platters. Meatballs, fuck yeah.

"Thanks for stopping by Birdie's earlier, Rex." She beams at me from the oven, wiping her hands on her apron.

"No problem." I give her a nod and move to the fridge. "Happy to help."

"I know my daughter is grateful as well."

I barely manage to hold in my scoff as I tear open a string cheese, eating half in one chomp, then pick up an apple. There's a strained tone to her voice that I don't want to look into. Miss Eda means well, but four months into my time in Winter Bliss, Thursday night dinners have started to devolve.

The closer it gets to Birdie's wedding in October, something inside of me has gone a little haywire. She and I bicker like it's an Olympic sport over the dinner table—whether a hot dog is a sandwich or not (it is), if narwhals are real (no way), and why *The Giving Tree* is not sweet but an absolute horror show (I had nightmares for weeks).

Her moms do their best to keep the peace between us. I'm not dumb enough to miss the new decor in the dining hall. They've been ramping up the positive messaging. *Throw kindness around like confetti* is handwritten on a chalkboard sign. Last month, Orla asked me to hang a framed art print that reads simply, *Happy Happy Happy Happy Happy* in rainbow colors. And just a couple days ago, a tapestry showed up in blue felt with gold lettering. *Think before you speak. Is it true? Is it fair? Will it build goodwill? Does it benefit all?*

They're basically trying to hypnotize us into good vibes. And it's about as subtle as a sledgehammer.

Normally, Birdie and I only interact at these Thursday night dinners. The best day of the week in my opinion, though I can guarantee she wouldn't agree. But with construction at both new Perkatory locations at a lull, I've had a slow few days and been in town more than usual. At first, I kept busy helping around the inn—cleaning ducts, adding some insulation to the attic, and installing a few new light fixtures. But today, Miss Eda asked me to take some big storage bins she'd bought on sale out to the ranch. Birdie can definitely use them in the garage, which is a disaster. But when I ran into the contractor for the cabins in the barn loading wood into a spare stall, I tried to get the rundown on how construction was going.

Nowhere, basically. The cabins are months behind schedule. Mother have mercy, the woman needs help.

"She's had a rough go lately," Miss Eda pats my forearm as I lean against the counter and dig into the apple.

The contractor was tight-lipped about why they were so delayed, only saying she'd been indecisive about next steps after the cement foundations were poured. It took all my energy not to rough him up to get more answers. But that's not my place, even though it's like having fucking fire pox again, an itch that won't go away, seeing her struggle.

"The only on-time contractors work for the mob," I say, trying to make a joke of the setbacks. "Delays are inevitable. Gotta bake it into the plan and then ride their asses."

"I have a feeling you're good at that." She chuckles and shakes her head. "You'll be staying for dinner?"

"I never miss your home cooking." I wash my hands and study her. Is she asking because she doesn't want me to come? Maybe my bad attitude is making Orla and Miss Eda uncomfortable. "Promise I'll be on my best behavior tonight," I say, laying my palm flat against the center of my chest over the solar plexus chakra. "The fire within me is mine."

It's a demon vow of responsibility for one's actions. I really need to stop getting Birdie so riled up over the stupidest of arguments. And I will.

The side door flies open. Birdie kicks off her shoes and rushes into the kitchen. Her purse thumps against her hips like choreography as she swings the fridge door open, grabs an apple, and spins around to face us. She's fresh-faced in jeans and a lilac button-down shirt.

"Rex." She always seems surprised to see me, probably annoyed that I'm still around. And even though I know she doesn't see me romantically, the slow perusal she gives me every now and then makes me hot under the collar all the same.

I can never look away.

To her, I'm sure it's just a juvenile staring contest, a battle of wills she finds annoying but can't kick the habit of engaging in. To me, it's the few fleeting moments I'm able to capture her attention. Where she really sees me.

My body reacts every time, skin growing hypersensitive and tight while a warmth floods my chest. Words escape me completely, just like when I was an idiot kid partnered with her in shop class. I can never find the right things to say. Almost always, they're the exact wrong ones.

Today, her hair is up in a high ponytail that's kind of lopsided. A dozen or more curling tendrils fall free. In the fading golden light she's a vision of chaos and sun-darkened skin.

"Nice . . ." Oh shit, when did I open my mouth? Why am I talking? "Nice . . . uhhh . . . hair."

She pats some of the flyaways on the side with a pinched expression and her trademark snort. "I know I look like a disaster. You don't have to point it out." With that, she strides into the half bath.

I look to her mom. "It was a compliment!" I whisper.

"Help me with the *kofte*." She opens the oven and gestures to the meatballs.

I sigh and pull the tray out, shaking them all onto a big platter. We bring that and the *mezze*—an assortment of salad, grilled veggies, and fruit—into the dining room where Orla, Old Ethel, and a gaggle of ladies in town for a charity 5k are seated.

When Birdie comes in, her hair is plaited down the back, which is also pretty, but I feel a stab of regret that she thought I was making fun of her.

No fiancé this week, it seems. I fold my napkin three times while stealing glances at her, trying to hide my excitement.

The running club are a bunch of moms and get on the topic of the best foods for picky eaters. My ears perk up.

"Grilled cheese." I point my fork at the purple-haired lady across from me. "Pro-tip: Use mayonnaise instead of butter to grill it."

While they titter over that, Birdie laughs and shakes her head. "Gross."

"Mayo's just egg and oil, miss ma'am. Nothin' gross about it."

"I mean, mayo is fine." She waves her hand and pops a tomato in her mouth. "Mixed with ketchup as a dipping sauce or sparingly used elsewhere, sure. But to use for toasting your grilled cheese?" The exaggerated face she makes is hysterical.

"I've never seen your mouth contort like that. Does it hurt?" I lean over to poke her cheek, making the table shudder. She swats me away. "Don't knock it till you try it."

She shimmies her shoulders and dips her meat in yogurt sauce. "Thankfully Mom makes the food around here, so I'll never have to be subjected to such cruelty."

"Oh, don't bait me like that, honey. I'll make some right now." I stand up and gesture to the group. "As a treat. A savory little snack. Who wants to try my world-famous grilled cheese?"

The table seems amused, even Miss Eda, which is a damn sight better than how nervous she looked earlier. "Take out the baklava when the timer dings, please."

"Maybe we'll have a moment of peace," I hear Old Ethel murmur to her sister who just chuckles.

"I can't let them eat that." Birdie stands up, throwing her napkin down. "I'll make them a proper grilled cheese."

"A friendly competition!" This is what I'm talking about. I race to the kitchen at the same time she does. We slide on our socks and get kind of smushed together in the kitchen doorway. With a rough shove, she knocks me back a half step.

I'm having an absolute ball as I grab a pan for me and one for her while she places an apron on and snaps some metal clips to keep her hair pinned back.

She looks so fucking determined, so happily hostile, that when I snap my fingers to light our two burners, the fire lets off extra sparks I have to blow out.

She grabs for the sourdough, and I nod that I want to use the same.

"At least we agree on one thing," I say. "A grilled cheese on sourdough? Paradise!"

She rips off a small piece from the butt end with her teeth and chews. "Homemade too. Nothing better."

When she spins to open the fridge and get some cheese, I snag the mayo from the front.

"Your funeral," she smirks.

"No, *yours*." Juvenile response, but oh well. I grab some of her mom's favorite breakfast cheese. It's got a feta-like consistency but if I mix it with some brie and American cheese, I bet it'll kill.

We both warm our pans and prep our slices. She sprinkles her buttered bread with some kind of herb seasoning.

"Cute," I say. "But it's not gonna beat the mayo."

"You're annoying." Her elbow jabs just above my waist. "And in my way."

"Not my fault I'm a big guy." I jostle her back just to hear her stomp and growl. In front of an open flame in a small kitchen, I really shouldn't have goosebumps, but being around her always makes me feel upside down.

She chops up some American cheese with efficient ferocity. "You know Gigi and Mimi are just nicknames."

"The horses? Short for what?" I ask. And why the change in subject? She must be trying to slow me down. I snatch the American from her and slice some for myself while she goes to town on a block of cheddar. Classic choice. Can't fault her there.

"Their real names are Gouda and Mimolette." She grins at me, a delighted evil slant to her mouth as she lays her sandwich onto the hot pan. "I know my cheese, Rex Perchaz."

Fuck, she named her horses after cheese. She really is the perfect girl. The smell of melted butter wafts between us as I place my sandwich on the pan.

"And I know my mayo, Birdie Lynn." I say, loving her cute snort in response.

We step back and cross our arms on a silent staring contest, except she can't hide that little smile. I'm gonna win this cook off, but it doesn't even matter, because I have what I want. Her letting loose a little. Having fun. Even better that it's with me. After a minute or two, she picks up the spatula and checks the bottom of her sandwich.

It's time. The first flip. A.k.a. the best part of making grilled cheese, choosing that perfect moment when the bread is browned just right but none of the cheese falls out when it turns.

We both manage with no casualties.

As our second side toasts, Birdie looks over at my pan and her expression clouds. "Hmm."

"Yours came out a little blacker. That's weird," I say in the most innocent tone. "Might have to scrape some of the burn off to be edible."

"Mind yourself. I'm just fine." She lifts a corner of her second side up to check the toast and turns her burner off first.

I leave mine on an extra half a minute before plating it up, brandishing a big knife, and cutting it into eight little bites. Everyone can have a taste.

"Cut yours?" I offer. She slides it over and grabs some colorful toothpicks from up high. Her shirt rides up in the back so I get a glimpse of the muscles along her spine and the dramatic curve where her waist nips in.

She stabs my pieces with red-flagged toothpicks. Hers get blue. The timer dings, so I grab the baklava. Birdie carries the big plate of grilled cheese samples and passes it around.

Even without the colored flags it's easy to tell between ours. Her's is the decidedly darker toast and I don't think the thicker slab of cheddar melted all the way through.

"Well, ladies?" I raise my hands. "Blind taste test. Which one's better?"

Still chewing, Miss Eda, Orla, and three of the ladies hold up mine. Only one prefers Birdie's.

"The seasoning on this is good," Miss Eda pokes at Birdie's "But this one is cooked just right. And you used the *beyaz peynir*, didnt you?"

Oh, that's what it's called. She puts that cheese in the eggs every morning and it's fucking amazing. I nod and bow.

"But that's too soft for grilled cheese." Birdie glares at me.

"Sprinkle it in with another one gets gooey, and voila." I wink at Birdie's mom, knowing a cook will appreciate the secret weapon. "Mayo has a higher smoke point, so you can grill the cheese even longer."

"Inspired," Orla says, finishing off both.

"You're not a fan of either?" Birdie asks her step-aunt.

"I'm lactose intolerant." Old Ethel puffs on her vape. "Thanks for nothing."

The door bursts open with a clang. Shoes go flying.

"I have news!" Randy bursts into the room like a wet blanket over a toasty campfire. "Oh, grilled cheese."

"Have at it." Old Ethel hands him her plate.

He chomps on mine first, naturally, humming and nodding. "Good stuff."

Birdie exhales noisily and moves toward him, straightening her shirt. "What's up?"

He has a bite of hers, then sets the plate down. Throwing one arm up in a theatrical flourish, he says, "A Wild Hearts Holiday."

"A what?" she asks.

It's August. What fucking holiday is he talking about?

He grabs her by the shoulder, like a dad would to his kid showing them the Grand fucking Canyon or something and uses his other arm like he's painting the words in the air. "A Wild Hearts Holiday: Your Solstice Retreat. We'll hold a formal catered dinner on the patio to celebrate the new luxury cabins. I'm going to run an A/B marketing test on the term 'tiny home' to see if that sells better." He shakes his head. "Anyway, after today's city council session, a bunch of bigwigs were at Lucky Magic Diner and we got to talking. Townsend said he and his wife would be in town over the winter and wanted a solstice event to go to. Something more elegant than the corny winter holiday events."

"Wait, the Chamber of Commerce guy?"

"Yeah, him. And his wife, who knows practically every-one. Skylla Flarelion was there too—the real mastermind behind the Emberlight Resort. I've been trying to get her ear for months. When she showed interest in the idea of the event, I knew I had to act. Your place has a Christmas tree farm. The fireflies always look amazing at sunset. And by December, the cabins will be booked up with rave reviews from our first customers."

"You think?" She has two level plots with foundations. That's not nothing, but it only leaves a couple months to fully construct and interior design two livable cabins before the autumn and holiday tourist season? I'm as doubtful as she looks.

"It'll be the *perfect* opportunity to show the most influen-tial tourism and small business players in Winter Bliss what the Wild Hearts Retreat can offer. I didn't have time to run it by you since I had to improvise quickly, but I knew you'd love it."

"I do love the holidays," she says, even though it's clear as fuck she's shell-shocked and just nodding along.

I hate it. Makes my leg shake. She's already got to run her ranch, a Christmas tree farm, construction, guests, and he's adding a formal party on top of all that?

"It's settled then." He squeezes her by the shoulders until she winces. "A Wild Hearts Holiday."

Birdie looks an odd shade of gray as she sits down, lost in her thoughts, so I pass the plate of baklava over. She grabs it, but I don't let go of my end until she looks up at me. "You alright?"

She tugs the plate harder and, before popping a piece of the flaky dessert into her mouth, breaks eye contact to stare at the tablecloth. "I'm fine."

October, Two Months Later

"To the happy couple!" A sparkling glass is raised in the air.

Champagne glitters in a sea of crystal as the crowd toasts, "To the happy couple!"

I throw back the bubbly liquid and relish in the burn as it flows down. That feels a lot better than the grim, dark emotion threatening to pound out of my skull. Tonight of all nights, I feel like an absolute shitbag.

"Thank you all for celebrating Rom and Noelle's engagement with us," Mom says to close the toast.

My brother is engaged. It's great or whatever, but that's not what has my mind a riot of radicalized hornets.

Birdie is getting married. Tomorrow morning.

"It's such a pleasure to be back in Winter Bliss seeing my son find his forever partner." She clears her throat, and it kills me that the first time I see my usually stoic mother overjoyed to tears, I can't share in the feeling. Dad passes her a handkerchief and she dabs at her eyes before sighing. "Enough with the waterworks. I know Rom has a speech prepared."

She hands my younger brother the microphone. He cracks his neck, readjusts his glasses, and locks in on the redhead he's loved since he was a kid. She's curled against his side, staring at him like he's the only person in the room.

"Noelle." He swallows, and I recognize the light tremor in his hand. He's nervous. As the middle brother and shy to his core, Rom was never one for the spotlight. He may be the smartest of us all, but when it came to public debate class, he muddled through, usually with my older brother to step in or me to offer some physical distraction. But being up there alone, expected to pour his fucking heart out to a packed room full of friends and family? This must be torture for him. When he doesn't continue, Noelle rubs a small circle, right over the center of his chest. He takes a shaky inhale and instead of clamming up, stammering, or handing the mic back as I'd expect, he smiles. Like, he full-on grins with all his fucking teeth.

What the fuck?

"Noelle," his voice is deeper. Louder, like some kind of actor body snatched my shy brother. "Meeting you was coming home."

I blink in shock through the first minute or so of the engagement speech. It's . . . a lot. Personal and endearing and heartbreaking in the sweetest way. Poetry this. Eternity that. The thing is, I'm happy for him. I am. But seeing a love like that transform my brother weirdly just intensifies the deep, dark fucking misery in my gut.

That same spark will never happen for me. I've only felt it for one person, and that's clearly a lost cause. I'll be honest; watching Rom and Noelle right now kind of stings.

Time to raid the appetizer table.

I slink away without catching my mom's attention. She's a keen old demoness, but thankfully completely glassy-eyed watching her son prepare for marriage.

And while Rom is happy as a clam being in Winter Bliss, I'm getting the fuck out of this town tomorrow. The next two Perkatory locations only need interior design to be launch ready. Managing two projects in under six months was pretty impressive. We came in under budget despite several setbacks. It was kinda fun to flex some old skills in flooring and custom carpentry when I had to pitch in for a couple contractors that flaked out.

Workwise, everything's good.

Emotionally, I'm a wreck.

Birdie's getting married. In the morning. Everytime I re-member, my fucking fingers go tingly and numb. At least seeing the engagement party from afar isn't quite so un-nerving. My family's joy is easier to take when I'm not sur-rounded by it, pressured to take part, to chime in, to smile. I don't mirror emotions well. I feel what I feel, and it always shows. I'm better in the shadows, supporting them by running errands and shit. Staying busy.

I make it to the front of the restaurant to see what's left of the finger foods. Another engagement party, another charcuterie board. And even the fresh burrata on a crunchy sourdough doesn't inspire a flicker of positive emotion.

I'm truly broken.

The door opens. A rush of crisp fall air washes over me with the hint of evergreen. Somehow, even before I turn, I just know.

It's Birdie. Alone.

She pushes the hood of her sweatshirt off and loosens the shawl at her neck, the one I know her mom made for her, her favorite when the night gets chilly after dinner. Her hair is down tonight, a mass of wild curls around her face that makes me ache. She rarely wears it like that.

Her gaze locks onto Rom and Noelle, and even though she's only a few paces away from me, as usual, she doesn't see me.

But my greedy fucking eyes take their fill of her. The soft light of the room flickers gold across the long slope of her nose, making her dark eyes sparkle. Her expression is strange though, something a smarter guy could write a sonnet about—tragic and curious and just this side of mysterious. In the end, the poor bastard would realize there's really no way to put her to words.

Her eyes are deep brown, but right now, they look black. True darkness. A demon's holiest color.

"Birdie Lynn." Her name escapes my lips without thinking, and she glances over. I can't fucking stop my stupid mouth around her.

Normally, seeing me, she'd straighten her back and bring her walls up, maybe say something delightfully snarky. I wait for it, the usual banter that makes me light up, but it never comes.

Instead, she closes the distance, tucking her hands in the pocket of her hoodie and watching me the whole way. With only a step between us, she stops and turns back to where my brother yaps on about true love.

"They're perfect for each other," she says quietly. Almost too quiet.

They are. Objectively and spiritually and on every plane of assessment.

I clench my jaw tight.

Why are you here? I want to ask. *You're getting married tomorrow and I'm not invited. Are you nervous? How is construction going?*

But I don't say any of that, because every time I speak, I say the wrong thing. Above and below it all, drinking in the sight of her, I know that this moment is it. The last time I'll see her before she's a married woman. Maybe the last time ever, if I can stay away from this goddess-blessed, blissed-out town long enough to forget the prettiest girl I ever knew.

When she turns to me, all I see in her eyes is the same joy my mom has. There's no trace of whatever haunted her coming in. Maybe the darkness was a figment of my imagination. Maybe I wanted to see something doubtful and hurt about her, as fucked up as that is.

"They're so in love," she says, trying to share her happiness with me, like she thinks I should be happy my brother is getting married. And, fuck, I wish I was, but I'm torn up over her instead. And that's the last thing I'd say the day before she gets married.

"Just like you and *Raymond*." I go for a joke that comes out harsh instead.

Her smile melts away. She inhales and straightens her spine, gaining a solid inch or two in height. "Is Randy such a hard name to remember?"

"It is for me." My teeth grind.

There's no darkness in her eyes now. No doubt. Just fire.

I love and hate it, because I draw it out of her, no one else, but it always pushes her further away from me.

Are you sure you wanna get married? That's what I asked all those months ago. That's what I should have fucking asked now, just once more, in a soft tone, not a sharp joke. Instead, I played the fool. It's the same question that's been on repeat in my mind all these months, the question I know the answer to even if she won't admit it to herself.

She's not.

She shouldn't marry a guy just because he's sorta half decent.

But Birdie has a spine of steel and is committed to a fucking fault, two things I've always admired about her.

She pulls a greeting card out of her purse and hands it to me. "Give this to Rom and Noelle, please."

I nod, jaw tight, willing myself not to say another stupid fucking thing.

"Thanks," she says, and with that, turns and walks back to the door.

Panicked, I yell out, "Congratulations."

Imbecile.

She doesn't even acknowledge me as the door swings shut behind her.

Chapter Five
Birdie

15 years ago

I egged him on.

"Awesome amphibians?" His voice is way deeper than most boys.

The day I acknowledged that Rex Perchaz exists, I brought this on myself.

Papers rustle and I barely suppress a growl, twisting around in my desk to snatch my magazine out of his giant grubby hands. It's brand new and I'm not about to let him get it all greasy.

"Looking for your frog prince?" He leans back, folding his arms behind his head. The school uniform is way too small on him. His arms are thick, and I can't ever figure out if it's muscle or fat. Probably both. Not that I look at him often.

His lips pucker and make a smacking sound.

Frog prince? Sure. If my frog prince was the beautiful *Thaumaturgus Amphibius Magnificens* from East Africa, featured on this month's cover of *Wildlife Unbound.* That frog is so rare, you bet your butt I'd kiss its red-and-purple spotted head if I saw one. Well, as long as I had an antidote ready. They're beautiful but also extremely poisonous.

I snatch the magazine back. "Gross."

As soon as I turn around in my seat, a better retort starts formulating. After vibrating for a minute, wishing I'd said something snappier, really stuck it to him, Mr. Slaytic pauses his demonstration of safety measures with electrical switches to grab more supplies for the room.

I hiss over my shoulder, "Kissing a frog *would* be infinitely more enjoyable than kissing you."

Ha! Got him. I wiggle in victory.

He leans forward, so close his breath tickles my hair, and whispers near my ear, "So you *have* thought about kissing me?" There's a smile in his voice. I just know it.

No. The word doesn't even make it past my lips as he wraps his finger around a curl. I feel the movement even though he doesn't pull or yank like my annoying little brothers do when they sit behind me in the car. Rex prefers to loop my hair around his fat finger and tug. He fiddles with it, applying enough pressure that my whole body tingles.

What was I thinking? I shouldn't have left it half down today. The day of shop class. The subtle motion of him behind me and the sound of him breathing makes everything inside me tighten, ready to snap. And now he's close enough I can smell him. It's just soap, I think, but it's nice. Clean. I think he must have gym class right before this.

My leg shakes. I can't take it anymore, so I sweep a hand behind my neck and snatch my hair over my right shoulder.

He always has this effect on me. Flirts with me as a joke.

And I always burn. Without fail, my cheeks flame. My neck flashed hot. If I could breathe fire, I would.

The way he always has that evil little smirk, I just *know* it's a trap. Because I'm the weird human kid in school and he's this tall rebellious demon who obviously doesn't care about rules or grades or doing anything the way they tell us to. Boys like him make meals of studious kids like me. Always poking at me. Big bully. He's just waiting for me to fall prey to the bad boy flirtation so he can turn around and laugh in my face. I just *know* it.

A warm gust of air floats across my exposed neck and ear. Except we're indoors and there's no breeze to be had. I know what he's up to now. Without even looking, I shoot my hand back to grab the drinking straw, one of his favorite implements of torture, and dig the kitten heel of my uniform shoe into the toe of his boot where it always creeps up under my desk.

Ever since I stopped ignoring him, fighting back is my only option. Because ignoring Rex Perchaz is impossible.

Present Day

As soon as the restaurant door closes, the night swallows me whole. Over the mismatched rooftops of Winter Bliss, fireflies twist in a twilight swarm over the lake. From town, the sight is little more than a flickering mass of rainbow lights, almost like a mirage, but if I was on the ranch, it would take my breath away.

Gosta fireflies are a rare, multicolored breed. They tend to stick together in family groups of similar colors, so up close you can see the small pods in similar hues as they dance around and between their neighbors of other colors. The rare off-color matches are mating pairs and easy to pick out—red and yellow or blue and purple or any other combination. It's like a little miracle when you can spot them. Love matches of opposites, I like to think.

Like Rom and Noelle.

"Lemmy, stop it." I halt and pull the prairie dog out of my hoodie pocket, his face to mine. "I know you think those are love bites, but they sure don't feel like it."

He was domesticated from infancy by a shady, unregulated animal shop off a back highway. I got hold of him when they closed down. And man, he's a cute little thing, even more so lately because of the tiny cast on his leg, making him look so helpless and innocent. But he's not. Those front teeth are no joke, and he's got no one but himself to blame for the broken leg.

I scratch his head and pick up a small branch off the ground, kicking myself for not bringing a better chew toy. He already ate tonight and I don't want him crapping in my clothes, so this'll do until we get back home.

Recently, Lemmy got stuck in the fencing I erected specifically to keep him out of the air vents. He's an escape artist and always looking for tunnels. But the fencing did its job, far too well, because he twisted himself up bad enough he broke his femur, saddling me with a $1,000 vet bill. At this point, I should just go back to school and become a vet myself with how much of a frequent flier I am. If the good doctor had a loyalty card, I'd be rolling in points. With a broken leg, he can't burn off his excess energy running around and tends to get into more trouble when left alone for long periods of time. So lately, he's been my little buddy wherever I can carry him.

For the last hour, he's been napping in my pocket, snuggled up, but usually he likes to poke his head out every chance he gets. It's why I didn't go too far into the restaurant.

With him safely ensconced back in my pocket, I can feel him going to town on the branch, so I rush down the street, eager to link up with Randy so I can get back home.

The streets are quiet. It's past eight, so people are where they plan to be for the night. I drove in to pick up some packages at my postbox and drop off a card for Noelle and Rom's engagement party. They weren't expecting me, but I wanted to go, and I'm glad I did.

They really are so in love.

Just like you and Raymond.

My exhale comes out like a growl as I quicken my steps and tighten my shawl, seeing Rex's stone-cold expression in my mind. That damned messy demon sets me on edge. Is Randy really such an impossible name to remember? Every word out of his mouth is a live wire straight to the bratty little girl who told him off in class. I can barely breathe around him sometimes. He's annoying. Brash. Unsettling.

And he's leaving Winter Bliss tomorrow. Mom told me offhandedly a few days ago. I pause on the sidewalk and look back. Was that the last time I'll see him? My stomach twists.

Maybe I'm hungry. I really should have picked up a plate from that engagement party. I forgot to eat dinner and just scarfed down some chips in the Jeep on the way over here. I'll stop by the diner before they close. To-go, since I'm sure a prairie dog isn't exactly welcome. The thought of some warm soup in a bread bowl is enough to lift my spirits though.

I love it here. Well, I love my ranch the most, but Winter Bliss is a close second. It's big enough that there are tons of great shops and restaurants, but small enough that if you frequent them, people remember you by name. Some folks hate the idea of moving back to their childhood hometown but for me, it was the opposite. Living in New York was suffocating. You can't see the stars. Having even a single pet is a production. I barely felt like I could stretch out. Even in yoga classes, we were packed arm to arm like sardines.

Having a prairie dog in my pocket? I'd probably be locked up for fifteen health code violations. Here, I get the odd stare if people notice, but it's mostly a live-and-let-live kind of town.

Moving home to Winter Bliss and buying my wild plot of land was the best decision I've ever made. I'm like a walking Hallmark movie heroine, down to owning a Christmas tree farm and getting engaged to a local guy.

And tomorrow's my wedding day.

I used to dream about quiet nights, living off the land, and having a simple life.

And I have it.

Don't I?

I hope Randy's okay. He hasn't texted me back since we video chatted over lunch about the wedding eve to-do list. He took care of all the town stuff while I took care of the ranch tasks. We're going to ride away from the reception on my two horses, so I got them groomed and all the food and supplies prepped.

And since we wanted the walk down the aisle to be the first time we see each other on the wedding day, we won't even stay with each other tonight. If I can catch him, we can have one final moment together before everything gets crazy tomorrow.

I try his phone again but it goes straight to voicemail. It must have died. He's been putting his back into all the logistics these last few days. As I turn the corner to his travel agency office, which he lives directly above, I see the light still on through the storefront window.

He really works hard. It's the first thing we bonded over when we met at a speed dating event in town. His work ethic and mine are perfectly aligned, and it turns out, our life visions are too. We love Winter Bliss and want to see it shine. Randy is at the forefront of the booming travel industry, connecting the local luxury resort clientele with small-town businesses. And I want to spearhead more awareness and protection of local wildlife. At times, those can seem like disconnected or even opposing goals, but my ranch hosting ecotourism is how we'll make it work.

"Hey! Randy, you here?" I call out as the door jingles behind me.

He's hunched over his desk and looks up, bleary-eyed, until he smiles. "Hey, you!"

We hug, and he immediately sits back down, pointing to his screen. "I know you said no honeymoon, but check this out. There's a last-minute package to Greece for a five-night cruise and three nights on land. Plane tickets are a steal."

"There's no way." I shake my head, hands wringing. That's eight days plus travel time. "The animals."

Lemmy takes the opportunity to pop out of my pocket.

"I thought something smelled weird." Randy looks at him with an exhausted expression, then back up to me.

"Fun fact: Prairie dogs have the most complicated language of any animal species ever decoded, including kissing to reinforce affection."

He pulls a cringe face that I think was meant to be a courtesy smile and sighs. "Listen, I could book the tickets for a couple days from now. With everyone at the wedding, I'm sure you can find people willing to feed the animals or whatever. They could cover the chores in shifts."

Normally, I'm a pushover with anything he wants, but the animals need a lot of specialized care that's hard to cover and the delays in construction have added hours of stress to my days and dozens of gray hairs to my head. I feel a grimace creasing across my face, the one I usually try to hide.

"Randy. There's just . . . there's no way. Not right now. There's way too much to do." I run a hand through my hair, pacing in front of his desk. "I mean, we could have maybe done a short trip over the summer if we hadn't gotten engaged on a whim."

Immediately, I worry that I hurt his feelings, but he just studies his computer screen with obvious disappointment before looking up at me like he's ready to say something when he stops.

"Hmm. Yeah." A strange look passes over his face as he glances from me to Lemmy. He swallows and stands, clasping my shoulder in an odd pseudo-embrace. I *do* have a stinky wild animal on my person. "You heading back out there soon?"

"Yep. Lemmy's up past his bedtime. Gotta make an early night of it." A morning wedding in town seemed like a good idea until I factored in all the prep time, then getting myself to the Hellfyre Inn. It's the practical choice for guests but not at all for me. I sigh. "Hair and makeup will be at the ranch at 4:30 a.m., then I'll need to get the horses loaded up. But I'm going to grab a bite to eat at the diner right now before I head out. You want to come with?"

"No thanks. I went to the sandwich shop earlier. Actually, Skyla Flarelion was there." He squeezes my shoulder and sits back down. There's light in his eyes for the first time all night. "She's really excited about A Wild Hearts Holiday. I wanted to finish off the PR flier for the event and email it over to keep it on her mind. We could be the most talked about holiday party in the county."

The holidays? I know it's still a couple months away, but I am seriously worried the cabins won't be done by then and a formal catered dinner will be all for nothing. But now's not the time to voice that. Or the small pang of sadness that he doesn't want to spend time together tonight, even if it's just to walk a few blocks away and get some food. Since getting engaged, our relationship has become even more distant than it was when we were dating.

I try to push it from my mind. Marriage is different than love, at least in my eyes. Everything about my life right now is laser focused on my responsibilities. I have a tree farm and animals I need to care for. That is more important to me than waiting around for some fairytale love. I'm practical enough to be satisfied with the best available option.

Good enough is good enough.

"I'm glad," I say. "About the event. And cc me on the email, please." Sometimes he forgets to include me in all these plans. I slide my hand into his for a quick squeeze.

His thumb rubs over my knuckles as he takes in the delicate henna design my mom and stepmom painted on my skin last night.

"Nice," he says. His smile doesn't meet his eyes.

While a bride's henna night is usually ladies-only, I tried to involve him in several other Turkish traditions my mom suggested. But every idea just sort of fell through. I mean, we've been busy. A few months isn't nearly enough time to splash out on everything my family would've wanted. It's fine.

"See you tomorrow," I say, and for some reason it almost comes out as a question.

"See you." He brings my knuckles to his lips for a chaste kiss. His nostrils flare and he grimaces. Oh crap, they probably don't smell great thanks to the wild rodent I've been holding all night. I back away with my fake-it-till-you-make-it smile working overtime. Randy's expression is like a mirror image.

We're both tired and nervous, but that realization bolsters me. We're in this together.

Chapter Six
Rex

"What's gotten into you?" Mom asks, trying to push some hair off my forehead, like if she looks closer at my eyes, she'll figure it out.

Fuck, she probably will.

"Nothing." I slam a folded chair into the rack and look away. Crap, I bet it's the way I'm stacking these chairs like they owe me lunch money that tipped her off to my rotten mood.

"I'm your mother, Rex. I know when something's upsetting you."

"I'm sick of this town, okay?" I flip the last table over and get to work collapsing the legs. "I did the job you wanted done, didn't I? I'm just ready to get home."

"You're all packed?"

"I had one duffel, and it's good to go." With all the tables and chairs in the supply closet, I slam it closed and head to the bar. Maybe a drink will settle my nerves. The champagne was a nice feeling. I need a nice feeling right about now.

She follows me. "Go back to The Deviled Egg, my emberling. Get some rest. We have a long drive to the airport tomorrow."

I grab an empty beer mug and catch the bartender's eye, nodding at the dregs of the last champagne bottle. "I'll take the rest of that."

My teeth grind together as Mom watches the bartender finish it off. Her eyes flare a deep scarlet, almost black. She doesn't want me to drink. I'm a well-known lightweight, not the tolerance anyone expects in a big guy, since I almost never drink. But my pride never quite makes the connection, and I have a habit of getting messy.

I chug the champagne. The burn registers, fast and delicious.

"He's done," Mom says. The bartender nods respectfully. She points at me. "Sleep it off."

U nder the Volcano is a cool tiki bar up on a hill that serves a damn good burger. Now normally, I do whatever my mom tells me, but I'm not here to drink my sorrows away. I'm here for answers.

Birdie's been quiet about the cabin construction the last month or so at dinners. That can't be good news. She'd be talking our ears off if things were going well.

Can I really leave Winter Bliss if she's in a bad spot? The only way to ease my mind is to hit up some local watering holes of contractors. I know the team lead of the construction crew she's got lined up likes to watch rugby up here from time to time.

"What's up, Oatmeal?" I slap his back.

As expected, the big, bald orc is watching a bunch of buff-ass ladies beat each other up on a TV over the bar. He helped me bust down a wall in one of the back rooms of Perkatory recently. Good guy.

"Rex." He nods before turning back to the screen. "What's up, brother?"

"How's work out at Birdie's place going?"

"Standstill." He shakes his head. "Foundation crew didn't realize she needed a septic system and utilities up there. Just laid solid slabs down. She's been sitting on it for a couple months now. Had to move her off my schedule until she makes a decision."

My leg shakes where I stand. Installing pipes under an already-made foundation is a nightmare. What the fuck is she gonna do? I know what I want to do—pitch in with Oatmeal's crew and help her avoid future blunders. But

I've got a nonrefundable one-way ticket home, and she's getting *fucking married* tomorrow. Facts are facts.

"Thanks, man." I pound a fist on the table, resolving to call Miss Eda in a few days for more info. I bet I could get Perkatory to fly me back to Winter Bliss for the grand opening of the next locations in a month or so.

My fists flex as I try to problem solve, but my mind is sluggish. It's probably that damn champagne kicking in. I need to soak it up with some greasy food.

"What'll you have?" The bartender sidles over.

"Top him up." I nudge Oatmeal with a nod of thanks. "And I'll have a nacho burger."

"We only serve food at the tables." His chin lifts to the tabletops behind me. "But I'll get it started with the wait-ress."

"Thanks, man."

Making my way through the dark dining area, I don't like how crowded the seating is, so I head out to the porch instead. A breath of fresh air would be nice. Growing up bigger than most, I became hyper aware of how much space I take up. Sometimes, for peace of mind, it's just easiest to stay out of people's way.

There's only one person outside, and I recognize his puny set of horns right away. What a twist of fate seeing him back here.

One of my two oldest friends.

Vale.

Last we spoke, he'd moved to Hollywood to play Thraxxius in a reboot of a popular sci-fi TV show. I watched it just for a chuckle, but ended up binging the whole series. My dude's pretty fucking talented. Keep meaning to call and tell him that.

Man, he's different now than when we were thick as thieves back in school. Fifteen years will do that to anyone. No longer a stringy little weirdo, he's got style. He leans a little closer to his single basket of tater tots and takes a big ol' sniff. Hmm, still a weirdo, after all.

"Are you gonna eat those or just eye fuck 'em?" I ask.

"Go get your own food," he snarls, whipping around, but when he sees me, he bolts up out of his chair. Shock is written all over his face. "Rex?"

I can't help but laugh. He was about to run me through for trying to snatch a couple cold tater tots. Vale was such a pip-squeak back in the day, but he's always had a fighter's spirit. The guy never backed down from a tussle. Trading insults was our typical hello.

"Mr. Hollywood." I step closer, kind of amazed we're nearly the same height. I used to throw him around, play-wrestling as kids. Just like my own brothers, I never took it easy on him, and he got better over time. Had to, what with all the bullying. He and Rom both had wicked stutters as a kid. We met in their speech therapist's waiting room. "I almost didn't recognize you, bro. I don't know how it's possible, but you got uglier."

He grins and, besides the horns, it's nearly the only familiar thing about him anymore. "And you got stupider."

He tips his head forward in the sign he's ready to tussle. Alright then, cowboy. Let's see what you got. We shove each other and lock horns. His are short enough, I'm not about to get caught. The muscle memory in how we play fight is automatic. He recognizes some of my moves but can actually counter them with strength now.

I feel . . . proud of him. Happy, I think, for the first time in a long time.

After a minute, I notice him breathing hard. He may work out with a trainer for the stars, but I work outside day in and day out. My stamina is on point. I twist him into an easy headlock, complete with ruffling his fancy hair. "Let me buy you a drink. I've got some food coming anyway."

This is how I want to spend my last night in Winter Bliss, hanging out with an old friend. End it on a high note.

"Rex!" It's my name but Vale is the one who lights up.

"I didn't tell you!" He elbows me. "Iggy's here too! Crazy, right?"

"What? Really?" I turn around and there she is.

A skinny, sleek-looking demoness grabs a tray full of shots and beer from a waitress and heads our way.

"Freak!" Her old nickname flies out of my mouth. Back in freshman year, she was the kooky goth kid into spiders and black lace veils and shit, Vale was the runt with the stutter, and I was the sixteen-year-old loser held back two grades. Total misfits.

Naturally, we three were the best of friends.

Now, they couldn't be more different. Iggy's in an all-black outfit, real put-together and walking with confidence, like she owns the room and we're just lucky to be in her presence.

It's damn good to see people grow into their own. They're two demons going places. Whereas, what am I doing? Odd jobs for my family business. Perkatory isn't mine; it's definitely not my passion. I just sort of hang around my successful family like dead weight.

Yeah, I'm gonna need that drink. Luckily, Iggy's got us covered. I steal one of her shots and grab the bowl of peanuts off the tray. She insults me with a grin and pours me a glass of beer from the pitcher.

We all chitchat for a while. The beer is tasty, so I have a refill.

Conversation with them is as easy as ever. Casual cursing. Talking shit. Nothing is all that serious. When the topic of moving back to Winter Bliss comes up, we each agree, that's a big fat no.

Not with Birdie running around married. Eventually she'll get all cute and pregnant, pop out a brood of curly-headed kids with big, pretty eyes.

Makes me sick to my stomach.

Time flies.

We talk about nothing and everything. I think I wrestle with someone else, but my mind keeps circling back to Birdie.

I can't believe she's getting fucking *married* tomorrow morning. How many hours to go now? I look at my phone. The numbers kind of blur together. That happens at night sometimes, vision just gets a little goofy.

Will she have wedding bells after the ceremony? That always seemed kinda nice. I wonder if I'll still be around town when it happens. I should want to leave early for the airport, but I kind of . . . I kind of hope I'm still around.

What if I came down the stairs tomorrow and saw Orla and Miss Eda dressed up all nice for the wedding? I'd give them the biggest hugs. And maybe, I mean, there's always a chance I could see Birdie again. Just once more.

I wouldn't say anything stupid this time. I'd be real nice.

An image of her in a wedding dress comes to life in my mind. She'd wear something lacy or linen, maybe both. Off-white, I think. Yeah, a warmer shade would look better if she was outdoors under the big oaks near Teapot Lake with her hair down. There's a perfect spot on her ranch where you could put out a few hay bales in a half circle and throw quilts over them for some color. Lanterns would hang in the tree limbs, and if it's right at sunset, the fireflies would drift by. It'd be an intimate ceremony. Magical, in a gentle sort of way. The animals could all be involved too, ring bearers and shit.

I laugh to myself. Fuck, I'd love to see that.

Thinking about her in a wedding dress doesn't even hurt.

Nothing hurts anymore.

Everything's just kind of hazy and nice. Real nice. My mind wanders through the prettiest daydream. Birdie in a wedding dress with flowers in her hair.

"You're so drunk, dude." Vale pushes my shoulder. I fall to the floor in slow motion.

Weird, that didn't hurt either.

"No way." I chuckle. Rather than try to regain my seat, I scoot back and let the wall hold me up. My horns rock against the wood. That's nice. Familiar. "Just feelin' good. My friend's getting married tomorrow. Wish I could see it."

"Just a couple minutes ago, you threatened to kill someone and we almost got into a bar fight. Sure you're *feelin' good*?"

"Wait, I did? Who?"

Vale just laughs. I think he's the drunk one. Silly billy.

"Hold on, who's getting married?" Iggy thumps my forehead. I snatch her wrist and growl. She bares her teeth right back. Shit starter.

"Birdie." I can't seem to remember much else, but her . . . I couldn't forget her if I tried.

"Your bird is getting married?" Iggy punches Vale's shoulder and they both giggle which turns into a chuckle that devolves into gut-busting chortles.

"What—oh, goddess—what's on the registry?" Vale struggles to get the words out because he's cackling like a maniac instead of breathing. "A double-wide cage?"

Iggy wheezes. "A sparkly pair of swings?"

"A *Home Tweet Home* sign?" Vale adds.

They're both basically choking on their own laughter. Couple of idiots.

My mind is stuck on something that feels important.

"Her registry! Fuck me, I never got Birdie a gift." I unlock my phone with my face since my passcode doesn't seem to be working and search for her wedding registry using voice commands. Nothing comes up. I know the address to her ranch. I'll just have to wing it and send something there.

"What's a good wedding gift?" I ask Iggy and Vale.

"Who's getting married?" Vale asks.

It's been all of five minutes. Dark Mother, they are really drunk. I don't even dignify that with an answer.

"I need options for the best damn wedding present you can think of." I point to Iggy. She's a girl, she should know. "Go!"

"A toaster."

"Lame." I point to Vale. "You're up, Hollywood."

"Crystal flutes."

"She lives on a ranch, dipshit. Birdie's not a fancy kind of girl. And anyway, what's she gonna do with those? Toast her lame-ass, limp-dick husband over dinner? Fuck that." I pet my mustache, thinking, when the perfect solution comes to me. "I'll shave off my mustache. She hates it! That's perfect. Real unconventional."

Iggy blinks at me. "I mean, it is ugly."

"Hey!"

"Like an overweight bug." Vale tries to poke it, and I smack his hand away.

"So who's got a knife?" I ask.

"Oh! Oh! I got one." Iggy bounces in her seat, a little too aggressively, so I grab the leg of the chair to keep her stable.

"Sweet. Give it." I hold my palm out.

"No, not a knife. Holy Darkness, I'm not a twelve-year-old boy trying to prove I have hair on my balls. Who carries around a knife for no reason?"

"Plenty of guys with hairy balls, thank you very much. I just packed mine up already and didn't bring it tonight."

"What I meant to say is I thought of a good present for your lady friend's wedding," she says.

I roll my arm like a crank, ready to hear their next horrible suggestion.

"A fancy showerhead!" She claps.

"Hmm." I imagine Birdie in the shower. Oh yeah, all those glistening curves. Totally nude. Yes. Yes, that's a good idea. Then I picture her fucking *husband* sliding into the shower with her, how he gets to see her like that, how he'd change the fancy controls of the showerhead so it's just a gentle mist coating her dark, curly eyelashes. All romantic and shit. I shake my head. "Fuck that. Her husband will enjoy it too much."

"You sure about that?" Iggy leans down so we're eye level.

I'm missing something and she can see it in my face because she boops my nose. It's a gentle boop so I don't retaliate with a bite. This time.

"All a guy's gonna do with a nice showerhead is set it to turbo blast and forget about it," she says. "But a woman? She'll find the perfect setting to pleasure herself with. If it's got a lot of options, she might even find two or three ways."

My body flashes hot.

Birdie's smart. And subtle. She would do that, wouldn't she? She'd read every page of the instructions and sneak away from that dingleberry asshat she shares a bed with. He'd be incapable of pleasing her, I'm sure of it. She'd turn on the shower and brace herself against the wall. Get comfortable. Let the sensation of a hundred jets of water slide over her skin until the room fogged up. She'd click over to her favorite setting, widen her legs, and move the showerhead into place. She'd take her time.

And *every* time she used it, she'd think of me. She wouldn't be able to stop herself. It'll be just like I'm there, right down on my knees. Holding her open. Drinking her up.

"Fuck yeah," my voice breaks a little. Best present ever.

"I know just the one." Iggy wiggles her fingers at me until I hand my phone over. She finds a showerhead in the blink of an eye and adds it to my cart. "Just enter her address here."

I focus real hard. Like really, really hard. Use the voice command, then edit the address by hand and reread it at least ten times before I hit the purchase button.

When my phone dings with a confirmation email, I jump to stand and put Iggy in a headlock. "You're a fuckin' genius, girl. I owe you one."

"So, you're keeping the mustache?" she frowns.

"Nah." I pat her back. "Birdie deserves two gifts, minimum. I'm gonna ask Oatmeal for a knife."

B efore I know it, the night air is pummeling my face in the most delicious way. My face feels cold and alive.

I'm a brand-new person.

Oh. My mustache is gone.

And my head is hanging out of an open car window.

I'm in a car?

My horns scrape the ceiling as I fold myself back in the cab. Iggy and Vale are here too. That's good. Those two goons would get into way too much trouble without me.

We're headed . . . somewhere.

Goddess, hopefully not The Deviled Egg. I can't rightly remember all the fancy steps Birdie taught me about how to sneak in all quiet-like.

The driver cuts us each a sharp look from the rearview mirror as the car slows to a stop. "This is your last chance. I'll give you ten seconds to tell me an address or I'm dropping you off at the town square. Pass out there for all I care."

Iggy purses her mouth and shakes her head.

Vale just laughs down at his phone. He's watching his own movie trailer, totally out of it.

There's no way in the Crystal Halls of the Underworld I would ever give them the address to The Deviled Egg in this condition. I'd sooner sleep on a public bench. Fine by me.

I always thought that haunted statue in the center of the plaza was cool anyway. Lots of pretty lanterns surround it. Kind of soothing, like a bunch of spooky night-lights.

I haven't seen it at night since I was a kid, so I climb out of the car and make my way in that direction.

The statue's imposing metal form looks pretty badass. Tall too. The historic dude stands atop a pedestal at least four feet above the ground. I knock on the base, then the foot of the statue. Marble on bottom and bronze up top, I'd guess. The impressive part of it all is the dozens of glass orbs filled with live flame. Every time I blink, the light swims and shifts.

Hmm, I might be a little toasted after all.

I trace the tubing leading into one of the lanterns, amazed by the craftsmanship. They're hidden well, but all these lines carry natural gas to each of the flickering lanterns. The two largest orbs are in the statue's upturned palms with a few at his feet and the rest spiraling above him in an arc. It's meant to look like he's summoning a mythic firestorm.

He fucking wishes.

"Alaric Infernus," I say, looking up at the founder of a bunch of historic shit in town, most notably the namesake of our good ole alma mater, Infernus Academy.

Most people know the truth about him now though. He was nothing more than a trumped-up snake oil salesman who made his money in a cascade of cons that led him to finally settle in Winter Bliss where he hid from federal agents until his dying day. Not that anyone back then knew that.

History has a way of revealing the villains given enough time.

"More like Asshole Infernus," Vale says. I nod at him. He gets it.

"Asshole Ignor-anus," Iggy adds.

"All-too-rich Doofus," I chuckle. You know what? This guy doesn't deserve such a cool-ass statue. "I bet I could melt off his face."

I hoist myself up on the pedestal and start climbing Alaric's larger-than-life frame. My friends are yelling at me. Encouragement, no doubt. How funny would it be to melt off the tip of his nose so he looked like a zombie while everyone walks through town tomorrow. *Surprise!* I laugh so hard, I almost lose my footing. A couple glass lanterns crunch beneath my feet. Whoops.

Everyone will understand. I have a job to do.

Improve Winter Bliss.

Unmask the real assholes—the slick, pretty boys who say all the right things, the guys who can trick even the smartest of people before fucking them over in the end. Guys like Randy.

"Fuck that guy," I whisper to myself as I put Alaric's bronze neck in a chokehold and rub my knuckles over his head like a noogie before punching him in the side, right where the kidneys would be. My fist meets metal. "Ouch,"

I growl, shaking out my hand. "Tough old bastard. Fuck you!"

"And fuck Infernus Academy!" Vale is up on the other side of the statue with me. When did he get up here? His eyes are glowing red. He only ever looked like that when cornered by bullies back at school, the school named after Alaric Infernus, whose own principal was a distant descendant and did fuck all to help Vale back then.

Okay, it makes sense why he'd hate this statue. And you know what? My buddy deserves a little payback. And I'm just the friend to help.

I snap my fingers until a bright-orange flame dances in my palm.

Vale does the same, his flame a vibrant blue.

We swirl our hands together, urging the fire bigger. Brighter. This feels so good. Right. So incredibly justified. Anger colors Vale's eyes and every harsh line of his face as the darkness and flames play off each other.

I know what it's like to be mad. To want the world to be different.

I want that for him.

I want that for both of us.

My vision grows gold and I know my eyes are glowing too, fire magic flowing through me stronger than ever.

Time for zombie founding father.

I slap my flaming hand on one side of Alaric's head until the tips of my fingers touch his nose. Within seconds, it melts at my touch. Rivulets of neon orange metal run down his face.

Vale roars and slams his flaming hand against the statue's chest.

He groans, as if in pain. Wait. No. Vale is fine. It's the statue that's groaning.

We're rocking side to side. The weight of both of us on the pedestal sets it off-kilter. The glass lanterns clink together. I slip and tumble to the ground, landing on my feet.

Vale falls too, still mad as hell. He throws a fireball straight at the statue's chest.

Uh oh. That was ill-advised.

Glass shatters and I smell gas just as Iggy shouts, "Get down!"

The ensuing explosion knocks me on my back.

But I don't go out cold.

I blink at the stars overhead that I can still see through the smoke. There are so many of them here, even in the middle of town. One of my favorite things to do as a kid was just lay in the backyard and stare up at the sky. There are way more constellations out here than the big city I've lived in the last decade or so.

I bet it looks even better from Birdie's ranch, out where there's no light pollution, just fresh air and evergreen trees and lots of ornery animals and an even more stubborn lady taking care of them all.

It's a real nice place, her ranch.

She should get married there, surrounded by everyone who cares about her, everyone she loves the most.

She deserves to have the best wedding day.

I hope tomorrow's nice for her, even if I won't get to see it.

Chapter Seven
Birdie

15 years ago

"One, two, three, four, five," Mr. Slaytic counts, pointing to each student's head in turn. "One, two, three, four, five. And one, two, three, four. Oh yeah, we have fourteen students. Eh, it'll be fine. Okay kiddos, so your final assignment is a group project."

I straighten my necklace chain, nervous, as the rest of the class groans in unison.

"Making deals, at its heart, is about cooperation," he says with a stern look around. "And even though this is a glorified shop class, it's my duty to ensure you're learning the real-life skills you'll need in the cutthroat world of small business. So your goal, as teams, is to create a handmade product you could sell at a local craft market. We've got four three-person groups and one duo. Who are the fives?"

I sit up straighter and raise my hand, only to hear Rex's chair groan behind me. Please tell me that doesn't—

"Oh good. Rex and Birdie." Our teacher smiles at me, and I try to parrot him, even though I'm swallowing down an internal scream. My final project—the make-or-break for me getting an A and staying on target for valedictorian—is with him!

Not *him.*

I close my eyes and let out the tiniest snort. It's all I'll allow before I compose myself. Pep talk time. You can do this. You can master your emotions around the giant oaf who irritates you more than any other living being.

Our teacher displays our names in the groups on the big screen and tells us to rearrange seating so we're with our partners. I clearly don't move fast enough, because before I can even get oriented, my desk and chair are being dragged to the side of the class. The outskirts, not the front.

I sputter and smack at Rex's arm.

He grins down at me. "Your name's Aylin?"

Weird. He pronounced it almost right. It's hard to get exactly correct for English speakers. Wait, how does he know my first name?

Oh, the class roster on the wall. *Aylin Badem (Birdie).* That's when I notice something even better as he pulls his desk alongside my left.

"Your name is Ramonarex?" I reorient to teasing him back, delighted to finally have the upper hand. "It's a perfect name for you."

His expression closes off, growing hard, as he slides to sit right next to me, practically shoulder to shoulder. Oh wow, he's really close, so close he's basically caging me in and I can smell his deodorant or soap or something. "Yeah? Because it's a girl's name? How original." He looks toward the rest of the class mulishly.

"What?" I huff. "No, that's stupid and sexist. You'd be lucky to have a girl's name."

"Why'd you laugh, then?" His gaze slides back to me, still wary.

"Because you're a pest." I poke his shoulder. "*Ramona the Pest.* The kids book?"

"Never heard of it." His tone is softer, curious.

"No wonder," I sigh and rearrange my notepad and pencil. "It's probably above your reading level."

He pokes my shoulder back. "Smart-ass."

"No cursing!" Mr. Slaytic grouses over his safety glasses.

With a mumbled apology, Rex leans the side of his body on his desk, facing me, basically blocking out the rest of the class.

"It's in honor of my grandma." His voice is quieter. "Ra-monarex."

"Oh. That's actually really cool. Aylin is my grandma's name too." I kind of feel bad making fun of it, but not enough to apologize. "I actually love it, but most people can't say it quite right. Nicknames for the win, huh? Birdie is mine because my mom's called me *minik kuşum* since I was a baby. It means *little bird* in Turkish."

"Cute. Though Aylin's too pretty to lose." He grins, correcting his pronunciation slightly after hearing me say it. I swallow, heart fluttering. Only my family really uses my first name, even then, not that often. "How about Birdie Lynn? It suits you."

My cheeks flame. No one's ever called me that before, but it does sound kind of nice. I don't hate it. I roll up my paper and tap his arm. "Yours does too, Rex the pest."

Wait, is this the first real conversation we've had with each other? I don't think we've ever actually *talked* before. And I'm just rambling about my name and my family and my feelings out of nowhere.

"I am kind of a pest, huh?" he asks.

"To say the least." I roll my eyes, happy to be back in sarcastic territory.

"But I'm your pest." He slow blinks.

I glance to the side. *Your pest.* Gah, the flirting again. It's the one thing that throws me off, and he must know it.

There's nothing to say to that, so I change subjects to the more important topic. Our actual subject.

"So what are we making for the final project?"

"Figured you could tell me. Be the brains of our little duo so we make a good grade or whatever."

I chew the inside of my cheek. "I'm so bad at this stuff, whereas you're a total savant."

"Sounds sexy."

My eyes bug out but I cover it with a snort. "You wish!"

His brows crinkle.

"Savant means you're like a genius with this handy stuff."

"It's just basic, easy shit." He pauses, glancing at the teacher, who clearly didn't hear that curse word. The way he's leaned his whole body sideways, he's like a big wall of boy between me and the rest of the class. Big horns. Big hands. Big blunt facial features. I've never really looked at him for more than a few passing moments, but his bright, fiery eyes are kind of pretty.

"Well?" he asks.

Well, what? I panic, worried that I was staring at him in a weird way.

"What am I building for you?" He smirks.

I bite my lip but hesitate. There's this one thing. An idea I just got today looking through my new magazine.

"You've got something in that big brain of yours. Spit it out."

Can eyes sparkle? I know demons' eyes light up and can even flicker, but I'd swear his are letting off infinitesimally small sparks.

"Birdie Lyyyyyynn." His whisper is singsong, teasing me because I'm staring like an absolute freak.

Oh, no. I'm finally succumbing to the flirting. He's a demon. Maybe he's using some kind of magic to hypnotize me. *No!* I shake my head. I'm in control here. With a huff, I grab the magazine in my bag, flipping to the first article. I can't look at him right now. I'm embarrassing myself. *Get it together, girl.*

"Something like this." I point to a new style of beehive. "But not for bees. For the Gosta fireflies. A habitat."

"People would buy that?" He's looking at the magazine, thank goodness, and not me anymore.

"Duh! Think of it like a hummingbird feeder or even how pollinator plants attract butterflies. Can you imagine how many people would love to watch colorful fireflies flitting around their garden each night?"

I've been secretly trying to attract them myself in our backyard treehouse with bits of yarrow and balsamroot I pick up on the walk home, since I've heard they like the pollen. I think it's working but a dedicated habitat where they could fly by during their nightly migration would probably help.

"Hmmm," Rex hums, looking at the magazine photos. "I'm surprised no one else ever thought of that." He scratches at the turtleneck he's wearing under our uniform sweater. When he pulls it down, I see irritated skin and dark ink.

"Is that a tattoo?" I whisper, shocked.

"Yeah. It sucks. I had no idea they'd be this fucking itchy."

"Rex!" the teacher barks. "That's a mark against you today. Mind your mouth."

"Mind your mouth," he mimics in a near whisper. "It wasn't my smartest move to let my goth friend practice her tattoo skills on my fucking neck. I'm such a dumbass."

Her? I swallow. Goth girls are so pretty. Maybe she's his girlfriend he makes out with on weekends or they crash cool parties and drink wine coolers. Rex could definitely fool someone into thinking he's old enough to buy alcohol. He's bigger than most adults I know. Sixteen with tattoos. I bet he got in so much trouble for that with his parents.

"Anyway," he grimaces. "So this firefly house. Seems easy enough. I'm good with a jig saw, and I'm sure you could make up a design with all your nerdy animal know-how."

Nerdy animal know-how! My fingers tighten around the magazine. Why does he flirt with me then call me a nerd? Is this all just a game? I can't ignore him completely, but I refuse to react. He won't get a rise out of me today. We have a job to do, and I'm getting that A.

I start writing down the structure of the final project and all the points we have to address in my notebook. I'll show him nerdy!

"So the customer market is admittedly small. It's only really a viable product in Winter Bliss or areas with a high population of bioluminescent fireflies. But the project goal is to sell at *our* local market. This fits the bill."

I glance over to see him nodding. His eyes track over my face like he's taking my measure. Does he hate the idea?

"Smart. Real smart, Birdie Lynn."

I bite my lips together to keep the pleased smile in, because I really want to stop reacting to him. And dangit, not only do I like that nickname, I also can't help that his compliment sets off butterflies in my stomach.

I kind of hate how much I like Rex Perchaz.

Present Day

My wedding day is perfect.

A clock ticks quietly in the corner. Each beat seems to reverberate overloud in the silence where Mom and I wait in the front parlor, closed off from the reception in the great room. It's a small crowd—just family and a few friends—so everyone must be settled and waiting. I glance back up at the tall grandfather clock.

Ten minutes to go.

Taking a breath, I exhale into my bouquet—a simple mix of hydrangeas, baby's breath, and roses—all white. The dress is pure white too and fits like a glove—a gauzy chiffon skirt leading up to a strapless bodice thanks to my itty bitty titties. The only wild card today was getting my two horses settled in the side garden. And even *they* have acted like little angels—well, big, smoke-breathing angels, but still—they are more than happy to munch jalapeños and carrots in a new-to-them patch of grass.

Everything's gone off without a hitch today. No mishaps at all.

The last thing we're waiting on is the groom.

No notifications.

I click my phone off, chewing the inside of my cheek, and set my bouquet aside. Randy hasn't sent a selfie or anything and neither have I, too superstitious about seeing each other before the altar. It's tradition but why? Seems like a recipe for anxiety. I did let him know that I made it into town with the horses then sent a second message once I'd gotten into the dress saying I'd see him soon.

Still no response. I bet his phone is just dead. That happens a lot when he gets overwhelmed. Totally normal.

Nothing to worry about.

"The most beautiful bride." Mom finishes securing one last bobby pin to my intricate lace veil. I let out a breath as I trace the scalloped detail along the edge, catching sight of the henna on the back of my hand. It's a Turkish tradition with a less-than-feminist history—representing the bride as a sacrifice. But we decided to embrace a modern take on it, because the beautiful part of a bride's henna night is the women in the family spending quality time together.

She picks up my left hand. Her fingertips trace over the dark red swirls and loops she drew while telling me the story of her wedding day, one I'd never heard. How excited she'd been to move to America with her new husband even though she didn't know him well. They married for a shared goal more than love—to make something of themselves in a new country filled with opportunities.

"Are you nervous?" she asks.

"No." I squeeze her hand and try to smile. I feel numb, if anything. Like I can't fully breathe all the way in. Like making eye contact with anyone is hard, especially her. I keep getting lost in my thoughts.

It's just wedding day jitters, I'm sure.

The fingertips of my other hand hover over my hair, held back with dozens of pins and the veil. I slide it into my pocket to stop fidgeting. The fabric is smooth and soft. The underwire contraption of my bodice makes my boobs look like a lot more than they are.

I feel beautiful.

And, I guess Mom is right, just a little nervous.

She recaptures both my hands in hers.

"I was supposed to make you cry when I was drawing the henna," she says.

"What? Why?" That seems odd, to *want* a bride to cry.

"The henna night gives a woman space and time to grieve the life she's leaving behind." Mom reaches up to hold my cheek, her thumb brushing lightly over the swell. "But you've never been a crier, have you? So secret with your feelings, even as a girl. Plus, you're not really leaving anything behind like I was. We have a nice life here, and I'm so lucky you live close. My day was so different. My mother and mother-in-law had me crying a river of tears. It wasn't until the henna was drawn that I really understood I'd be leaving them for good. My whole family. Others I loved."

She doesn't speak of Türkiye as often as she did when I was a child, especially since her mother passed away and she stopped making trips as often. It strikes me that I don't really know her as anything other than what she is to *me*—a mom. Not a young woman who left people behind. Someone with past heartache and losses before I was even born.

"Are you glad you got married and moved here?" I ask, thinking of her painful divorce with my dad.

"Of course I am." She laughs. "Even though our marriage ended, your father gave me so much. We grew apart, but not before we built each other up, in a way—our new life in a new country. Maybe it wasn't everything we'd imagined on our wedding day, but you and your brothers? We cherish you. I wouldn't change a thing."

I nod, catching the flare of relief that she doesn't regret *me*, not realizing that maybe I'd been wondering that for a while.

Their divorce wasn't easy on any of us. I was a teenager trying to focus on getting into college, and my two brothers took the news hard. The pressure to be perfect, to not be any kind of burden, seemed to suffocate me after their split. My family only came to Winter Bliss for vacations back then, but after a few trips, Mom fell in love with the town. And then with how much Dad traveled back to New York for work, they grew apart. She wanted a life of her own. To avoid a custody battle, Dad's only requirement to agree to let us live in Winter Bliss full-time was that we attend Infernus Academy, a private business school he felt was equal or better to the schools in New York City.

Still reeling from their divorce, I threw myself into academics, the one thing that seemed to bring any light into my dad's eyes. I even graduated a year early, going on to live with him in the big city through my master's degree then spending several years on Wall Street.

But one trip home a couple of years ago, a single tour of my stepmom's family land, and everything changed. I'd always loved animals, but it wasn't something my school—or my dad—encouraged academically. It was a curiosity. A pet interest. But Orla's property was unique—a struggling Christmas tree farm home to several local endangered species. The barn was in disrepair, and she couldn't afford the rising taxes, so she planned to put it up for sale, even though the land hadn't left her family in over two hundred years.

I used the majority of the money I'd made in my early career to buy it from her instead, determined to carve out a protected space for animals in an area slowly being encroached upon by private developers. The bonus is that she and my mom were able to use that money to open The Deviled Egg.

"Most of all, I'm glad that you don't *need* marriage." Mom smiles at me. "You have the freedom to choose it for love."

Tears prick my eyes, and I have to blink to keep them back.

"*Kuşum*, are you okay?" She bends to try and catch my eye, but I sniff and pull away.

"You know marriage isn't always about love," I whisper.

Mom says nothing. When I look over, her brows twist together, surprise evident in the wrinkles that sprout between them."You already have it all—an education, a home, and work you are passionate about. The only thing you *need* is love."

She doesn't get it. What I need is stability. Someone who won't leave me at the drop of a hat for a life of passion and excitement.

Someone like her.

The air squeezes from my chest.

My mom is everything to me, but *this* is something I've never quite connected the dots on. She's the one who left Dad after all.

I look to my hand in hers. They're so similar, down to the shape of our nails. But in so many ways, as people, we aren't. I shouldn't have said anything, shouldn't have opened up.

My emotions have never been convenient or easy to deal with. They've never really made sense to her. She's warm and open and passionate and loving. And she's right. I never cried much, either as a child or a teenager during their divorce. There was enough crying between her and my brothers. If I did as well, the family would have fallen apart. Instead, I learned from my dad. Be strong for those around you. Emotions are a luxury for those who don't carry the burden of holding a family together. Push them down until they're forgotten. Soldier on.

Is it really so wrong of me to marry Randy because he's the best choice?

Our goals align. We both care about sustainable eco-tourism in Winter Bliss and we each have strengths to support the other to make that happen, to grow together.

I focus on the design she and Orla drew on my hand. The blood-red ink is a mix of fire and flowers. For the first time, it strikes me how similar the flames are to the tattoos Rex has climbing up his neck, the specific way they curve and point. Maybe they were subconsciously influenced by their long-term guest. He's been like a tornado in their inn these last few months and drives me up the wall half the time, but they've never laughed more since having him around.

It's a sweet thought.

"There's a smile. Much better." Mom pats my cheek. "Sometimes love takes time."

I take a deep breath and sigh.

Sure. Maybe.

I click my phone on and only see notifications of photo tags on social media. My brothers are total hams, trying to coerce Dad into a selfie with begrudging success. They all look so handsome.

Still nothing from Randy.

I text him a single red heart emoji just in case he still has it on him or he just got it recharged, hoping for dancing dots or a heart back or an impromptu whispered phone call, even though that's not really his style.

It's a waiting game now.

Orla ran out to check on him and make sure everything was ready. She'll be back any minute to let us know when it's time to head down to the start of the aisle where Dad will be waiting for me.

The clock ticks along. How is it so damn loud? The sound makes something inside me jolt with every click. My leg bounces.

"There's still time." Mom pats my hand, still in both of hers. "It's good for the bride to be a little behind schedule. Guests running late have a chance to settle."

Everyone's waiting on me. No pressure.

Mom's grip squeezes mine. I shake my head and refocus on her. She looks concerned, like she's inspecting me.

"Are you certain you wish to marry?" she asks.

I rear back. "Mom."

Everyone's here. Even with it being an intimate ceremony, we still sunk a bunch of money into the day.

"It's not too late," she says, hurriedly. "You are an independent woman with everything going for you. You should only do this if it's something you really want. If you *know* it's right. You don't have to set—"

She stops, looks behind me, and freezes.

The door creaks open and closes quietly. I turn. Orla stands there in an elegant column dress of gold satin, hands behind her back. Her tall spiraling horns arch proudly up from her silver hair, braided with white and gold ribbons.

But her face is a mask of tension. She says nothing.

The clock ticks. How is it getting *louder*?

"What's wrong?" I ask, looking to Mom, who's watching her wife, something silent passing between them. "What?" I spin back to Orla. "You went to find Randy. Is he okay?"

At the mention of his name, my stepmother's eyes blaze black and red, spidery glowing veins lighting up her temples. She's angry. For a demon, Orla is extremely even-keeled. Stoic, even. I've almost never seen her upset.

"Where's Randy?" I ask quieter, noting the squeakiness to my tone and the tremble in my jaw.

He's my practical, small-town fiancé.

He wants what I want.

We're a match.

Yet he hasn't answered a single text or call since I spoke to him last night.

My stepmom walks up to me and lays a hand on my shoulder. "He's not coming."

No.

Are you certain you wish to marry?

NO.

That's the real answer to Mom's question, the same question that I've asked so many times over the last months of planning and stress. I've asked myself and discarded the question, again and again.

No.

I wasn't sure about getting married. I didn't even particularly *want* to. It was Randy who thought it'd be a good idea.

"Where is he?" I ask Orla, wide-eyed. I want to throttle him! Or, no. I need to talk him into doing this, even just for show. My whole family is out there. His too. I can't face our families alone. What would I say?

My *father* is out there. He never wanted me to move back to Winter Bliss and work on a ranch. Adding this failure to that still-healing disappointment, how will I ever look him in the eye again?

No.

I need to find Randy so we can get this ceremony done and quietly annul the marriage after a respectable few months and the first holiday season of renters is in the books. This isn't good for him either!

"Where is he?" My voice is almost a screech.

"Greece."

I laugh hysterically. "Greece?"

The honeymoon he wanted. The trip he'd been sending me social media videos clips and articles and mock itineraries and deals on excursions that I just had to see. What do I care about Greece when I have 300 acres, animals that depend on me, a construction project in complete disarray, and no help from his corner?

Not going along with his honeymoon idea is the only time I ever put my foot down with him. And it wasn't even a *no*; it was a *not now*.

The shocked laughter leaves me feeling oddly light. Like I dodged a bullet.

I didn't even want to get married. That's clear now. *What was I thinking?*

He left me here, alone, with everyone I know and love dressed up and thousands of dollars of food and bills to pay.

The money.

Oh no, there's so much money on the line. We were getting married and building those cabins with the last of my savings to try and put Wild Hearts Retreat on the map.

My hands start shaking. My breath stutters, chest growing hot.

This can't be happening. I put everything into this plan. Randy books the reservations. I host them.

On my ranch. Home to all my animals and wildlife that are only just now really thriving. My ranch—the one thing I know without a shadow of a doubt that I *do* love.

I gasp and double over, tears blinding me, falling down my fingers and palms, making the henna designs look glossy and brighter—a brilliant red, like fresh blood. I heave for air, trying to hold onto a single rational thought while all I feel is cold, desperate panic.

The cabins are just . . . a money pit at this point. Can I even afford to finish them if there's no travel agent to bring in renters?

I'm not one to cry, but right now, I'm a sobbing mess.

"Birdie, breathe," my stepmom's voice sounds far away.

"*Minik kuşum.* Oh no, don't cry."

All the anxiety spiraling inside of me clashes with the shame of knowing my mom is watching me have a complete breakdown. I don't act like this.

My father is down the hallway. Everyone I care about will see me like this. They'll know what a mess I really am.

What a failure.

There are so many wedding gifts we've already received I'll have to send back. My mind tries to start a damage control list. How does one, logistically, control getting jilted at the altar? There's no way.

It's a disaster of the highest order.

The tears won't quit, and my fingers come away a little black. The mascara trailing down my face must be hideous.

No one can see me like this.

I don't cry, and this is why. It hurts. It's ugly. It's so incredibly embarrassing. It makes everything worse. But sobbing through the full body-and-mind meltdown is the only pressure release valve that keeps me breathing.

I glance up and, through the tears, see my mom's panicked face.

I haven't seen that face since they first got divorced and my brothers had a fit, tearing up their room and thrashing as she tried to hug them. Being twins, there were two of them, so I got down on the floor and hugged them too. She was so scared back then, just like she is now.

This will break her heart. This will embarrass my dad.

I can't change the fact my groom didn't show up. But I also can't let them see me like this. I can't face the pity in their faces.

The clock clangs, several loud, discordant sounds that are supposed to be a top-of-the-hour tune. It's harsh and ugly, echoing through the room and straight through to my bones.

"Your mom and I just need to talk for one second, Birdie." Orla pulls my mom up. They go just outside the door and whisper to each other. Mom can't even close it, keeping her hand clutched to the jamb.

They have to *deal* with me.

No, no, no. I can't do this, can't stay here anymore, can't be the burden and disaster they all stare at.

I jolt to stand, look around, and make the only rational choice. Leaving through the door won't work. My moms are there, trying to figure out how to handle their basket case daughter.

No. I hate it.

I race to the window facing the garden and fling it open, gather my skirts, and heave my body through the opening.

No one can see me like this.

It's not time to get married.

It's time to get my ass out of here.

Chapter Eight
Rex

Well, *this is embarrassing.*

I hang my head, rubbing my wrists because I know what's coming—handcuffs. It's what usually happens when I let loose.

Absolute disaster. Unholy chaos.

After exploding ole Alaric Infernus into tiny bronze bits, the police took the three of us into custody and straight into the drunk tank. I got a few hours of shut-eye in our cell before the door burst open with a clank that would've woken the dead.

It's the crack of dawn on a Saturday, but this demoness bailiff is all business, reading us the riot act about our crimes and their consequences.

"You've been charged with vandalism, criminal mischief, aggravated criminal damage, negligent and reckless use of fire, and conspiracy to commit property destruction."

Sounds about right from what I remember.

Vale puts on his charming actor face and sidles up to her. I'm not saying he shouldn't try the flirt tactic; he's a good-looking guy nowadays. I'm just saying I wouldn't bet money it'll work on this particular demoness.

Short and stocky, the bailiff's dark hair is graying at the temples and her thin looping horns are decorated in arcane engravings. An old-school Devout probably, not one to be impressed by a pretty boy from out of town. She'd be the sort of demon to keep to traditional practices, which you tend to find a lot of in Winter Bliss. Though demons are in the minority worldwide as far as people groups go, the volcano here has been a historic hot spot for us.

Vale tries his best to talk her into letting us go, but she closes her file folder with a harsh snap.

"You have three options, and you must decide as a group: trial by judge, trial by jury, or plead your case before the daemon tribunal. Which will it be?"

"A trial?" Vale gasps. "Th-that's s-so extreme!"

I can't imagine something like this would be great PR for his new movie.

"The tribunal." I stand from where I was slouched against the cinder block wall and approach the bars. "We choose that."

"Hold on," Iggy says. "Is that better for us? I don't want to get disappeared down a deep, dark hole, never to be seen or heard from again."

"That can't happen," Vale snorts. Then turning to the bailiff, he asks, "Can it?"

"A daemon tribunal is not bound by predetermined sentencing guidelines," she replies. "Under tribunal law, the judge has full authority to issue any punishment he deems fitting to the crime."

"Okay, yeah, but there's an upside." I step in. She's not telling the full story. "Like all things demon, a tribunal's rulings are kept private. They never share records with outsiders, not with other cities, the state, nobody. We'll serve whatever sentence they give us, and once it's over, there'll be no record of it anywhere except here in Winter Bliss. As far as the rest of the world is concerned, it'll be like last night never happened."

Iggy asks her questions about background checks and employers.

I turn to Vale.

"Sounds good," he says reluctantly. His eyes dart between me and the bailiff.

"Excellent." Her demeanor brightens, eyes alight with a golden gleam. "I'll contact the judge immediately. He likes to adjudicate these cases as quickly as possible to keep everything hush-hush."

I nod. The judge can throw the book at us, but there's no way it's gonna be that bad. It was a statue for fuck's sake. We didn't kill anybody. Barely harmed ourselves, to be honest.

The bailiff pulls out her cell phone and sends a quick text before grabbing a stack of bright-orange fabric from a cabinet. "Change into these jumpsuits. We just deep cleaned the tribunal court, and you all smell awful." Her phone pings and she lights up. "The judge is on his way. Chop, chop!"

We're dressed in identical ugly orange, shackled with handcuffs and fire-stop gloves, and marched into an elevator within minutes. The cramped space grows cooler and cooler the farther we travel underground. The ancient court. As a hot-blooded creature, I feel instantly on edge, vulnerable. It doesn't help that my hands are restrained. We're led into a huge dark space that looks more cavern than courtroom. Black rock walls, rough-hewn and shiny, surround us, and there are honest-to-goddess torches along the walls. We pass several rows of benches for an audience as the bailiff sits us behind a long table at the front.

The minutes drag on, and I hear rustling behind us, a handful of people taking seats. Fuck, we have an audience. I'm feeling less hopeful the longer I watch the fire flicker strange shadows in this cold, creepy room. The shifting light highlights engraved reliefs of demons in various forms of torture and agony. How many sons of bitches in the olden days were sentenced to be cast into a lava pit or have their fucking horns cut off for petty crimes?

Maybe this was a bad gamble. Why the fuck did my friends listen to me? A daemon tribunal! This could go very, very wrong.

My forehead drops to the tabletop and I rock my horns side to side, just to feel the responding thunk on the hard surface.

Perfect timing for another major life fuckup.

I spend months obsessing over an engaged woman, then the moment my parents come into town to watch my younger brother fall in love with a woman *not* already engaged to someone else, I blow up a statue in the middle of town.

Right on cue, Rex.

Once the family loser, always the family loser.

"ALL RISE FOR THE HONORABLE JUDGE SILAS GRIMSHAW!"

I jolt. Fuck, old girl has a set of lungs on her. Iggy elbows me in the ribs as she stands. I lumber up, my limbs protesting the whole way. My whole body feels like a bruise stuffed into a too-tight jumpsuit. Despite the fact I chugged water from the drinking fountain on the way in like a dying fish, it hasn't helped the hangover.

An old demon, skin tone a dark purple-red, in a long velvet robe takes the high seat. He looks like my high school wrestling coach, complete with a disapproving frown.

Yikes. This isn't looking good.

"The ancient court of Mount Winter Bliss is now in session," the bailiff shouts again before slamming some kind of ceremonial staff three times on the ground. My temples pound to the painful, sluggish beat of my pulse. "Please be seated and come to order."

The judge is silent, staring us down one at a time, starting with me. My butthole clenches, but I do my best to stare back with a blank face. If I look away, I'd come across as guilty and weak. If I look upset, I'm guilty and angry. If I try to put on the waterworks, I'm guilty and lying.

What I really am is hungover and regretting every decision I made last night. I think. At least, the ones I remember. I couldn't care less about the statue, but I really do miss my mustache.

I've been in trouble with the law enough to know it's best to stay quiet. Never speak up. That's just self-incriminating stupidity.

Vale takes the opportunity to stand up and launch into a dramatic monologue. I shoot him a death glare even though he's trying to fall on his sword and take all the blame. For an actor, he's going fantastically off script and the judge is not having it.

I stand up and use my elbow to try to shove him to his seat which just ends up in us tussling until the bailiff and judge are both banging their respective noise implements, shouting, "ORDER IN THE COURT."

Guess we're fucked then.

I plop to my seat and glare at a torch along the wall, watching the flames dance. Something about the curving shapes reminds me of Birdie—her hips in motion, her sinister little smile right before she tells me off.

What time is it?

I glance around but there are no clocks. I think it was half past nine when we left the jail cell, which means her wedding is about to start. She's getting married. Real soon. Which means right now she's probably sitting in her wedding dress, fixing her pretty hair or putting on the last touches of makeup.

She's starting her life while mine is falling apart.

Goddess, I'm such an idiot.

"Guilty on all counts," the judge says once the noise quiets down. "Your deplorable actions have not only scarred the heart of our beautiful town square, they've also disrespected the memory of a legendary figure, a great man."

"A great asshole," Vale mutters.

I have the presence of mind not to pick up the insult train.

"As punishment befitting your shameful crimes, you are hereby sentenced to twelve weeks of probation and two hundred and fifty hours of unpaid labor."

I groan and drop my head on the table with a rough thunk.

Fuck! I'm stuck in Winter Bliss for three more months.

The idea of being trapped in this town for that long while Birdie is a frequently fucked newlywed is some ninth level of torture. There's no way I'll ask for an extension to stay at The Deviled Egg. First, I can't afford it if I'm on some free labor contract. Second, as a local criminal, I'd just embarrass Orla and Miss Eda. Third, I can't see Birdie in the blissed-out honeymoon stage.

Even I have my limits.

Homeless on a park bench it is. Maybe I could stuff a sleeping bag in the storeroom at Perkatory without Rom noticing.

"My wife! She needs me," Vale shouts.

Wife? He isn't married. I know that for a fact with all the dating he does in Hollywood. The more he and the judge talk, the more confused I get. His wife owns a therapy clinic in town? But he hasn't been back to Winter Bliss in years. Then, a thin human woman I've never seen before walks forward and stands next to Vale, claiming to be his wife. What the actual fu—

The judge bangs his gavel and the bailiff responds with her staff. The clanging echo makes my eyeballs ache. I drop my forehead back to the table just to feel the cool table on my pounding skull.

Soon after, the bailiff leads us out of the ancient court and back up the elevator. We're uncuffed and told to change back into our singed and smelly clothing then dropped in the small, dingy office of our new probation officer—Gertie Dale.

Gertie sounds like Birdie. Easy to remember.

The stone-faced orc lady shows us these metal rings that clamp on our horn. They can track our location to make sure we don't leave county lines, don't drive (our licenses are suspended), and don't go anywhere that sells alcohol.

Nice. Just great.

She explains that the biggest requirement of our probation is volunteering for 250 hours, about twenty per week, with any local community project willing to take us on, which means we have to find someone to sign off as our Community Service Compliance Officer. That person, our handler so to speak, will wear a metal bracelet thingy that helps them track our hours.

Working for free is a shame to demons, declaring us worthless, essentially. I swallow. My parents will be mortified. There's no way I can show my face around Orla and Old Ethel during my sentence either. But I can take the hit to my ego. For a demon, I've always been a loser. Nothing new.

Gertie gets through the whole spiel, fits us with our red blinking horn clamps, and makes us sign some paperwork before handing us our own manila folder along with the bracelet for our volunteer leader person. They have to swear in or some shit and start logging our hours by Monday. Any weeks we miss come with a huge fine.

Yadda yadda.

Final-fucking-ly, we're let go. I tear out of there. My phone is dead as a doornail, but I'll check in with Vale and Iggy later.

Every demon for themselves, and right now, I've got one goal—grab my bag at The Deviled Egg before Miss Eda or Orla get back from the wedding. I'm sure I'll see them around town in the next few months, but I can't face them today. Soon enough, they'll hear gossip that I made a total ass of myself, and I'm sure they'll be glad to have me in their rearview.

I sneak into the B&B from the back just like Birdie showed me. My duffel bag is right inside my bedroom door. Man, I'm gonna miss this cute-ass place. The wallpaper is a warm yellow with flowers, the comforter is the perfect thickness, and those pillows are made with real deal goose down feathers. Those ladies really know how to make a house feel like a home. And despite me living here for months, the room still smells good, like fresh sheets and the warm wax from a recently burned candle.

It feels like every second I stand here, I'm polluting their perfect house more with my smoky clothes and body odor.

Mother Below, I'm a wreck.

My mom is still in town too. Realizing I have to explain why I'm not going back to the airport with the rest of the family sends me into a mild panic. Fuck!

I rush into the bathroom and take the most efficient shower of my life. I don't have time for a full shave but use my clippers to even out the absolute hack job I did to my glorious mustache. I decide to keep the scruffy five-o' clock shadow already coming in since it kind of blends together and looks half decent now. Toweling off, I pen a quick note to Miss Eda and Orla on the back of a receipt.

I got into a spot of trouble, and even though I'll be around a little longer, I'll stay out of your hair. Thank you ladies for being the best host moms in the world. I didn't deserve a hospitality that felt so much like home, but I sure appreciated it.

Big hugs, Rex

I leave it along with a $100 bill on top of the dresser, wishing I could give more, but money is gonna be tight working for free for the next three months. With a longing glance at the kitchen after I head downstairs, I barely resist raiding the fridge, opting to pick up an apple from a bowl at the dining table instead.

Then I'm out the back door and headed to the only place I can think of—the library.

My best bet is to beg my future sister-in-law, Noelle, to let me work for her. I can haul boxes or build shit or whatever. Oh, maybe she'll even let me drag a cot into a corner of that big closet in the back to just sleep there. It smells like a bunch of old books which is kind of gross but I could set up some air fresheners or something. Pine air fresheners. It's better than an alleyway, at least.

I'm just down the first two blocks when a flash of white falls out of a window.

I blink and rub my eyes, taking a bite of my apple. I haven't eaten much of anything this morning. Is this a blood sugar crash? Am I hallucinating?

Because that curvy little lady picking her way out of a bush sure looks like Birdie.

Birdie in a wedding dress.

Her veil tangles briefly on the windowsill before she struggles free and hurries up alongside one of her horses.

Unable to stop myself, I edge closer. She's only a couple buildings down from me as she quickly unties Mimi, the younger of her mares. Gigi, the mama, is right beside her. Two picture-perfect Umbran horses, all gray hide with rock-mottled bellies, lavender hair, and black horns. And they're both saddled up with some frilly white decorations along the leather. Cute.

I guess the bride and groom are meant to ride off into the sunset on them. Though that doesn't seem to be what Birdie's doing now.

It's still morning.

She just jumped out of a window.

Her movements are halting and quick.

I stop in my tracks, dumbstruck, questioning again if I'm hallucinating, dreaming something impossible into existence. Last night, I imagined her like this—pretty and glowing in a wedding dress with her animals—but the reality is not quite what I had in mind.

Is she . . . running away?

My chest rises and falls as I sink deeper against the wall holding me up, unable to look away.

With the grace of a skilled rider, Birdie hops up on the slat of a fence, grips the pommel, and jumps into the saddle. A vision in all white, her veil and dress gust around her like clouds in slow motion. Her skin glows in the sunlight and that strapless top is doing her every favor possible. Fuck, she's a stunner. As her face turns my way, looking down the street with wild eyes, a light rain starts, little more than a mist, even as the sun shines above.

The gods are kissing the earth. That's what demons call a sun-shower. An omen of good fortune.

Without a backward glance, she leans forward and steers Mimi out the garden gate and onto the empty one-way road in the opposite direction. The street is silent except for her lightly clopping hooves. The horse dances sideways for a moment, a little jumpy all of a sudden, before taking off in brisk trot.

"Aylin!" a familiar voice calls out as both rider and horse wind up into a canter. "*Kuşum!*" Miss Eda only makes it a few feet out of the front door before stopping. Her wife and Old Ethel come out next.

Gigi grows antsy, stomping and snorting as Birdie and Mimi race off. I come up beside the older mare with a hand on her flank, sidling up and talking low to calm her. I try to feed her the rest of my apple. She takes one bite then shakes me off, yanking at the reins keeping her hitched to the garden fence.

"Shh, girl. Your baby's alright. Birdie's got her. It's alright, sweetheart."

Her eyes flash to me, and I try to pour all my energy into calming her. Umbran horses are emotional creatures. Bred for the volatile environment of living on volcanic mountains, they can withstand high heat and are faster than fast.

"You think she went home?" Birdie's mom asks the other two, still not seeing me. "We should follow in the car."

"Don't do that," I call out.

The ladies all look over in surprise.

"Birdie looked upset," I say. "And these horses are easily spooked by their rider's emotions. Mama here wants to catch up with them." I pet down Gigi's nose, keeping an arm slung over her neck to try and calm her. "A car won't help, but she might."

Birdie's mom hugs herself. Orla takes her shawl and puts it over her head to shield her from the rain.

"You can ride that thing?" Old Ethel grimaces, lifting her hand over her brow to keep her vape dry.

I nod, jaw tight.

Gigi's a damn good horse, I want to bite back at the old demoness. She's only stomping and snorting up a smoky storm because she wants to get going. Instead, I shake off my irritation, knowing it'll only upset the horse, and start to untie her from the post.

But first, I need information.

"Why'd Birdie run off?" I ask, keeping my eyes averted, trying not to get too hopeful. I imagine her finally coming to her senses and leaving that slick-haired douchecanoe in the dust. At the eleventh hour, sure, but a win's a win.

"Randy never showed up," Orla says.

My body and mind lock up. *He* jilted *her*? I glance to see all three women glaring, the two demonesses eyes ablaze with fury.

My chest lights with no small amount of my own. That smelly waste-of-spunk loser!

I crack my neck, slowly leading Gigi out of the garden and onto the road.

How dare he? Birdie as a pretty runaway bride makes total sense. But him leaving her?

I want to light his car on fire. Throw rotten eggs down his chimney.

My vision goes dark and wavy. I'm sure my eyes don't look quite right. They always turn creepy as fuck when I let the rage take over.

Gigi hops and snorts a thick plume of smoke, so I hold her face and bring our foreheads together. When her eyes find mine, her third eye is open—a shiny deep-black with a ribbon of orange fire in the middle.

The third eye only opens in times of acute distress. One of the Umbrans lesser-known abilities is the strong emotional bonds they develop with their riders, especially in times of crisis.

Her body language tells me she's more than ready to race off to chase after her daughter, but the eye tells me we're bonded.

Let's. Fucking. Go!

My anger is hers. My nervous energy is hers. The tiny flicker of hope that I can catch Birdie once and for all is hers too.

The realization rattles me in a new way. If Birdie's heartbroken, her horse may be too. That's a different kind of emotion than anger or fear. All of those can sharpen the senses of the horse.

But a heart sick horse is dangerous. They're not above landing themselves in a whole heap of trouble, even life-threatening.

I imagine Birdie bucked off with a broken neck in a ditch and everything inside me finds a new purpose. *That's not fucking happening*. It's up to me to stay in control if we're going to get them both back to the ranch safely.

I grip the reins tight under her face and lock eyes once more, resolving as much to myself as to the giant beast of a horse magically connected to me.

"It's you and me, sweetheart. We've got this." I give her another firm pat, round her side to grab the pommel, and fly up into the saddle. Testing out my seat and control, I lead her in a circle around the women watching me slack-jawed.

"I'll find Birdie, ladies. Don't you worry." With a brief nod, I squeeze my thighs and tap my heels. Gigi doesn't hesitate.

We're off like lightning with two runaway girls to catch.

Chapter Nine
Birdie

I lean forward and sit deep with a tight hold on the reins. Yet for the first time today, I can finally let go.

The rush of wind covers my sobs. The hoofbeats pound over my racing heart. Every meter of land we pass brings me closer to home.

When I breathe in deep, it's filled with the comforting scent of grass and leather and horse. Mimi's huge, warm body carries me away from everything that hurts, like I weigh nothing, like my feelings and hers are the same, like I'm not a burden at all but a small part of her powerful form.

This is what I needed. To be something else. To disappear completely.

Together, we tear down the road, just running and running and letting it all out. As we approach a turn, she veers onto a dirt path. There's a network of trails off-road, and several of them lead to the edge of my property. So I let her go. Rather than slow down on the rougher terrain, she keeps the same pace. And as my body maintains the calm needed of a rider, I let my emotions run wild.

The cool, misty rain mixes with the salt of my tears. I close my eyes and let Mimi sprint as fast as she wants, wherever she wants.

I let out a furious scream I can barely hear.

He left me! The stable, small-town guy I thought I could trust with a stable, small-town future jilted me at the altar, even after I did everything right, everything he wanted. And now I'm careening toward a future with no plan.

I feel like I'm circling in a wastewater whirlpool right before everything slips down the drain. It doesn't matter anymore. Nothing does. I'm not in control anymore. Have I ever been?

Mimi whinnies and lets out a choking plume of smoke from her nose. She's riding so hard she's trembling, like her fast-twitch muscles are going haywire. And her smoke-filled exhales seem much too quick.

I lay my palm at the base of her neck and realize she's burning up. Under my fingers, her mane starts to glow, from gray-blue to a luminescent orange. And with it comes more heat.

What on earth?

She darts right suddenly and I catch a glimpse of one of her eyes, pure orange and lit from within. No pupil in sight. The color of her mane continues to transform before me, blazing a heat that's borderline uncomfortable. This isn't good.

"Mimolette," my voice catches, hoarse from all the crying, barely audible above the wind and pounding beat of her hooves. She veers left suddenly, and we're half sliding, half stumbling down a hill. I screech and dig my heels into the stirrups.

Instead of slowing down when she reaches the bottom, she shakes her head, the now fully glowing mane sliding along my skin like a sunburn, and speeds up.

A voice shouts behind me. I spin around and almost fall out of the saddle, seeing a flash of my other horse, Gigi, and a demon.

Is that—

"Mimi, please slow down," I cry out as she jumps over a fallen branch and I struggle to stay on, descending into a new type of panic. No matter how much I pull on the reins, she ignores me. "Please."

"Fuck's sake, woman."

I know that voice. It *is* him.

"Rex!" I whip just my head around. He's closer now, coming up on the left which makes Mimi skip further right. Her hooves kick up rocks that tumble off the side of a cliff.

A cliff?!

We skirt around a section of brush and then we're headed straight down again. An incline so steep I nearly topple over the front of her head, my chest and stomach instantly hot from brushing against her mane. The side of my bodice snags in one of her horns before I manage to dig in and lean back enough to stay on.

Only to see we're headed toward a steaming body of water. A familiar, if infamous, sight. The deadly Sula Hot Springs.

I've never been this close to the half dozen pond-sized pockets of turquoise water that boast the hottest recorded temperature of any hot spring in the West. They stay that hot because they border an active lava pit.

The Sula Hot Springs will kill a human on contact, either from the scalding evaporating mist or the skin-melting water. Or both.

"I'm gonna die," I whisper.

We're headed straight toward a translucent white mist that's about to turn me into goo. Still more than fifty feet away, the first blast of singeing, sulfuric air slams into me, causing an immediate, full-body sweat. And Mimi powers forward, fully intent on jumping in. Even her legs are glowing, hooves on fire as they pound against the hard-packed dirt trail.

"Oh shit, I'm really gonna die." My last thought is that at least she seems impervious. Maybe she'll survive even if I don't.

Just before we reach the edge, she rears back.

A rider on horseback emerges from the mist, leaving the shallow edge of the steaming water in a dramatic splash. A giant horned figure with black flames on his neck on a blue-gray horse with flaming mane and hooves.

"Gigi," I gasp out my mama horse's name. And Rex, her rider.

Both have pitch-black eyes with an orange flame center like they're completely connected—body and mind—as they rise from the bright-blue water, framed by the neon lava flow behind them.

It's like something out of a beautiful nightmare.

No, a dangerous dream.

I'm flung back as Mimi bucks, only managing to stay on the saddle by pitching my weight to counterbalance and grasping her mane with a burning hand.

Rex and Gigi work as one, still dripping with steaming water, first with a full-body block to the left when Mimi tries to dart that direction, then they spring right. Focused in purpose, they force us backward, one stuttering step at a time.

With clucking noises and a mastery of horsemanship I didn't know he had, Rex leads us into a flat clearing surrounded by blackened trees. Every twitch in my nervous

Mimi is responded to by Rex and Gigi as if they're of twin minds to soothe her.

In a last effort to escape being corralled, Mimi surges again. I grip the pommel with a white-knuckled fist. Her reins start slipping through my hand, so I glance left.

Rex is off horse and on foot next to us, sliding the reins slowly toward him.

"Be careful!" I shout.

"Says the renegade runaway bride," he says, while keeping his eery orange-black eyes trained on Mimi.

"You spooked her."

"Did not," Rex says.

"We were fine until—"

"Shut that pretty mouth of yours, Birdie Lynn." His jaw clenches, nostrils flaring. "We need to calm this horse more than you need to yell at me. Her third eye is open, and you're her bonded rider."

"That-that—" I stammer. Her *bonded rider*?

"She feels what you feel," his voice is calmer now, like a lullaby. "How about you take a deep fucking breath?"

That's just a myth. An old wives' tale. But when Mimi's head swivels left toward me, I see the truth in the glow of her wide-open orange eyes. It's not just the two. Her third eye is open, and she's dancing on her feet, as flighty and upset and confused as I feel.

Did I cause this?

Rex wraps his fist around her reins a second time and eases closer. Raising his free hand, his fingers start to glow, ember yellow-white at the tips fading to orange-red and black down his palm. A shower of sparks float in the air.

I exhale in wonder. *Incredible.*

Mimi settles slowly, ears perking up and forward, stomps going softer. She's nervous but curious. Maybe I am too. Our breathing connects. Her tongue licks out and catches the first spark. When she huffs, I sigh. Our deep inhale is shared, filling me down to my bones.

I've never seen her third eye open. It's beautiful. A small black flame is visible in the center. She's completely enthralled by Rex's fire magic and, it seems, also bonded to me.

"Good girl," he says at the same time I do. His hand moves slowly toward her mouth as he feeds her more shimmering specks of fire from his palm. "Sweet girl. You're alright." He rubs her nose. Grown calmer, all the frenetic stress that's possessed her since we sprinted out of town is nowhere to be found in her giant frame.

My heart squeezes knowing that I did this. I put her in danger, both of us, because I completely lost it. My chin trembles, but before I start crying for the second time today, I'm pulled out of the saddle completely.

Rex throws me over his shoulder.

"How dare—" I shout. "Put me down!"

"And let you try and kill yourself again? I'll pass. You're sticking with me, honey."

Honey?! I growl and ball my fists into his white shirt, which only reminds me how huge and strong he is. Gah!

Am I relieved to be alive? Sure. But I'm also a total mess—upset and annoyed and uncomfortable and a thousand other emotions. Why is it *Rex* of all people who has to see me like this?

"Up you go." He throws me like a sack of potatoes into Gigi's saddle and jumps up behind me before I can even get my bearings. Her mane is already shifting from bright orange to lavender gray again. His fists grip her reins above mine. He's also holding Mimi's reins, who's settled in beside us, letting her mom nuzzle up and down her neck.

"I got it," he grunts.

I tense, but let the reins go in favor of the pommel.

"I'm not a bad rider," I whisper.

"Just an emotional one."

I growl.

"Easy." He laughs, though neither of our emotions seem to rattle the horses. Maybe we cancel each other out. I clearly have no idea.

"You're a good rider, Birdie Lynn," he says after making a clicking sound to get the horses moving in a slow walk forward. "That's clear as day. Just maybe think twice before racing out of town with a broken heart . . . on an Umbran horse."

Not my finest moment, I'll admit, but it's little wonder the possibility didn't occur to me. I didn't realize there was truth to how affected they can be by emotions. They've never reacted like this before.

Do I keep my feelings *that* tightly held?

Already, my chest is tense as I work to control my breathing and straighten my posture. I didn't even have to think of it. It's usually so easy to just close up. No more pesky emotions. But today, right now, it's harder to do.

I almost hurt my horse.

I almost got myself killed.

I was jilted at the altar by my fiancé.

And to top it all off, the guy I've been avoiding or fighting with for months is the one who showed up to help?

The scream inside me rattles around my stomach and up my throat but stops short. I *cannot* lose it again. I just have to keep it together a little longer.

My fingers flex on the pommel until the knuckles go white and I can feel the sunburn-like sting on my palms. This is so awkward. I'm damp from the rain in a torn wedding dress with my veils twisted around an arm somehow, sharing a saddle with the man who does nothing but set me on edge. My heart pounds erratically with some mix of adrenaline, embarrassment, and . . . relief.

Rex is cool as a cucumber as we make our way onto my property and find our way to the barn. Well, he's not *cool*. He's overly warm, blazing that signature demon heat behind me, all around me. I'm practically sitting in his lap. His legs are snug and firm, right alongside mine. His big burly arms cage me in, resting lightly on the tops of my thighs. Even his cheek slots right alongside mine.

And though we don't talk—he stays blessedly silent—his every measured exhale is right next to my ear. His chest rises and falls like a living mountain behind me.

He feels secure. Good. *Safe.*

I don't like it.

Before I know it, we reach the horses' paddock. Rex hops off first and catches my waist to steady me as I slide down too. Immediately, I work to untack and groom on a frenzied autopilot.

"I've got it." Rex removes the curry comb slowly from my hand. "I'll get the gear off and you can give them a good cleaning soon. Not right now though, okay?"

I glare at him, and all I see is a gentle concern.

Oh no. *Oh no!* He's right. I'm too emotional. I could set them off again, put them in danger. My lungs squeeze.

"I've got it," he repeats, his tone even quieter, like he's calming me. Rex is *never* this nice to me. I don't *like it!*

"Fine!" I race to the house on foot. My heart rate works back up to a breakneck pace, the heat rising within me once again. All the emotions of the day choke to get out, and I don't know how much longer it will be before I explode.

Chapter Ten
Rex

15 years ago

It's the last school day before winter break. Since all the group projects were dragging ass, Mr. Slaytic gave the whole class an extension so we could turn in our final product today. Birdie and I could've been done a week ago, but I've been making the final touches to our firefly habitat stretch on purpose. The more we have to do, the more time she spends with me after school trying to get it perfect.

It's been the best week of my life, and I don't want to miss a second of it.

But time's almost up.

We're out in a field behind the gym. She insisted on testing out the habitat since we have another hour before Mr. Slaytic locks up. She wanted to get video evidence it works with real Gosta fireflies to support our final report. It's almost sunset, and I know I'm gonna be in deep shit with my parents, but this is more than worth it.

"Did you see that?" Birdie looks up at me, eyes aglow.

She's worth it.

"We caught one, huh?" I play dumb because I know what's coming.

She elbows me in the stomach, and I'm a freak, because I love it. I tease her every day, hoping for a little poke or shove. It's a game. "We're not *catching* them, Rex. You know this! We're enticing them, letting them know they have a safe place to visit during their nightly migration from the volcano down here to eat. Lots of yummy plants, little guys!" She raises the small structure that looks like a mix between a birdhouse and a beehive up in the air. A lone red firefly flits into one of the entrances. "Ah! Are you getting this?"

Right. Fuck. I'm on camera duty. I take a video of her holding it up, smiling back at me every time a new little bugger circles around her. I keep accidentally focusing just on her and kind of missing the firefly habitat, but I think Mr. Slaytic will get the idea.

A cool mist starts to fall from the sky. I click off my phone with a curse and tear off my jacket, raising it overhead to cover Birdie and our project. The weatherproof paint sup-posedly needs forty-eight hours to fully dry and I'm not about to lose her A+ over a technicality.

"Why the fuck is it raining?" It's cold as balls. It should be snowing.

"The volcano let off some steam earlier. It is technically snowing but because of the warmer air still in the atmos-phere, we get rain instead of snow." She's grinning ear to ear as more fireflies join us in my makeshift leather jacket tent, probably trying to shelter from the rain like us. "We also get new *Gosta Lampyridae* friends."

After my time on this project, I know now that's the Latin name for these rainbowy fireflies she's obsessed with.

"Such a nerd." My elbow knocks in, touching her shoul-der.

Her eyes flit to me finally. "Why do you call me that?"

"Nerd?" I ask, and she gets that sharp look about her that lights me up. "You're the smartest person I know, and that's saying a lot because I have some brainiac brothers."

"Oh." She looks down then back up. "Smarter than your girlfriend?"

"Girlfriend?" I laugh. "Uhh, no. Don't have one of those."

"Oh." This time, her tone is higher pitched as she looks away.

Wanna be mine? I should've said that, but the moment passed too quick and she seems kind of off today. I flick my tongue out to taste the air, having become more familiar with her subtle emotional scents. She's happy—about the project, I'm sure—but nervous too.

Maybe I'm making her uncomfortable because we're so close, hiding from the rain.

"This project will get you an A, no question," I say, trying to put her more at ease. "None of these other blockheads put nearly as much thought into the assignment as you did."

"And you! You built it." Her brown eyes flash red, green, purple, and yellow reflecting the new fireflies surrounding us. She watches them and sighs. "This is so cool, Rex. Maybe the coolest thing I've ever done in my life."

"We make a good team," I say. When she looks at me again, it feels like we're getting closer and closer, but maybe it's just my imagination or the fact we're trapped under a jacket trying to stay dry.

"We do." Her eyes cross when a pink firefly lands on her nose. After it flits away, she refocuses on me. "I still can't believe we *made* this. It's amazing."

You're amazing, I want to say but I'm a fucking dumbass and all I do is stare at her. It'd probably come out gross and pathetic anyway.

"Rex. Reeeex," a distance voice carries from behind Birdie, but thank fuck they haven't seen me yet. My parents are here. I've successfully dodged them all day but time is well and truly running out now, right when I'm finally getting somewhere with Birdie after weeks of flirting she always takes as fighting.

I quickly sidestep, shepherding her and our project behind a nearby tree, trying to hide just a little longer.

"Listen, Birdie Lynn."

She looks up, alarmed by the sudden movement and how much closer it brings us. She smells so nice, and I get lost in her eyes again, completely forgetting what I'd planned to fucking say. How do I tell her that last night I overheard my parents saying they'd save money by pulling me and my brothers out of Infernus Academy. While normally, that'd be music to my ears, after a semester tugging Birdie's hair in class and actually getting to fucking talk to her, I kind of don't want to go. But the closer I eavesdropped on their conversation, the more things went from bad to worse.

"I won't be here next semester," I say.

"You're . . ." She swallows and licks her lips. So pretty and kissable. What would it be like? She'd probably hate it. "You're transferring to the public high school?"

Ugh. I wish that was it. Could there be worse timing in life? I'm the unluckiest guy in the world.

"My family is moving away." I look sideways at my parents before pulling the jacket over on that side more to fully hide us, just for another fucking minute. "It's like, a thousand miles away or some shit."

"Oh."

Is it my imagination or does she look a little sad about it?

Fuck it. Let's just go full corny. I've been working myself up to saying something nice. *Just do it, dumbass.*

"I just, I mean . . ." Dark Mother Below, this romantic shit is hard. "I wanted you to know that doing this cool-ass project with you and, well, even meeting you, when you aren't yelling at me at least or even sometimes then, errr, it's been really ni—"

Birdie's lips meet mine and I nearly trip backward in shock. She's up on her tippy toes, her fingers grasping the collar of my uniform sweater with one hand. The feel of her nails scraping my chest lights something dangerous inside me.

She's kissing me! Birdie is kissing me!

Fuck yeah! I groan at how soft her lips are. They taste like minty goodness. Oh wow, her mouth is *wet.* Am I doing this right? Her whole body is plastered to mine and it feels super warm, in the best possible way.

Fuck, the habitat is wobbling at her side, so I drop an arm to help her hold it. Our fingers interlace and that does things below the belt I'm a little nervous she'll notice.

Whoa, fuck. Is that her tongue? This is completely insan—

I'm wrenched away by the horns. Only one demoness has the strength of a hundred fucking bulls when it comes to yanking me around.

"Fuck's sake, Mom!

"Don't you curse at me, you tricksy little emberling. Making out with a girl when your father and I have been searching high and low for you for hours."

She rambles on as I stumble backward, but I completely tune her out, twisting to watch Birdie. This is it. The last look.

My leather jacket is tented over her head and she's clutching the firefly habitat in one arm with the fingers of the other tracing a line back and forth over her lips.

When she smiles and does a small wave, I grin like the demon that made the first deal.

Life may be turning to shit fast, and me the unluckiest bastard to ever live, but that moment? That was *perfect.*

Present Day

I kick off my shoes in the mudroom and drop my duffel bag beside them. Feels weird, like I'm trespassing, seeing as I've never been inside Birdie's house before. But I just need to make sure she's okay.

That horse-chase-near-death-experience was some crazy shit and she was not in a great frame of mind when she stormed out of the barn.

I find her hunched over the sink with the tap on full blast, splashing her face. Then, she twists her mouth up and starts guzzling water from the spout full tilt. I can't help it; she's such a cute fucking mess it makes me laugh.

In a flash, she sees me and straightens like a deer in the headlights. A wreck, is my first thought. Black makeup streaks down her cheeks. Her hair's a disaster with that lacy veil hanging on by a thread.

And she's also just as beautiful as the first day I caught sight of her in the school hallway. The afternoon she kissed me in that field. The night we reconnected over a plate of cheese.

"What happened to your mustache?" she asks, before snatching a towel off the counter to dab her face and neck. My gaze follows the motion like a caress.

"Oh, that." I chuckle, my fingers making the motion to pet the facial hair that's no longer there anymore. Weird question, but okay. "Funny story actually." I take a step inside her colorful kitchen full of orange, blue, and yellow tilework. "I'm happy to tell you all about it if you tell me what happened back in town that set you off."

I know what her moms said, but I need to hear it from her. Still doesn't make any fucking sense.

Her gaze narrows and she casually picks up a serrated bread knife from the counter.

"What's it to you?" She points it at me, then turning it on herself, slips it along the inside of her dress on the side.

Alarm bells scream in my head as I close the distance and wrench it out of her hand, letting it clatter further down the counter. "What's it to me? My fucking friend almost got herself killed on some suicide ride into a lava pit and now she's brandishing a knife at herself."

She barks out an angry laugh. "I wasn't trying to kill myself! Then or now. He left me! Jilted at the altar, if you must know. There! That's what happened. No word, no warning. Up and left me in the middle of this damn construction project that was *his* idea, that I can barely afford and don't have the energy to oversee. Supplies are clogging up my barn and with the holiday season coming, the Christmas tree farm is about to go into high gear." The rant stops as she slumps, then continues, defeated, "He left me. Everyone was waiting for nothing. Nothing except to witness my humiliation. I just had to get out of there."

He really did it then. That slimy fuckface left *her*. I'm gonna throw a rock through his window.

Birdie lunges for the knife again. On instinct, I twist her back to my front and pin her arms down with one of mine.

"Let me go!" She thrashes for a moment before glaring up at me. "And for the record, we aren't friends."

My grip tightens for a moment, wanting to fight her but doing my damnedest because I'm trying real hard to be the good guy today. Get her home safe and make sure she's okay. She's a heartbroken mess, and it'd be a dick move to argue with her right now.

"Please." She slumps, the fight leaving her. "I need to get out of this dress. I can't breathe and it's making me itch. That's what the knife is for. These ties are double knotted and I can't even begin to know how the clasps at the back work. I just want it off." Every inhale makes her chest swell against the lacy edge, but it also makes me notice how, despite the strapless top making her petite tits looks fucking incredible, her skin does seem irritated.

"My knife is better." I let her go and pull the Damascus steel with rosewood handle out of my pocket. Pressing on a hidden button, the blade snicks open.

When I hand it over, her arms bend back but her hand starts shaking when she tries to slide it under the criss-crossing ribbon.

"That's sharp as fuck," I say, imagining her cutting herself.

"Thanks, Captain Obvious." Her lips pinch as we make eye contact. "A little help . . . friend?"

I take the knife back. "Turn around."

Despite the long ride across open country, her hair still smells amazing. Of course it does. I sweep it over one shoulder and try not to get too excited by how soft it, or her skin, feels. I slide the back of my hand under the fabric so the blade has enough room to safely work. I have to focus, because even that small contact of my knuckles grazing her shoulderblades feels fucking good. Entirely forbidden.

Goosebumps prickle across her skin. She's probably repulsed. Her chest and shoulders rise and fall like she's sprinting for her life. Damn, this dress really must be a death trap.

The blade cuts through the ribbons like butter. I get a better look at the fabric underneath held together by an elaborate mass of metal clasps I can't make any sense of.

"You sure you don't mind this thing getting cut up?" Ribbons are one thing but this will ruin it.

"Positive." Birdie answers immediately. "With the wedding on short notice, this dress wasn't even one I really wanted, just the best option I could find."

Best option. That's what she called that twatwaffle turd the first time I asked if she really wanted to get married. I take my time cutting through the fabric, going slow enough to avoid the delicate bra or whatever she's got on underneath.

"I didn't really love it. Not like you're supposed to," she adds, almost absentmindedly. And even though I know she's talking about the dress, I imagine that what she's really saying is that she never loved that dirtbag she almost married. That he was the best option and she's recognizing her mistake, that maybe she's not heartbroken, just embarrassed and freaked out.

But that's a dangerous line of thinking for a demon like me watching a scantily clad Birdie step out of the wreckage of her wedding dress. She raises her arms to make quick work of the veil. The tattered white mesh lands on the trash heap of her dress.

"Happy now?" she asks, turning with fists at her hips.

Happy? Uhh, yeah. The visual comes to me in slow motion, one of those sights you never forget. From her hips down, she's wearing a form-fitting, shiny little skirt, but it's her chest that makes me freeze. A tight little bra-thing pushes up her pointy dark nipples like they're framing a work of art. It's completely see-through.

My mouth salivates at the sweet treats on display.

"I bet you're just wriggling with glee." She steps forward and pokes my chest. "You were always saying shit about the wedding."

No defense there. And I'm definitely pleased but not quite for the reason she's thinking. I shrug and try to keep my eyes up.

"You never liked him, did you?" she asks, accusation in her tone.

Him? Oh. Fuck. That guy. Why are we thinking about him right now? Waste of limited brain cells. I play dumb. "Who? Ryall?

The anger leaves her in a burst of surprised laughter. She shakes her head, making her already wild hair look even bigger, like a cloud of curly, soft perfection.

"Ass," she mutters with the hint of a smile.

"Yeah, no," I say. "I really fucking didn't." *He had you,* I think but don't say. No better reason to hate anyone.

"I thought so. Had a feeling." Her gaze trails over me. She did? Does she know why though? Probably not. I'm just the jerk who opens his mouth and annoys the shit out of her. Why stop now?

"Asshole vibes."

"Takes one to know one?" She smirks.

"Fair." My eyebrows bounce. I have my moments. And if she's joking around, I'm happy.

"I bet you've never jilted someone on their wedding day, though."

"Innocent as a lamb." I raise my hands and pinch two fingers together with a teasing voice. "I'm only a little bit of an asshole. Nothing like that guy."

"Fuck him," Birdie spits.

"Yeah, fuck him," I egg her on.

"Fuck you, Randy!" she cries out, louder this time.

"Fuck. Youuuuuuu," I crow at the ceiling, a big breath between each word.

She's grinning now as she balls up her fists and lets out a full-throated shout like we're playing the *who-can-say-cock-loudest* game.

"FUCK! YOU!"

Oof. Something about seeing the tendons in her throat flex and her face go red gives me a half chub. Maybe I'm a sicko, but I don't think so.

She taps into something for me that I've never felt with anyone else.

As far as demons go, I'm a shit one. Never been good at all the clever manipulations we're taught from an early age. But what other demons describe as that gut instinct they feel to make a deal—the sensation of bliss in that tantalizing possibility—I swear I feel it with Birdie.

But it's not about a deal. It's more primal. It's fire. Hers. The one she's hiding no one else can even sense. But *I* can. And the desire to see the flames lick up to the sky, to coax them into a bonfire that everyone can finally see is an impulse too heady to ignore. So I never do. I stoke it. Every chance I get.

"Feels good, huh?" I ask after she shouts one last time, her voice cracking at the end.

She nods.

We're both breathing hard now.

After the crescendo of shouting, a silence stretches, charged with tension and, unless my senses are mistaken, the faint honeyed taste of her arousal. I lick the air and my bottom lip to be sure. She watches the movement. My heart beats like the drums of the underworld, like change is imminent.

It's right now.

"Fuck him," she whispers. Her stare turns dark as she steps closer until we're nearly flush, chest to chest. Just a scrap of a human woman, looking so fierce and fuckable, I want to fall to my knees.

It's usually stupid to say what I'm really thinking, but I'm just high enough from her energy and leftover adrenaline and the big dangling *what-if* in my mind ever since I first saw her jump out of that window in her wedding dress.

I say the stupid thing.

"Fuck me instead."

My hands stay glued to my side, just letting the words hang between us. It takes a couple seconds for her face to change. Her breath hitches.

Do it. I stay still, like a predator with eyes locked on its next meal.

Fuck me.

"I mean . . ." She exhales, then even quieter, "Yeah. Why shouldn't I?"

My lips tip up in a smirk while a rational part of my brain tries to sound the alarm. This is wrong. So fucking wrong to take advantage of her in a vulnerable state. It's not what a good dude would do.

A nice guy would be gentle and caring, self-sacrificing to a fault. Resist the heat of the moment.

A nice guy would give her space.

But from that first day in class, strong-arming to get the seat behind her then doing any damn thing to get her attention, I know myself better than to believe I'm capable of any of that hero bullshit.

That's just not me.

When it comes to Birdie, I've never been the nice guy.

I take what I can get. Every glare. Every hot exchange. Every stolen moment.

My last hesitation dies when her fingers tuck around my belt buckle.

According to her, we aren't friends.

It's about time I leaned into it.

Chapter Eleven
Birdie

We clash together like swords in battle. Our mouths bite more than kiss, exploring in a hungry crash. Everything with us is a fight. Why should this be any different?

The thought, oddly, makes me want to laugh, some frantic joy trying to bubble out as he grabs my face with both hands and sucks on my bottom lip. The way he does that, then tilts to stick his tongue down my throat, reminds me of some slavering beast who hasn't eaten in years.

I'm enveloped in his solid heat, completely surrounded. My fingernails latch onto his forearms and scrape down. He groans as he dominates my mouth. I haven't kissed many demons, but wow, his mouth is hot. His tongue is longer, thicker even, than I'm used to. And God, his hands are big. Our size difference has never been more apparent.

Fuck me.

What an unexpected solution.

The kiss grows deeper, more frantic. I have only the haziest memory of our first kiss all those years ago. It was so innocent compared to this, the first time I threw caution to the wind. He was moving away, and I had nothing to lose.

It's the same now. Rex doesn't live here. He's leaving, just like before. No one needs to know. What's one more impulsive moment?

But I'm not a teenager anymore. I need more.

I refocus on his waistband, rip open his belt, and shuttle down the zipper, sliding my hand over the bulge covered by briefs.

"Fuck." His breath gusts out. I've always secretly liked how much he curses, how free he is with words. With everything. Not that I'd admit it to him. And now, as his lips travel across my cheek to my ear, he exhales out the curse again when I cup his balls and trail my fingers up. "Fuck, Birdie. What're you doing to me?"

To him? *He's* the force of nature. He's the demon who says and does whatever he wants. The guy who always says *fuck the rules.* I need that energy right now.

He grabs my face again, bringing my attention back to his shining black eyes. A single, wild flame dances at the center of his pupils.

"What do you want, honey?"

My breath hitches, a surge of surprising emotion crashing over me. It's such a simple question—what do I want?—one I rarely consider, not when I planned that rushed wedding, not when I agreed to build those stupid cabins, and not when I smile and nod to whatever everyone else wants *all the fucking time.*

"I want to feel." The truth comes out before I know what I'm saying, and it scares me a little.

His jaw clenches and a hard look passes over his face, then I'm in the air and placed on the cool granite countertop. We're eye to eye, and he still surrounds me, caging me in with his giant arms.

"You weren't taken care of, were you?" His voice is dark gravel, and before I can even answer, he shakes his head. "It doesn't matter. What matters is that you are now. I'll do it."

His rough hands slide over my silk slip. The calluses catch in the fabric, so he tucks them under and urges my legs open. His gaze snares on my chest, the attention making my nipples tighten in the tiny, tight bustier I didn't remember until just now is totally see-through.

"I could eat you right up." One of his palms glides up the inside of my thigh while the other yanks down my top with barely concealed violence, ripping the delicate seams in the low V. "But I need to suck these titties first."

The urge to laugh again emerges then turns to a gasp as his overheated mouth makes contact with a wet noise. I buck as he latches onto one nipple then darts to the other, using his thumb to stimulate where his mouth isn't. One hand grips the base of his thick horn while the fingers of the other end up tangled in his hair, instinctively holding him to me.

He groans then pops off. His hair is a mess and he's grinning like I've never seen before as he catches his breath. His thumb notches under my chin to make my lips available for plunder again, a bite and a suck between heavy exhales. God, the sounds he makes are unhinged. He hunches back down to latch back onto one breast, then the other.

It makes me crazy. He's always made me so crazy I can barely think around him.

"So quiet, honey."

Am I being quiet? Because he won't shut up.

"Nothing mean to say? Now that I'm sucking your nipples in the clothes you almost married some other asshole in."

I exhale in surprise and yank his head back. "You're evil."

"There she is." He chuckles and shakes me off, traveling back up my chest to suck at my neck.

He likes it when I'm a little mean, and I'm just now realizing how much fun it is to tease him back.

"You smell." I bite at his ear, tasting the salt of his skin.

"You like it, though, don't you?" He takes a deep inhale while licking his lips. I remember that demons can sense arousal along with other heightened emotions—something between a scent and a taste. "And for the record you smell too."

"Evil," I gasp.

"You smell, but good. Real tasty. Pretty Birdie sweat." His nose trails up my throat as he licks my skin to follow the path. Under my slip, his fingers move from squeezing my thigh to pressing over the gusset of my panties, firmly, mapping the flesh underneath. "Can't wait to lick you everywhere. I bet there's nothing sweeter."

I lean my cheek against his horn and hide my smile. He's so brash, but somehow it's working. Everything about him works for me right now. Maybe I needed to match his natural chaos to see him in a new light, where everything about him makes sense. He's honest. He's funny. And the chemistry is explosive.

"I wanna feel something too." His fingers slide under the fabric and through my arousal. Without preamble, he sinks one thick digit inside.

"Look at that," he says and slides a second alongside, made far too easy by how wet I am. I wait for him to tease me. When we make eye contact though, it's just puppy dog eyes full of awe. "You are perfect, aren't you?" His fingers move in and out, press up. "So perfect. A smart girl with good grades. A pretty lady with polite words. But now . . ." He grips my neck with his free hand, holding me still, like he won't let me look away. "Now I see a new side of you." I'm breathless, waiting on every word. "A needy little slut."

I suck in a breath, jaw dropping. My arousal ramps up, and I hate how hot it makes me, how sure I am he's eating up every reaction.

His tongue flicks out to taste the air again, and an evil half smirk returns.

"Desperate for me, aren't you?"

"Pig." I smack his shoulder and try to wiggle free which just makes his smile widen, grip tighten, and fingers sink deeper. His thumb passes over my clit and I jolt. Determined to make *him* feel something, I pull his hair. And now he's grinning. I want to demand he take it back, *shut up*, but I can't. I won't.

"I'm right, aren't I?" He licks my lips now, tongue traveling across my cheek. It's obscene and absolutely should be gross but it's really, really not.

I growl at him and wrench his face back to bite his bottom lip. Suck it. Dig my nails into his cheeks. That'll shut him up. Stupid, sexy demon giant.

"You're my hot little slut." He speaks against my mouth and crooks his fingers inside me. His thumb circles my clit with heavy pressure. Everything clenches tight. "My perfect girl."

The meanness and praise mixed makes me crazy. I'd scream if I could, but I'm frozen in bliss, incapable of saying anything, only feeling. Trembling and pulsing. Desperate for more as he works me over with those thick, talented fingers.

"Can't admit it, can you? That you need me that bad." He chuckles at my ear, barely a whisper. Not that anyone else can hear us, but it still feels too secret what he's found out. The truth of what I am and what I want. "That's okay, honey. I'll give it to you anyhow."

In a move that really should take more effort, his grip moves under me. I'm hoisted up and pressed against the fridge. My legs lock around his waist. We're chest to chest, plastered together.

And while I'm a sweaty, nearly naked mess, he's still in all his clothes, feet widening for a stable stance.

My hand slides down his unzipped fly and under the waistband to finally feel his bare cock. It's thick and hot to the touch. Glancing down, the skin glows! Some inner light morphs, pulsing slightly with his heartbeat. Demons exhibit a large variety of traits, not just the horns but tails, wings, claws, and . . . well . . . this.

His cock is almost like a lava lamp. The more I fist and pump, exploring the ridges and folds of skin, the brighter neon-red and harder he grows.

I want to feel him inside me. Closer.

Using my legs, I wiggle and work to push his pants further down. He positions himself in the crook of my hips, bare with only the scrap of my thong between us.

The ambient light of his skin casts a red glow between us. "You ready?" he asks.

So ready. I can't wait another second to fall deeper, grow wilder, be different.

"Fuck me," I say. It's what he wanted. This was his idea. But it's my turn to demand. "Do it."

He tugs my panties to the side, and then he's there, luminescent angry-red cock sliding up and through my folds. The sound is crude and wet. He's hard and hot and silky soft at the same time. Skin on skin. I sigh, my eyes going half-mast as the heated sensation of his perfect, glowing cock sends a rush of warmth through me. My arousal makes the way I rock on him an easy thing.

"You feel that?" He bites my upper lip and nips my nose before placing chaste little kisses over my cheek.

I nod and rotate my hips, trying to catch the tip, desperately chasing his mouth but he never gives in.

"So hungry, honey." A sliver of smoke gusts from his nose, like a bull enraged. "Feel more of me, then."

He notches at my entrance. I arch. He presses. Every inch gained is slow and sure. He glides in a fraction then back out, making determined progress with each thrust in, his big muscles flexing and tight.

We exhale together, our breaths sawing in to match. And even though I can't see where we're joined now, I can hear it—the fluid sounds, a groan, my panties ripping, lost to the floor. I get greedy and bite his lip, wanting his mouth on mine again, the full-body experience. Feel it all—taste and hear and touch and see.

His horns frame the light from the window with only the bright fire of his eyes glowing in the shadows. He's a demon god, entirely focused on my devastation, dragging me deeper into darkness. I should be frightened but I'm not. He makes me feel dangerous instead.

A wild creature like him.

Free.

I tip my hips as he shifts slightly, roots deeper. There's so much pressure and pleasure, I can't speak. My hands shake, frantically clawing over his chest then scraping up the dark tattoos of his neck. I anchor my grip behind his neck and hold on for dear life as he shuttles me up and down, faster now. We're on a slippery slope driving straight off a cliff. I hug tighter, hiding my face at his neck, watching his pulse beat rapidly, feeling the steam coming off his skin as he overheats.

He jolts deep inside me and slows, voice shaky. "I'm—fuck—I'm too close."

I take up the motion, almost there myself. With the added friction of his hairy belly on my clit as I move, the edge is coming.

"Me too. Keep going. Fuck me, Rex. Never stop."

Oh. Those last two words light a new fire inside him. A feral growl rumbles out as he smashes me further against the fridge and ruts me with abandon. My breaths shudder as I come in a full-body rush of sensation. And he keeps going. Every smack of his hips extend my aftershocks, like my body *needs* to squeeze the cum out of him.

With a trembling quick movement, he turns, dashing dishes off the counter to set me back down. He pulls out, aims his bright orange-red cock at me, and unloads all over my bare pussy.

Seeing a giant demon shake and whimper with his glowing, pulsing cock in his hand is almost as much fun as feeling it inside me. I'm grinning as he finishes coming down. Still breathing hard, he softly nudges just the tip through the mess, up and down my entrance and over my clit until I'm so ticklish or so far outside my head, I finally let go.

I start laughing.

He glances up, surprised, and in a blink, joins me in a fit of laughter as he leans one hand against the counter to catch his breath.

I close my legs around his hips. He squeezes my thigh then moves to grab a paper towel, wetting it with warm water, before cleaning me up as best he can.

"Sorry about the clothes." His gaze stays busy anywhere but my face.

I think about the torn, discarded clothing around the kitchen. The off-the-rack dress, the itchy underclothes, the tissue-paper veil. None of it I really wanted.

"All things considered, it was the best thing that could've happened to them."

He glances up with a little smile. "Yeah?"

"Fuck that dress."

He nods, shoulders relaxing. It's like an unspoken *we're good* about what just went down. All his teasing cockiness from earlier is gone. Rex and I aren't exactly close friends, able to talk through our feelings. Not that I talk through my feelings with anyone, but I get the sense he was worried I'd completely freak out on him.

I jump off the counter and pull an apron over my front for respectability's sake. I'm not embarrassed at all, weirdly. Should I be? If anything, I feel *good*. Dirty and disheveled, for sure. Tired, yeah, but in a relaxed way. It's like my body and mind needed a hard reset after the wedding this morning. The almost wedding. Ugh. I push it from my mind.

Nope. Not going there. One crisis at a time.

Rex's hand trails down his face as he watches me carefully. The way his fingers frame then drag down his mouth reminds me how he'd do that to fiddle with his old mustache. The mustache that was hiding some seriously plush and sexy lips that will now haunt my wet dreams. I almost wish he still had it, not that it matters.

"You'll need a drive back into town, huh? What time are you leaving today? Is that why you shaved?" I snicker. "I bet your mom hates it. And what is this blinking thing on your horn? If it's decorative, it's kind of an eyesore."

"Damn, twenty questions already." He scratches the side of his nose nervously then leans both arms straight on the counter. "First of all, my mom likes my mustache just fine. I think. She's never commented on it, anyhow. And . . ." He pauses and drums his fingers, gazes darting away. "Well this horn clamp and my lack of facial hair is courtesy of some poor decisions last night. They're kind of the reason I'll be staying in town a little longer."

Huh? He shaved his mustache and bought weird electronic horn jewelry which means he can't leave town. How does that make sense?

He *has* to leave, just like before. This was a freak occurrence, a one-time thing before we're both on our separate ways to nice, normal lives.

"Earth to Birdie." He snaps his fingers in front of my face. I swat them away.

"Ugh. Stop. You're not . . ." My voice cracks. "You're not leaving town?"

His features show his annoyance. "Don't be so heartbroken about it, honey. Yes, your wham-bam-thank-you-ma'am is sticking around. I got into a bit of mischief last night which landed me twelve weeks of probation and some shit I've got to sort out."

"Th-that's almost three months."

"Up through the holidays, yep." The p-sound pops.

"And you're staying with my mom?" I feel breathless. The mortification if she found out what I did today is huge. On my wedding day. With Rex, her long-term guest.

"Uh, no. I checked out. Actually, I . . ." His voice trails off.

I exhale the biggest sigh of relief.

When Rex is quiet for too long, I notice he's looking around my home like he's inspecting it, more curious than he should be. He turns to me with a dazzling smile.

"Funny coin-ky-dink, Birdie Lynn. I actually need a place to bunk up for a while."

"No." The harsh word is immediate. Absolutely not.

"My probation involves me volunteering somewhere. I just need to find a local willing to vouch for me." He pulls out a paper and a metal bracelet from his pocket and sets it on the counter. "There's some legal shit to agree to but it seems like a pretty sweet deal for the person in question. Three months of free labor from yours truly."

No, I want to say, but I hold my tongue.

After listening to me rant about how Randy left me high and dry and I'm running out of money to finish the cabins, I think Rex knows why. A volunteer means free labor, something uniquely shameful to demons, not that he seems to mind. Rex is insanely skilled at building things if our time in shop class and the little I know about the work he does for Perkatory means anything.

"Seems to me you could use some help around here," he adds.

He's not wrong. The ranch would definitely qualify, considering all the animals I care for on the nonprofit side.

"By the silent treatment, I take it you're thinking about it." He grabs a bag of my favorite snack—chili jerky—and shovels some into his mouth as he eyes the living room. "Got a guest bedroom back there?"

"No." I snatch the bag from him and throw it further down the counter. Rex in my home? After what just went down. After the way we fight. "No way."

"No to the guest room or the whole idea of using a strapping demon with animal know-how and construction expertise for free labor through the holidays?" He grabs a breakfast bar from the container. I allow it. "That is your busy season, isn't it?"

It's easy to forget he's a demon with his casual nonchalance and blue-collar sensibilities, but I think he's just more clever about it. Rex may not be a wheeler-dealer in boardrooms, but I see the instinct flare to life, the anticipation at finding an opportunity he can twist to his advantage. How much of our kitchen romp, the way he licked his lips and devoured me, was only taking advantage of a vulnerable woman in—

"No." I shake my head. That crazy choice went both ways. We enjoyed ourselves. Thoroughly. I pause, recalling the procedures of demonic negotiation like the back of my hand. Even if I do see the plus side of having a free ranch hand during the busiest time of the year, I have to stay firm with him if I'm going to seriously consider the idea. He needs to understand my first requirement. "You can't stay in the house."

"My probation says I can't drive, and I'm damn sure not walking eight miles round trip from here to town. Don't have the money for lodging anymore anyway." One big muscly arm sweeps across the room. "Thus, I have to stay here. You get to boss me around. I'll do whatever you want. Ride me rough if you need to." His eyes flare at that. "But my one and only condition is that I live here."

"It's a one bedroom."

"One bed, huh? Sounds cozy." When I don't snipe back at that, he sighs. "I get that you find me hideous and would never in a thousand jillion years fuck me. Oh, wait." He smacks his forehead and laughs. "That's not true at all. You can't resist me, can you?"

I growl. He grins.

It's not customary to show vulnerability in a negotiation, but boundaries are important.

"I need space."

I'm standing here in tattered underwear and a dirty apron with my life falling apart. He has to see this as a reasonable boundary. His eyes tighten as he inspects me, calculating his next move.

"Where will I stay then?"

An open question instead of the traditional counteroffer. It's a calculated step in the direction of what he wants. By assuming I've accepted his help, he's giving me a carrot and letting me make the next move.

He insists on staying here, but I can't have him in my home.

"The barn."

He laughs. "With the animals. That's how it is?"

"The barn is the only option." I shrug. "There's a fully functional bathroom and I could find a way to make you comfortable."

"I'm sure you could." He watches me with open hunger that gives me pause.

Another boundary he needs to be aware of.

"It can't happen again." I say, needing to be sure he knows this was a one-and-done fit of passion. But worry creeps up, because Rex has never been good at following rules. "You know what? Maybe we shouldn't even—"

"No. We're doing this." His eyes flare.

"If I'm meant to vouch for you in a legal matter, what if someone finds out what just happened? If the judge asks—"

"If, if, if. What would you say?" he cuts me off. "That we rawdogged against your fridge on your wedding day?"

"Rex!" I throw a dish sponge at him, which leaves a wet splat on his boulder-like chest.

"Yeah, no. We're not telling anyone about what's between you and me. It's no one else's business. End of story." What a demon thing to say. Still, his assurance eases a lot of my anxiety around the topic. He claps his hands then rubs them together. "So before I agree to this proposal, what am I doing, boss? First project. Hit me with it."

Before he agrees? This was his idea! And *boss*. Ugh. He's so annoying. "I guess the cabins. If you can manage it."

"Oh, I can." Then he blurts out the most ridiculous thing. "Problem is, you hate those cabins."

"Pfft. What? How can I hate something that doesn't exist, that's supposed to bring in a lot of money?" Even saying that leaves a sour taste in my mouth. Money would be nice, but if I pump the brakes now, I could still keep the ranch afloat with the tree farm. Maybe.

"I think you know they're more trouble than they're worth. You've been fucking miserable for six months."

Since I got surprise engaged and talked into this whole nightmare. Why did I ever think that Randy was my best choice? That luxury cabins are what my ranch needs? I hate the rich people my dad always glad handed growing up. It's at least half the reason I left finance to begin with.

"I do hate those cabins." God, that feels good to say. "I never wanted them to begin with."

Rex's eyes glow as he leans closer. It's the same look he had when he encouraged me to scream *fuck you*.

"They were his idea," I continue. "You know what, yeah, fuck Randy." But the rational side of me kicks in quick with a heavy sigh. "It doesn't matter. I still have a big load of wood and supplies in the barn already paid for. And two cement foundations. I mean, maybe I should just finish the job."

"Sunk cost fallacy," Rex mutters. How does he— "How big are the slabs?"

"Uh, twenty by twenty."

"No electric or plumbing yet?"

Stress starts to close up my throat thinking about contractors again. How they were supposed to install utilities but Randy didn't explain the project well enough and then the slabs were just done and I've been sitting on my hands for ages. All I can manage is to shake my head.

"Good." He cracks his neck.

"Good?"

"Yeah. So you've got two sites with four-hundred square feet of nice level space to play with. Need another barn?"

"On a hill that high up? No."

"What goes good on a hill?"

A big binocular to view the wildlife all around the property. That's ridiculous though.

"There's something going on upstairs," he says. "Spit it out."

"It's silly."

"I like silly things." He grins.

I roll my eyes. "The only time I really go up there is in the evenings. I ride the horses sometimes around sunset to wear them out."

"Umbrans love steep elevation."

"Yeah, exactly. Fun fact: they evolved on volcanic mountains with goat-like hooves." I smile. "So anyway, you can see the surrounding area for miles. I was thinking . . . binoculars. Really heavy though, like the big metal ones at roadside spots and state parks. I bet it could see all the way across the lake and into at least two nearby wildlife habitats—the owls and the otters. Oh, the fireflies would probably love it too if there were more wildflowers up there."

"So an observation deck with some fancy equipment."

I can see it so clearly. An overhang for shade. Lots of seating. Maybe a hiking trail leading up there. Oh, and big educational displays explaining the terrain and the local animals. There's more ideas already filling my mind, but I'd need to do some research.

"You should see the way your eyes are shining right now." Rex gives me finger guns. "That's a winner. That's what you're doing with the wood pile."

"Yeah?"

"Well, not you. Me." He winks.

"What about the other cement pad?"

"Geez, Birdie Lynn. One project at a time. Trying to work me to the bone already." His eyebrows dance.

I shake my head with a grin.

"You'll think of something, boss," he says.

This demon simultaneously makes me want to laugh, scream, and slug him. Even still, there's a bright feeling inside that tells me this just might work out.

"So you agree?" I ask, getting us back in negotiation territory. "You work for me until your probation is over. I let you live here and vouch for you with the court."

He gives me a lingering look before standing to his full height, arm outstretched. "I accept."

I run through the scenario one more time and see no downside. That's not quite true, but the benefits far outweigh the temporary awkwardness.

"You're going to be put to work." I grasp his hand. His thumb brushes over the henna design my moms made—the same shape of his flame tattoos—and the corners of his mouth tip up. That small caress sends a sparkling sensation up my arm. With a steady voice, I try to keep us on track. "I won't be easy on you."

"You never are." He looms over me, moving one step closer to slide his forearm up and along mine, the position of a demon making an ironclad deal. "It's one of my favorite things about you."

His eyes blaze black and red with hints of swirling gold. Veins along his temple darken as his magic strengthens, telling me he's taking our agreement as serious as death.

Vouching for him in court is one thing. Paperwork.

This is a true demon pact. We're agreeing to spend three months together.

My fingers squeeze around his strong forearm.

"A deal is a deal," we say together, sealing our fate.

A FRENEMY IN NEED
FANTASY SPRITE STUDIO

Chapter Twelve
Rex

One month later

I'm thinking about growing back the 'stache

IGGY

You're an idiot

VALE

Bro . . . no

y'all suck :/

VALE

Why do you want it? This must be coming from some deeper motivation.

wtf dude, did a shrink body snatch my best bro?

IGGY

Yup. His fake doctor wife. But V asks a good question. Why do you want that hideous thing back on your face?

VALE

REAL doctor. Fake wife.

it's sexy :/

IGGY

Says who? Have you asked the vag you're hoping to push broom how she feels about bristles?

Are you stroking out, freak?

Vale

What Iggy means is that a well-man-
icured mustache can work for some
ladies. Sometimes. That's not what you
had. Just go with some scruff and call it
a day.

Iggy

Who are you trying to impress with a
hairy upper lip anyway?

Birdie obviously

Iggy

a birdie, huh?

(¬‿¬)

Vale

Nooooo

brb

laughing so hard I can't breathe

(o_o) ┌∩┐

she's a PERSON you deviants!

Iggy

Ohhhh. THE Birdie. The one you bought a showerhead for, right? Did she love the detachable head? Oh, did she let you drive it? ;)

On second thought, keep the details to yourself.

"I know the service is good up here, but how can you look at your phone with all this?" Birdie turns in a half circle, arms upraised, hair down, and cheeks flushed.

We hiked up the short trail from her house after lunch so I could show her the final touches of the viewing platform. One month in, and it's done and dusted.

"Right. It's beautiful." I clear my throat and try not to think about her in the shower, but as the skirt of her sundress lifts higher, the fantasy eats at me. She has such glowy skin. But wet? Mmmm. I scratch my hairy chest, wishing I knew.

Birdie's made good on her boundaries, I'll say that. But boundaries were meant to be tested. I think someone really smart said that once.

In light of that, I work shirtless. Exclusively. It doesn't matter that it's November and the cold winds of winter are blowing in. I'm a demon. I run hot, hottest when I've got a goal in mind—seducing the pretty human I'm working for. She hasn't cracked yet, but I catch her watching me when I'm digging holes or chopping wood or riding one of the horses. That spark is still there, I can feel it.

She makes her way over to the big-ass metal binoculars, the kind you might see in a zoo or along the edge of the Grand Canyon. Her fingers trace over all the shiny new details, from the eyeholes to the joints to the metal arms connecting it to the base, allowing the telescope part to tilt and swivel any which way. Sunlight shines in through the slats of the pergola's roof I built overhead for shade and protection. I used more of the wood to make some long benches and a couple seven-foot tall weather-resistant signs. She's getting some educational posters and shit to put in it soon, once I get some plexiglass sheets to protect them. I also found some smaller boulders nearby that, with the help of the horses, I was able to finagle into place for extra seating.

But it's the jumbo binoculars that are the real centerpiece of the platform. The box it came in called it a *viewing scope*. It had a photo of them on the Empire State Building. Heavy as shit, come to find out. Took me two full days to install to my satisfaction. Fucker was expensive too, but Birdie came into a surprise payday a couple weeks ago when my actor buddy, Vale, rented the ranch to shoot a televised interview with him and his new fake wife. He's in some holiday romcom movie coming out soon, I guess. It's a long story.

Birdie wants to buy a couple more of the scopes but she's gonna wait to see how it holds up in the elements first. Smart girl.

She bends over and the gust of cool air lifts the hem of her dress in a flutter of fabric. She's wearing tights, but she's built so thick from the waist down, they're almost sheer over her plump thighs and the curve of her ass. Unless I'm seeing things, I think she may only be wearing a thong under that.

I bite my fist.

After our kitchen romp, Birdie informed me she got tested for STDs, worried that Randy left because he was cheating. Her results ended up coming back negative. As did mine when I checked. Demons and humans can't normally conceive the old-fashioned way, so taking her bare isn't as much of a risk. Now, it's all I can imagine, my cum leaking out of her, filling her up again and again.

Being around Birdie every day is a delicious form of torture, specifically designed for me. If the judge knew, he'd be thrilled. He wouldn't have bothered with community service. He'd have ordered her to do exactly what she's doing. Fuck me like a sexual tornado then refuse to touch me for the remainder of my sentence.

I had that one fast-and-furious taste of her, buried deep inside all that heat with her wide-open eyes full of emotion showing me her entire world.

Totally open to me. Finally, my chance.

Then . . . nothing.

Even after all the oohing and aahing over the finished project, not a swoon in my arms, not a smacker on the lips, not even a full-body hug. Nothing but very animated thank-yous. Okay, that's not nothing.

And I can't say I don't understand her reasoning for distance. I do.

I just have a counterargument. *Fuck it* is my argument. Hasn't quite resonated with her yet.

"Looks pretty snazzy, huh?" I ask, trying to get a few more gasps and compliments. I'm eating that shit up.

"Rex, it's incredible!" She comes closer, curls swirling in the wind, never looking more beautiful. I played some small part in that, in seeing more of her smiles and less of the tears. Not that she lets me see her crying. Birdie Lynn is real good at keeping her feelings hidden, but I hear her sniffling all the same. I don't think she's used to sharing space with anybody, so her walls are lower out here than the months we circled each other back at her mom's over Thursday dinners.

"Ow! Shit!" My ankle stings like it got chopped with a tiny machete. "What the f—"

"Lemmy, no!" Birdie tugs the leash connected to her prairie dog's tiny harness back. For a few glorious seconds, I forgot the little shit was up here with us. He's getting some mobility back in his broken leg and has been connected to her like glue lately.

"Baked potato rat," I whisper. He hates me for some reason.

She kneels down to pull him back. "I'm sorry. Did he break skin?"

I pull up my pant leg but it's just an angry-looking, dark imprint. "I'm fine."

The fact she's nearly always got one, if not half a dozen, animals surrounding her hasn't been in my favor for the seduce-the-daylights-out-of-Birdie-Lynn mission. And this fucker is one of the worst offenders.

A squawk precedes the arrival of the horny wood owl. Speak of death itself.

"Sunny!"

Her feathered friend was released into the wild months ago but still drops in for treats and pets. Apparently, she wasn't supposed to hand-feed them, so now they have a name and are basically part of the family. She scratches their head and their dark eyes flutter closed. But the second I move closer, it pops back up and cocks its head to the side, regarding me coolly. I can almost feel their venom singing through my veins, and they haven't even bit me yet. The threat and intention couldn't be more clear. I've gotta find some animal allies, and these two aren't it.

Birdie coaxes Sunny to fly off and turns back to me.

"I'll never be able to thank you enough. Seriously." She ties Lemmy to the viewing scope and rushes to her big backpack. "I almost forgot! I have a surprise for you." She digs around and pulls out a tall rectangular box. It looks so familiar.

Then it hits me. "Holy Darkness."

"Yep." She grins. "It's our shop class project. A little worse for wear, but only because it's seen good use. I wanted to install it up here somewhere."

"You kept it," I whisper, taken back to that winter afternoon years ago, how I'd put off that last coat of paint just to have another day with her.

"Of course." She looks at me like I'm crazy as I close the distance. "The first thing I did when I moved into the property was put it up on my back porch."

My chest squeezes as I stare at her. Those midnight eyes suck me in every time. The fact I can't kiss the fuck out of her right now is so unfair.

"I can build you another one," I finally manage to croak. "A bigger one. We could do it together." Mother Below, I sound pathetic, and maybe she sees it because her eyes shift away and she squeezes me in a hug. Not a full-body one, but a careful side hug since we're both still holding the structure in a hand.

I take a deep breath. My thumb traces the faded design of a window she drew on the side with Sharpie, remembering how I sourced the white ash from the scrap pile after she did some research and realized it'd be the most attractive for the fireflies.

Dropping my face to the top of her head, I inhale the scent of her hair, just letting the moment breathe.

"This just feels *right*," she says. "It's all like a dream come true."

I know she means to say turning this cement slab into a viewing platform is her dream come true, but fuck it, I'm reading more into it. We work so well together. Surely she's starting to see it.

"Making decisions for yourself isn't half bad, huh?" I squeeze her side.

"I guess not." She squeezes me back and turns her face to my shoulder. "You smell, by the way."

Swiftly, I grab her hair in a fist and tug until she's looking at me only to see a sassy slant to her smile. "That so?"

Minx. Joke's on her, because after our little romp I know she *likes* the way I smell. I know more of her secrets every day.

"You should really start wearing shirts. The first snow will be any day now."

"Mhmm." I think she's playing hard to get.

She pats the palm of her hand on my belly before shoving my arm off and stepping back. Still, I catch the swallow as her gaze drifts slowly away from my body. I'm a big boy, soft where other dudes are Dorito shaped, but she likes what she sees. Even if she won't admit to it easily.

When it comes to Birdie, I don't forget a thing. She's never once said that what we did was a *mistake* or a *regret* or even *wrong*. Inappropriate, sure. Inappropriate I can work with. Birdie's a rule follower, through and through.

I basically strong-armed her into our demon's deal, giving me the chance to volunteer at the ranch. I need to bust my ass to show her it was the right decision, that she's getting nothing but good out of it. I need to make the rules work for me. Not my specialty, but with this twist of fate in my favor, putting Birdie and me in daily contact, I'll do whatever it takes to have another taste of her.

"Alright boss, what's next?" I set the weathered habitat on a bench and brush some nonexistent dust off my chest before pointing to the right with both arms. If I flex a little, who's to say. "We've got that other cement pad to do something with. There's still plenty of wood left, but if you want a full cabin I'll need about a truckload of supplies." The two sites are only a couple hundred feet from each other.

She bites the inside of her cheek and I know there's something on her mind but she just needs the confidence to say it.

"What about a tent?" she asks.

I nod, even though I have no idea what she's getting at. Tents don't need wood and would blow off the hill with a strong wind, but I don't want to negative Nelly her when I know there's more to the idea.

"Have you ever seen the fancy glamping-type ones?" Her hands move in swirling motions and the excitement starts bubbling out. "I've been doing some research and it's not too expensive, good for the outdoors, and a really versatile option for a multifunctional space."

"Nerd." Always with the big fancy words.

She rolls her eyes "Okay, so if we make a permanent frame from wood and get it secured to the foundation, it'll be really stable. The canvas fabric on the sides could be utilized in different ways. I'm thinking half-open with a flat sunshade, it could serve as an outdoor classroom for kids' field trips or community groups, giving them easy access between here and the viewing platform. But, we could also fully close it in if visiting scholars need to stay overnight, like for longer research trips. Can you imagine? Helping *real* wildlife research? Getting to chat with them over dinner on the patio?"

She's practically vibrating and I want to pinch her cheeks so bad, but by some strength of will hold back. "Real smart, Birdie Lynn."

"Oh no." Her jaw ticks side to side. "The barn's bathroom is way too far. People would need a toilet at a minimum, for accessibility. Maybe it wouldn't work."

I'm not about to let her second guess herself now.

"Ecotoilets are simple as shit, pun intended, and don't need running water," I say. "Plus, for overnight stays, the researchers can rough it with a camper's sink and bag shower if they don't want to clean up at the barn. You could always give the horses or those lazy blacknose goats a workout carting up a couple jerricans of water."

She grins. "Fun fact: Goats were among the first animals to ever be domesticated, likely over 9,000 years ago. Plus, you're right. They could probably use the exercise."

"Nerd." I poke her nose. "Sounds like a good fit then. I can figure out how to rig a clean and gray water setup that's easy to manage. No frills, though."

"No frills is fine. You really think it'd work?"

"Fuck, yeah. People love that zero-waste, eco-friendly shit, especially if they're all morally upstanding animal lovers like yourself."

"Morally upstanding?" she teases, poking my side.

I shrug. "If the shoe fits."

"Like your shirts clearly don't?" She sticks out her tongue, but can't hide her smile. I try to pinch it but she dances back.

Man, oh man, Birdie's a tough nut to crack when she sets her mind to something. And that something, right now, is *not* fucking me. I did get a hug just now though. Progress is being made. Maybe it's time to push.

"I'm a hot-blooded, virile, young demon. Shirts are un-necessary."

"You're thirty-one Rex."

"We both are. Age is a state of mind, honey." And she didn't say I wasn't virile. I waggle my eyebrows at her. "Anyway, laundry's a bitch when you live in a barn." If she'd only let me sleep on the couch, get a little closer—

"It was your prerogative to live on property. You agreed to that deal. Besides, you have free rein of my washroom and kitchen as long as you give me a heads-up."

Because she doesn't want me sniffing around when she's scantily clad or naked or showering. Speaking of showering . . .

"You ever get that showerhead I gifted you?"

"Showerhead?" She blinks for a second then makes the connection. "Oh! When that came in, I thought you bought it for the barn bathroom. For yourself. I put it in there."

"It was a wedding gift."

She rears back. Shit, maybe I shouldn't have brought up the whole getting jilted thing.

"I-I gave back all the wedding gifts already," she stammers. "Um, just keep it. Install it in the barn or mail it home or-or it's probably still in the return window. I could check online to initiate a refund and drop it by the—"

"It's for you," I interrupt, stepping closer. "I bought it for one reason and one reason only." I grasp a curl and tuck it behind her ear, letting my thumb rub along the delicate curve and pinch the satin-soft lobe.

"Why?" she asks, quiet as a whisper.

"So you could jill off in the shower and think of me."

Her jaw drops. "Even when . . . You didn't!"

I grin. "You know I did."

"Evil!" She snorts and smacks my chest. I grab her hand tight and place it, palm down, over my heart.

Flirting with this woman is always a dance on the razor-thin edge of disaster and delight.

"Your kind of evil?" I bend lower and run my nose along her hairline. Fuck, she always smells so good, a night-blooming flower you can only catch once in a blue moon. The kind you wait for. Her arousal coats my throat and tongue, so thick in the air between us it's making me crazy.

Just before my lips brush her forehead, she steps back.

"I have a power dynamic over you." Her hand falls from my chest, and for the first time today, I feel cold. Half naked. "It can't happen again. We need boundaries. If this is what you really want, to volunteer here."

"It's not what I want." My jaw clenches. I take a breath when she makes a sharp inhale, needing to set her straight. "I don't mind the work, Birdie Lynn. I'll work like a dog for you, sunup to sundown, but it's not what I want. What I *want* is you. That smart mouth of yours, that wet pussy on my face. I want to fuck you in every room of your house. In your car. Outdoors. Doesn't fucking matter as long as I get another taste of that fire you're hiding."

She shivers, breaths going short. I don't think Birdie's familiar with the kind of intensity I feel for her. It's new for me too.

"But boundaries are what *you* need, hmm?" I ask. "Space?"

"I think-I think it's the best idea."

I huff, and maybe I'm crazy but I see a crack in the wall she's got between us. It's not what she needs. The way she stuttered or the bland way she described boundaries as *the best idea*. It reeks of the way she called Randy her *best option*. For once, the reminder doesn't eat at me.

Birdie's practical to a fault. Thoughtful. She doesn't let herself have fun or feel much of anything just because. I aim to change that, but I also need to be patient, let her come to me. I can't help but leave her with a rational argument though.

"You're not my supervisor. We're doing each other a favor. As equals. A bargain between two adults. And if I recall correctly, our deal didn't involve intimacy between us at all. That was never on the table. Your exact words were '*You work for me until your probation is over. I let you live here and vouch for you with the court.*' That's it. That's all we agreed to."

She takes it in, swallows, and her hand lifts up. For one stupid second I think it'll land on my cheek, that she'll lean in and—

Buzz. Buzz.

The bracelet she wears as my designated Community Service Compliance Officer lights up in green, as I'm sure the embarrassing clamp on my stupid horn does.

"You've done way more than twenty hours this week. Maybe you should take some time off," she says with a courtesy smile. Her opposite hand fiddles with the bracelet like it's a physical reminder of the barrier between us, even though that's hogshit. "I didn't want to forget to log your hours today. Doing it online is a pain."

"Government websites are trash."

"True."

And we're back to small talk. Cute.

That's okay, though. We've made progress even if I pushed a little too far just now. I've got time, plenty of time to win her over. My phone beeps.

"It's my brother," I mumble. Again. He keeps pestering me about final prep for the new Perkatory locations. Easy shit he could answer if he just did a web search. I explain that the designer needs to use drywall screws for hanging the art instead of nails. On a whim, I send him a few photos of the completed project with the viewing scope. "I've really gotta get him up to see this sometime."

"Maybe you'll find a shirt for the occasion?" she jokes, bringing us back to the comfort zone of snarkiness.

"Not a chance." I tuck my phone away again. I'm made of tougher stuff than that, especially when I've got a woman to woo.

Sleeping with her was probably a mistake. To be fair, we didn't sleep at all. We fucked and it was glorious. Naw, screw that. I'd do it again in a heartbeat. If it goes down as my most epic fuckup, I have zero regrets, though winning her over again will be complicated.

She's not in a place to take me seriously, not that I'm a serious guy who deserves her by any stretch of the imagination. *Who says she'd even want you?* the asshole in my head whispers. *She fucked you because you were on your way out of town. You were just the wrong guy at the right time.*

I shake of my head, telling that part of me to fuck off. My penance continues. I'm going to be a fucking good guy for once.

"Would it be okay if I invited him over sometimes? Maybe after I finish the fancy tent idea."

"Of course!" She looks around at the wooden structure, the empty education sign, and the viewing scope at the overlook with a small smile. "Especially since I took you away from your work at Perkatory. Oh, and Noelle! They should both come out for a visit. Maybe dinner or . . ." Her eyelashes flutter, and she looks away. It takes me a second to realize what has her retreating. The reason she hasn't left the ranch in over a month.

"The last time they were out here was probably that fucked up surprise engagement, huh?"

She shrugs more than nods, but that's a yes. She hasn't stepped foot back in Winter Bliss and is dodging her friends' calls. Her mom comes by with groceries, but Birdie isn't ready to talk about much with anyone.

My first probation meeting is in a couple days. She offered to drive me but looked so fucking anxious I told her I'd take Mimi instead. The younger horse can always use the exercise and it'll help test how she does without her mom for a longer trip.

Probation terms say I can't drive a car, which makes horses fair game as far as I'm concerned. And I've sworn off alcohol altogether. Fuck that shit. I make enough bad decisions dead sober.

"I want them to come visit," she says. "Especially to see all the work you've done. I just—It's so embarrassing. Did you know that night was supposed to be a relaunch of the ranch as Wild Hearts Retreat?"

"Corny name."

"Rex!" She swats me with the back of her hand and I grab it again. At this point, she should know that's what's gonna happen. My thumb rolls over her knuckles, and she doesn't snatch it back, just keeps talking. "It was my idea. The Wild Hearts part, at least. The *Retreat* was Randy's, a way to market the cabins to the kinds of high-end tourists he was trying to attract. That dinner was a way to get our name out there with local friends. The engagement was just, well it was a business decision more than anything." She shakes her head.

The idea of that doucheburger and Birdie together is like a fucking rusty sword through my spleen. I can't help but sneer, my heart squeezing with rage at what he did to her. And still, radio silence from the chucklefuck. It's been weeks and he's supposedly still in Greece, living it up. *Snot-nosed cockbag.*

"You really hate the name?"

I glare at her. *Randy? Of course.*

"Wild Hearts?" Birdie asks with a small voice. "I actually wanted to call it Wild Hearts Sanctuary. That's probably even cornier."

A sanctuary.

Fuck. That's exactly what this place is.

And *Wild Hearts* was her idea. The realization makes my chest ache. She probably meant the name to symbolize every stinky, broken animal she comes across that she tucks into her pocket and makes whole again through early morning feedings and late-night research and mounting vet bills that all get covered on a shoestring budget.

Wild Hearts Sanctuary.

I see the name in a new light.

She's the beating, bleeding heart of this place, the one who gives everything to those who have no chance of survival otherwise. The one who makes them strong enough to be wild again, gives them a safe place to heal and grow.

Damn. In a twisted way, maybe I'm one of them. I'm living in her barn for fuck's sake. I needed her help and despite being an absolute moron ninety percent of the time I'm around her, she took me in.

But if there's one thing I'm sure of with Birdie? She doesn't pity me. Or the animals for that matter. Her goodness is straight from the heart. And every little confidence she gives me, each tender moment, like this one right here, is a gift. A treasure I sock away. Something I refuse to fuck up now.

"No. I get it," I say, my voice scratchy. "A sanctuary is exactly what this place is." I squeeze her hand and bring it to my lips. "But the wildest heart out here is yours."

And I'll be damned if it won't be mine one day.

Chapter Thirteen
Birdie

As the days grow shorter, I wake up a little earlier. The sky is still an inky purple when I bundle up and head out to check on the smaller animals. My busy season officially starts on Friday, the day after Thanksgiving, when families descend on the ranch to cut down their Christmas tree.

And I still have so much to do.

By the time I've seen to the rabbits, ferrets, prairie dog, and chickens, the sky's brightened to sherbert pinks and oranges. I make breakfast for three—one portion for me and double for Rex. Sometimes he'll shuffle into the kitchen early in search of caffeine, but usually I bring it to him. The demon works hard, well over his required twenty hours per week, but man does he love to sleep in.

Reluctantly, I've come to admit that Rex has been a huge help. Not only has he taken on my two special construction projects, he's also a natural at tree trimming, and does most of the chores for the bigger animals in the barn.

For the first time in a long time, when I go to sleep at night, I feel like I can breathe. Even with the holidays approaching, my tasks are manageable and the ranch isn't only being held together by duct tape and a dream.

I finish off my eggs and toast, package up Rex's, and jump into the Jeep just as dawn is truly starting to glow orange and yellow between the mountaintops. I fix my hair in the rearview mirror and pop a stick of gum in my mouth. If I'm wearing some lip stain, new overalls that hug my ass just right, and a warm red sweater that makes my skin glow, who's to say?

As I drive, I glance over at the hill where the new tent recently went up, though I can only see an obscured view.

Today, Rex promised he'd show me the progress on my multifunctional tent. After that, we'll do a quick drive around the property to distribute extra food pellets for the wild animals using the feed dispenser on the back of my Jeep. As winter approaches, I like to make sure there's enough for the deer, sheep, elk, and occasional moose that roam the ranch, especially since several of them are threatened or endangered. Finally, we'll finish trimming the last acre of Christmas trees before I'm officially open for business. The major pruning happens in the summer, but right before the holiday season starts, the entire tree farm gets one last round with the chainsaw-like hedge trimmer so they have that perfect triangle shape.

Naturally, wielding a deadly mechanized tool is Rex's favorite thing to do. What takes my other seasonal employees a day to do, he can bust out in a couple of hours. And even though working shirtless is dangerous, he refuses to put one on. Wood chips and sharp metal be damned.

He's an obstinate demon. And kind of a genius.

I can't help but smile as I pass the field with half a dozen giant tractor tires scattered about. While frost covers most of the ground, I have a section of land heated geothermally that stays grassy year-round. Last week, I found all my goats tied to the tires via crude rope leashes. Thinking Rex was mistreating them, I gave him a piece of my mind before he explained it was a way to test out rotational grazing without setting up big temporary fences.

The whole setup—ropes scattered around big tires—looks janky as all get-out, but it worked *and* cut my hay bill by half. When the herd had properly decimated their circles, Rex painstakingly flipped each huge tire to the next field over.

All that sweaty, muscled back in service of feeding a few ornery goats. It was a sight to behold, I'll say that. Not that I should be mooning after my shirtless criminally-inclined volunteer, but, well . . . I kind of am. And I can't seem to convince myself it's a bad idea. I'm just looking, after all. Even if those looks come with the hottest sensual memories of what his touch felt like.

I park outside the barn and open the group chat that's been popping off this morning. Since my stepmom's family started the farm decades ago, I always hire her siblings, nephews, and nieces as seasonal staff for trimming and cutting the trees. However, since Rex is absolutely killing it on the prep side, they get a break this year.

I sent them a reminder that we're opening on Friday, bright and early, and what shifts I need covered.

ORLA

> You sure you don't need extra help in advance? I can come this week anytime. Just let me know.

ETHEL

> You know I'll hold down the register. Don't worry one bit.

KVETA

> Will we be sharing some shifts? Miss you.

SIMON

> Sign me up. I'm here for you, girl.

There's no outright pity in their messages, but I can sense their concern like whispers in my ear, getting closer and closer. I haven't seen any of them since my not-wedding day. My mom has come to visit but only briefly. Seven weeks of missed family dinners. I know I have to face them all this week, and I will.

The truth is, Rex isn't only saving me money by pitching in, he's helping me continue to avoid, well, everyone. My hermit behavior has to end.

It's just that every time I imagine facing their pity, I clam up. *I don't need your sympathy* I wish I could shout! *Wipe the entire debacle from your minds!* But I promised to come over for Thanksgiving and Mom's already been dropping hints about all the other holiday events coming up. With the tree farm opening, I have to be ready to actually face people.

A Wild Hearts Holiday.

I let out an ugly loud exhale of relief as I slam my car door closed and move to the barn, happy at least that it's one less thing I have to worry about. The only upside to getting jilted is not having to deal with that stuffy, catered, $300 per plate dinner for the rich and well-connected of Winter Bliss that Randy was planning.

That was all him. I'm over it. From now on, all I care about is me, my ranch, and what I want to do with it.

Fuck Randy.

I open the barn and check in on the stalls. I see Rex must've woken up earlier to feed everyone, then fallen back asleep. That's his typical routine. When I finally make it back to his makeshift bedroom, a raised platform of hay bales and several layers of old quilts, I stop and lean against the low barrier blocking off his space from the rest.

Before I start clapping to try and rouse him from his snore-filled slumber, I let myself just look. He's honestly breathtaking. A perfect male specimen, at least in my eyes, with his overwide chest and messy hair, the rounded swell of his belly with sweatpants riding low. Lying down, somehow his neck seems even thicker than normal. Inked up with those sexy tattoos.

It's not a crime to look. Maybe a little creepy, though I know he would encourage the attention. He flirts shamelessly but never pushes too far. I'm the only one with boundaries in this strange partnership we've got. Restraint is my defense.

There's just one problem. Day by day, it's all falling apart.

The urge to jump this demon's bones is reaching critical levels. He's sexy and huge, sure. But anyone with a pulse would understand my plight seeing the way, right this moment, he's cuddled up with a three-month-old goat drooling on his naked chest. Rex's hand is so big it cups their furry little rump like a football. When the little guy fidgets, Rex does too, like they're some kind of interspecies father/son pair.

The resemblance is sort of uncanny. This particular goat kid has no need of hand rearing. He's not the runt of the litter. If anything, he's the not-runt, the biggest of them all, so plump and greedy for milk that his mom frequently singes him with a blast of fire to try and give his siblings a chance to eat.

Naturally, Rex felt for the hungry guy's plight and has essentially adopted him as his own. The cuteness is almost too much. I take a breath and shore up my defenses.

"Rise and shine!" I sing out with a gentle clap of my hands.

On a dramatic groan, Rex peeks at me with one gleaming orange eye, before closing it and shifting the goat higher up his chest for a kiss on the head. Oof. I bite my lip at the adorableness.

"Your mistress is a real ballbuster. Works me nonstop. Can't even sleep in." He cracks open the other eye to peer at me. "Dewdrop needs his beauty rest, boss."

I try to restrain my smile. "His name is Baaaaash."

All the goats have long-vowel B-names because it's fun. Except Gumdrop, their mom, because she was already named when I got the property.

"Bash?" His lips curl in disgust. "After Bandit and Beth and Billy and Borat, you have to admit your creative juices are running low."

"Dewdrop's kind of whimsical for him, don't you think?"

The kid in question blinks awake, and I'd swear he's judging me.

Rex snorts smoke which the goat copies immediately. "Who says you can't be whimsical with a little meat on your bones? Dewdrop deserves a special name, like his mom. He likes to lick the dew off the grass in the morning. It's the cutest."

I barely restrain the urge to laugh, the sensation warming my chest as my cheeks twitch to smile. Rex is so annoying sometimes, but when he's goofy with the animals, my loins quake.

"He's even litter trained." Rex stands up and makes his way over to me. With his eyes locked on his little buddy, I have another chance to take in his massive frame. Ugh. The shirtlessness must be stopped. "A real gentleman he's turning out to be. Good instincts with people too."

"You mean because he likes you," I tease. Most of my animals find Rex frightening. Not that I blame them. It's probably the prey instinct in the face of a giant male demon. He's kind of an apex predator in the scheme of things around here. For a moment, I'm reminded that he's leaving the ranch in only a few weeks. "Bash really shouldn't be sleeping with you."

He looks hurt, and hugs the fluffy goat tighter. "It's almost winter, Birdie Lynn. Have a heart. And his name is Dewdrop. Get it straight."

I roll my eyes. "Get dressed. I want to see how the tent is going and then we've got that last acre to hit."

"Yes, ma'am." He drops Bash, err, Dewdrop, in the goat paddock on the way to the bathroom. When he comes out in blue jeans and nothing else, I hand over the food and coffee. Cracking it open, he closes his eyes on an inhale. "Mmmm. You're too good to me."

He's a hungry demon with a long day of tree trimming ahead of him. It's the least I can do. As usual, he inhales his breakfast in three minutes flat.

"You really should wear a flannel at least for the trimming, Rex." It doesn't matter how many times I try to warn him about basic workplace safety, he's just obstinate about the shirtlessness.

"I wear goggles." He throws two pairs of battered safety eyewear in his backpack. "Good enough."

"Don't say I didn't warn you when you slice off a nipple."

He grimaces and covers his chest. "Don't put that out in the world, Birdie Lynn."

I shake my head to hide my smile.

"Let's go, big guy."

"That's what she said . . . once upon a time."

I'd like to say his puppy dog eyes have no effect on me, but I'd be lying. And even if it's only to myself, I'm trying not to do that anymore.

By the time we hike up the hill that the second foundation was built on, I'm practically shaking with excitement when I see the tent in all its glory.

With a cry of joy, I rush over to feel the canvas fabric in my fingers. Even early in the morning, the moisture doesn't stick at all. And the zipper enclosing the entrance is perfectly flush with a lower barrier which I can see would keep the warmth in for someone camping overnight. It's totally dark and empty inside except for a few heavy-duty trunks, until Rex unties a couple of flaps that act as windows.

The sunlight pours in, and even more, I'm blown away, breathless at seeing it put together. My fingers trace over every little detail as I race around and babble out each of the specifications I know by heart after painstakingly researching the setup.

How the fabric is taut against the wooden frame and every corner. How three of the four sides are capable of being propped open to create a shaded learning space. How the fourth wall houses the climate control and simple bathroom/kitchenette, meaning up to six researchers could camp on cots for extended stays. The roll up dry-erase board fits perfectly along one side. There's a small wooden table that can fold out to six times its size, stained to match the tent frame and the collapsible bench seating tucked into one corner. Everything is custom constructed to serve the two purposes I wanted. Education and research.

It's perfect.

"You don't hate it, huh?"

I spin to find Rex leaning against one of the support posts, arms crossed, looking nervous. How could he even—

"It's the most beautiful thing I've ever seen." Tears well up instantly, and I cover my mouth to hold in the happy sob. *Get it together, Birdie!* I rush over and smack his chest. "It looks even better than the photos!"

"I made some modifications." His mouth tips up on one side, almost bashful. "Improvements, I think."

"You think!" I beat my fists jokingly against his bare chest, and when he tentatively pats my back, I give in and go for a bear hug, working through the surprising fit of crying I'm going through. My words come out through hitched breaths. "With everything else going on— I never really let myself believe— It didn't seem possible. I still don't know if these two sites will even become anything, but—"

"Of course they will." He squeezes me tight while one hand cradles my head. "You're a force of nature, honey. All your dreams are just a step away."

That just makes me cry more. I let the hope sink in, trying not to doubt that what I want with the ranch could one day become a reality. That this place could be an epicenter for education about the fragile, incredible ecosystem right here in Winter Bliss.

"I gotta up my game," he rumbles beneath my cheek. "I've mastered making you angry. We can add crying to the list, but smiling? I'm rusty with that one."

I snort then pull back and let loose the smile I try so hard to hide around him. I can't even remember why anymore.

"A hundred billion smiles and yours is the best." He pinches my chin. "Just makes me happy to see it."

I can't help but needle him. "There's only about seven billion people in the—"

"Shut your piehole, smart-ass."

I fall back into his chest and giggle.

"No, no, no. Look here." He lifts my face back up and pokes my cheeks until I laugh again. "There we go, Birdie Lynn. Prettiest smile that ever was."

He opens one of the flaps to show me how he set up the clean and gray water, fully outfitted with a camping sink, small outdoor shower, and ecotoilet. There's a simple foot pump faucet and the toilet uses sawdust to compost with no cleanup necessary. They're both incredibly easy to use and maintain.

Just as he's explaining how to take a shower over the two-foot square cedar plank platform using a water bag, I get a phone call. While he finishes rigging that up to demonstrate, I sit down on the wood slats and look at my screen.

Incoming Call - Randy

I blink. It's been almost two months of radio silence. I hit the End Call button with shaking hands. How? Why?

A text pops up.

RANDY

Please answer. It's important.

The phone rings again and I feel lightheaded. He's like the freaking ghost of Christmas past from that Scrooge story. Something about seeing his name after weeks of imagining my future unfolding without him brings me back to who I was *with* him.

Compliant and completely tuned out.

When that call goes unanswered he calls a third time.

I do it. I hit the green button and bring the phone to my ear. Still, I can't seem to utter a word. There's movement on the other end, until finally he breaks the silence.

"Birdie?"

I make a humming noise in answer. What the fuck is wrong with me? *Speak! Yell at him!*

"Hey. So . . ."

I swallow.

"The Wild Hearts Holiday PR package I emailed out the, um, the night before . . ." he trails off.

"You left me," I fill in the gap quietly.

He sighs. "Yeah. So it's bouncing around with some big players—the mayor, school superintendent, and Chamber of Commerce leadership. It's generating a lot of interest. We've gotten some calls about—"

"You're back?" I gasp.

"No. I'm still traveling, trying out the digital nomad life. I snagged that honeymoon package on such a steal but you were adamant about not going. Call it cold feet or mental health crisis, I don't know. I'm a travel agent who's never traveled!"

My jaw grinds. There's no hint of apology, just a—*this is what I wanted and you didn't get in line.* He left me to go on vacation.

"I never cheated on you or anything. I still, you know, I care about you."

He does? How? Knowing he didn't cheat is a cold comfort. Every word over the line seems to numb me further. I feel myself breathing and blinking, but can't say anything. At my continued silence, he prattles on.

"Anyway, my sister's been holding down the fort. We just found out that the holiday event flier was shared in the local country club newsletter and uh . . ."

I groan and rub my temples, imagining the rich and fabulous of Winter Bliss and surrounding areas chitchatting about the formal evening affair they were promised.

"How are the cabins coming along?" he asks.

I scoff. Back to business, then. I clear my throat. "They're not. There aren't going to be any cabins."

"Oh." His voice pitches up. Did he really assume I'd just be a good soldier and continue partnering with him in the vacation rental business after he left me at the altar? "I'll let Susie know to reach out to the email list that signed up as interested in bookings."

"You do that." My tone comes out even, which is better than how shaky I feel. *A Wild Hearts Holiday.* Something about it sticks in my mind. "Forward me your email about the event. What the newsletter saw." As expected, he didn't cc me on the message and I have no idea what's been promised. He mentioned the superintendent and the mayor were interested, both people I have in mind to reach out to about the new educational direction of the ranch. Would canceling the event leave a sour taste in their mouths right when I want to pivot to something new?

"What do you want to do about the holiday event?" he asks. "My, well to be honest, my reputation is on the line with this, especially if I'm putting out the word the cabins aren't happening."

His reputation? Unbelievable.

"It could be a great networking opportunity for you," he picks up, talking faster. "Hey, use it to promote your little tree farm. Or hell, pivot to a fundraiser. Put out a donation jar for the animals. You know, I'd be happy to manage the ticket sales remotely and set aside a portion for your non-profit."

Little farm? Donation jar?! My teeth grind at the minimization of everything I do day in and day out. The assumption he'd control all the money. How his energy picks up the moment he thinks he can convince *me* to do work for him. *Him!* I hold back from laughing like a madwoman, from snarling out a curse.

Fuck you, Randy!

All my desire to hear him apologize evaporates into thin air. He clearly doesn't give a shit. And the truth is, I get it. I don't give a flying fuck about him either. Not a day has gone by that I miss his presence. That should have struck me as strange before now. The only thing he brings up is a reminder of my humiliation, of what a fucking pushover I've always been.

There's something scratching at the back of my mind though—a seed of an idea about the holiday event—but I'm too blinded by the cacophonous anger and bone-deep sadness that I spent so long dating this asshole!

Rex yanks the phone out of my hand and whispers darkly into the receiver.

"Riddle me this, you Gumby-looking cockwaffle. How does it feel to know you ruined the best thing to ever be placed in your clammy, shit-stained hands? I hope it drives you to drink a gallon of dish soap in the stupid hope you could ever wash away the shame. I hope your family whispers about you behind your back until you're on death's door, alone in a musty nursing home because they all know you're a rat-faced hosebag who doesn't deserve to breathe the same air as Birdie. And if I ever see you in a dark alleyway—"

With my heart in my throat, my wits return and I snatch the phone back. I stare at the screen and bark out a relieved exhale when I see Rex accidentally fat fingered and put the call on mute when he grabbed it from me.

"Birdie? Still there?" Randy's voice is tinny.

I turn away from Rex. His energy is too addictive, the desire to repeat everything he just said with my own colorful spin is far too tempting. But I need to be smart right now. Maybe I can salvage that holiday event. I just need some time to think.

"We'll talk soon, Randy," I say, tone flat. "Send me that email."

After hanging up, I set the phone aside and hang my head in my hands.

The crazy thing is—I don't even cry. I can't. Maybe I only cry when I'm happy? Is that broken of me? Or maybe it's not me. Maybe it's the dynamic between me and Randy. I'm closed off to most people, but with him, I shut down in a way I've never really realized until just now. I go numb. I turn inward. I accept the bare minimum, and part of that's on me. My brain rationalized our relationship into practical bite-sized compromises that seemed sensible at the time.

But now, on the whole, I wonder why I was always the loser, the one who did the work, the one who had to sacrifice?

I think Rex is talking—his voice sounds so far away—but there's so much static in my mind, I can't hear anything else. Deep down, was it safer to accept good enough than hold out hope for what I really wanted? Something right. Someone perfect for me. It's a chilling thought, making the numbness spread to my arms and legs.

Good enough was a better option than dreaming. It meant a comfortable way of life. No one could hurt me if they never got close enough. I can't go back to that though—

A deluge of water shocks the air out of me. Soaks through my clothes in an instant and puddles into icy mud beneath my feet. I inhale and exhale, watching my hair hang in a lumpy, dripping curtain all around my face. My whole body freezes in the cold air, but inside?

Inside of me, something dangerous flares to life.

"What the *fuck*?" I jump up in a whirl of droplets, fists balled, to find Rex with a jerrican of water poised above me.

"I tried—I asked if you were okay." He looks, frankly, a little shocked at what he did, frozen in place. "You were so quiet and still. It freaked me out."

"So you—" I sputter through wet lips. "You doused me with gallons of ice-cold water?"

"Okay." He nods, cranking his arm at me. "There you go. Get mad! Let's call that pencil-dick asshole back and read him the riot act."

I growl.

"You're the asshole! I'm SOAKED!"

His face goes blank. He drops the container and takes off running.

"Oh no, you don't!" I spring after him, slowed down by the fact my clothes are heavy and wet. His lead grows. For how big he is, the demon can run.

"Ramonarex Cohl Perchaz!"

He heads for some old stone steps that lead down to Teapot Lake. When he reaches them, he spins back with a smirk on his face. "You know my middle name."

"You're fucking smiling? Oh no, sir. You won't be smiling when I get a hold of you."

"Promises, promises." He grins and disappears down the stairs, but his voice carries. "Use the f-word one more time, Birdie Lynn. I'm bricked up."

That annoying demon! That insufferable scamp! I have no idea what I'm going to do to him when I catch him, but I better make it good. As he's scurrying down toward the water, a few steps before the dock, he slips on wet stone and falls over the edge. I don't see him land but I hear a splash.

"Rex!" I scream. My mood changes in an icy flash.

He could be knocked out cold. He could be bleeding or sinking to the bottom. I see a patch of white churning water near a section I know is deep, so I dive in. Underwater, I find him nearby, thrashing and looking disoriented, so I grab him by the horns, and swim backward to a shallow section.

We pop up at the same time, panting, and I keep tugging his arm until we're both able to stand on the lava rock lake bed.

My hands skate over his face, his neck, then yank his horns this way and that, but I don't see any blood. "Did you hit anything? Hurt yourself?"

"Just my pride." He grimaces.

"You dummy!" I pound my fist on his chest. "You big stupid jerk. You never run on a wet surface like that. You could have killed yourself!"

His face softens into the ghost of a smile. "I thought you were gonna kill me anyway."

"Don't you dare smile!" I growl and pummel his chest with both hands. His wet, naked, hairy chest. "I hate you," I say with no conviction.

His hands fall to my shoulders, then pull me closer by my back. "I don't think that's true, honey."

"It isn't." My forehead hits his chest. Why am I tearing up all of a sudden? Why am I always crying around him? Maybe I *am* broken. "You scared me."

His hand holds the base of my skull while the other fists gently under my chin. Slowly, he lifts my face. I still won't look at him. The silence extends, until I can't take it anymore and make eye contact.

His gaze is pure black with a dancing flame of gold in the center, just like when he rescued me on horseback.

"I'm sorry," he says, steady and heartfelt.

An apology. It's that simple for him. A genuine apology, the likes of which I couldn't even get from the guy who jilted me.

This big chaos monster may be the only guy who's ever cared enough about my emotions to even see them. Anger, sadness, joy, and fear. Not just that, he relentlessly drags them out of me. Even if I'm kicking and screaming.

He always has. And right now, *wanting him close* is all I feel. Why should I deny it?

I grab him by the back of the neck and demand a kiss. There's no other option anymore. I hate fighting my feelings so much. For once, even if it's only for a few weeks, I want to just let them be, maybe even follow them every once and a while.

He groans and clasps me to his chest, pulling me up with an arm under my ass. I loop my legs around his waist. Instead of messy and fast like before, he takes his time. I take mine, tracing his full lips with my finger, feeling the prickly stubble down over the bump at his throat as he gulps.

"Kiss me again," he whispers.

I oblige. Our lips meet again, gentle and soft. Warm and wet. We open and taste, learning each other for long moments in a totally new way. What it's like to be at peace with Rex instead of at odds. Our hands explore, tongues dance again and again. When we break to catch our breath, there's a furrow between his brows.

"He wants you back, doesn't he?"

"No." I shake my head. "Far from it."

His gaze darkens. "Fucking dick—"

"Stop it." I peck his lips once. Twice. Kiss him into submission until the grumbles die out and he'll let me explain. "He called, wanting to convince me to do the Wild Hearts Holiday thing he'd planned—that formal dinner for rich people a few days before Christmas."

"Fuck that." Rex rears back, his grip on my ass tightening. "Fuck him. May his business die a slow and debt-riddled death. Bad riddance, asshole."

I giggle. "Right? So that was basically my first instinct. But then, I mean, what if I did host a fun holiday event? Cut Randy out completely and just do it my way. Nothing fancy. Free admission. Have it be the open house I've always wanted for the animal side of the ranch. My moms could cook all the traditional demon solstice snacks over an open fire. We could have all kinds of fun Christmasy activities, like a holiday petting zoo, some crafts, maybe a kid-sized snow sleigh pulled by the goats."

"That sounds like a death trap."

I laugh. "Okay, fair."

"Otherwise, why not? Smart idea, turning lemons into lemonade."

I sigh and hug his neck, laying my forehead against his. "Talking with Randy was . . . Well, it was the wake-up call I didn't know I needed. I think I'm ready to show my face around town again. More than that, I want to get the message out about the new improvements, let folks know I'm open to field trips and educational events. I think A Wild Hearts Holiday might be the right move."

"Fuck yeah." His shoulders bounce as he squeezes me tight. "Let's do it."

"You're in?" I laugh, just as a snowflake lands on the tip of his nose.

"All in, honey."

Chapter Fourteen
Rex

"You should really get a mold assessment done in here." My nose tickles as I eye the age-yellowed tiles of the office ceiling and the faux wood paneling everywhere.

The formidable orc woman sitting across the desk from me doesn't move a muscle, except for a slight snarl above one of her tusks. My probation officer, Miss Gertie Dale.

"Sorry." I hold up my hands. "You should really get a mold assessment done in here, *ma'am*."

She closes her eyes slowly and takes a fortifying breath. "Mr. Perchaz. Stop avoiding the issue at hand."

"Yikes. That's my dad's name. Rex is fine."

"Rex. Focus." She steeples her fingers and leans forward on her elbows, fixing me with an ice-cold, zeroed-in stare. "You're working too much."

I make a funny sound with my lips. "Come on, now. I think this horn tracker doohickey is on the fritz. Half the time my compliance officer checks me in and out, it blinks red. Like, really fast. It's kinda freaking her out. Can I get a newer model?"

"It's not broken. It's a valid error message when you log over forty hours a week. I've tried to explain this to you." She sighs and shuffles through some paperwork on her desk. "You're working too much." With a manicured green finger, she slides a report with my name at the top over to me, pointing at a bulleted list. "Twenty-one hours per week is the average needed to complete your probation on time. In your first month, you averaged forty-five. Per week. That's too much."

I smile. *Fuck yeah.* Working my ass off for Birdie. I store the number away in the back of my mind. That should impress her. Get me a few more kisses of gratitude.

"Hey." She snaps, drawing my gaze back up. "That's a problem. Your only saving grace is that in November you got down in the single digits average per week, so the total is evening out, but this week, your hours are in the fifties."

I rub my jaw, thumb scratching through the scruff. The lower hours were when I was helping trim and prep the trees for the farm to open for the holiday season. Lately, her family's been helping run the Christmas tree business while I spent time fixing her fences. Too many of the goats have been getting loose and giving Birdie heart palpitations.

"I'm a model citizen, what can I say?" I hold my arms out, like I deserve an award. "She's running a real important animal rescue and it's my job to take care of the big guys in the barn. I do what I can to keep them safe. You really want to jeopardize animal safety?"

"Why did the hours lower last month?"

"Tree trimming. She pays me for that since it's part of the for-profit side of the ranch. For the animal-welfare side, she just kinda forgot to use that bracelet thingy to log my hours most days, but I have to admit, I like reminding her. Sometimes it leads to—" I stop myself. Fuck, I was about to spill the beans about how often my clocking in and out leads to cornering her in a barn until we're kissing like crazy. *Bad demon! That's private fucking business. Get your head on straight, asshole.*

"I can have a chat with your CSC Officer to ensure she understands the importance of—"

"No," I growl. Birdie still probably thinks us bumping uglies is inappropriate or what-the-fuck-ever. Talking to Officer Gertie Dale is gonna snuff out my fragile chance with her real quick. I lean forward. "This is between you and me."

"You said she forgets."

Smoke curls out of my nostrils. I fucked up, running my mouth as usual.

"I forget." I put a hand over my heart. "The work is mostly independent, so that shit is my responsibility. I'll do better." My temples heat, the demon instinct to turn this situation back in my favor is close. "But think about it. If you convinced her to log more of my hours, wouldn't that make the problem worse?"

"True." She props her head on one hand and assesses me. "So stop working so much. Keep an eye on your total service hours balance on the website and adjust accordingly. If you're over forty hours in a week, the tribunal has no procedures for how to compensate you."

"That website is shit," I grumble, then her last sentence flickers back through my awareness. "Wait. I'm trying to read between the lines here. You're saying Judge Grimshaw has to cut me a check for any hours I work over?" I grin and lean my elbows on her desk. "Now that would be something. Really stick it to the man."

"No." She throws her hands up. A defensive posture. I'm onto something here. "What I'm saying is the tribunal has never been faced with a demon criminal who likes to work for free as much as you do. Our system is coded to accept up to forty hours per week, but because of your projected trajectory, leadership is looking into international labor laws and starting an internal audit of the time card system.

They've been holding weekly meetings to discuss a remedy."

I laugh. "That's fucking ridiculous. I'm volunteering. Non-demons do it all the time. It's, like, my free choice or whatever."

"You know as well as I do a daemon tribunal doesn't see it that way. Especially if you're clocking in and out in their system of record. I told the judge I'd speak with you. Convince you to stop sending our technical team and executive leadership into a tailspin."

I fold my arms in front of me, debating. While it would be a gag if the ancient court had to send me a magical bag of golden money or whatever, they could just as easily put Birdie on the hook to pay me for the hours, and fuck that.

"Work. Less," she repeats. "You only have eighteen hours left before you reach your quota. We *will* find a remedy to stop you from logging too much."

Ugh. Eighteen hours and I still have almost a month left. Working less means losing the twice-daily reminder I give Birdie to lift her delicate little wrist up to my horn. Most days, with the tree farm in full production mode, it's the only time we're physically in each other's presence.

Some days, it leads to running my nose along her forearm which turns into little pecks and nips at her skin and then we're making out in a haystack. I'm loath to give up a single opportunity to distract her, even if it's just one more time. Every volunteer hour counts.

"How the fuck am I in trouble for working too much for a good cause?" I grouse. "This is some bullshit."

She sighs. "You and your two friends are giving me more trouble than any of the hardened criminals I've ever dealt with!"

"Pfft!" I bulk up my shoulders. "I'm hardened. I've done time."

"And I've seen your record, tough guy. You haven't spent more than a long weekend incarcerated, and then only for petty crimes. Drag racing. Tagging. Public indecency at a water polo event."

"That was a misunderstanding."

She gives me a quelling look. "I'm not buying that you're some hardened criminal, Mr. Perchaz."

"Rex," I grumble.

"And anyway, if you are a reformed model citizen as you say, you can learn to start following the rules and work less."

Fucking relentless, this lady.

"Eighteen hours for the rest of my time barely covers morning chores. I've got way more to do than that." In my mind, that's only a couple workdays. One or two chances max to seduce Birdie in close quarters.

"Then do good on your own time. Take a few days off, for fate's sake."

I scratch my forehead then rub my temples. Fuck. Even if I did explain the limited hours to Birdie, that I can only formally log a few more hours for probation and can keep volunteering off the books, it'll just remind her of the truth—my end date, when there's no more reason to stay on the ranch.

I refuse to leave early. I've gotta draw this out. Or go over. Or . . . something.

We've just made a breakthrough together, an unspoken truce that's also become a hunger for more. My chance with her is *now*, and I refuse to fuck it up.

In the two weeks since I fell into the lake, we haven't gone beyond kissing, but the slow burn is burning. Something between us is building, not a crazy fluke she can laugh off. It feels real this time.

"What's really going on?" Officer Dale asks, her perceptive blue-green eyes narrowing at me.

Well, fuck, I'm not about to give her my whole life story. What's between me and Birdie isn't any of this orc's damn business. I shrug and shake my head. Play dumb.

"When I get bored, I burn things."

She blinks at me slowly with no expression, then heaves a weary sigh and mutters to herself while clicking at her mouse and staring at her screen. "I'll be glad to see the backside of you."

"That's what she said."

The look she cuts me is unamused. Over her head I see the clock tick to the top of the hour. It's five-o' clock somewhere. And that somewhere is right freaking here. I slap my knees and stand up.

"Listen, this has been a barrel of court-ordered fun, but I've got chores to do and a showerhead to install. Priorities."

She stares me down.

"None of that's on the clock. Promise." I put my hands up and back toward the door. "Today's my day off. Mostly."

She blinks at me again, so I relent with some reassuring finger guns.

"Work less. Message received."

She lifts her chin to the door. "Get out of my office."

I salute her. Being respectful of your superiors is important. "See you next month, Officer Dale. The pleasure was all yours, I'm sure."

Lucky Magic Diner is on fire.

Not literally, though my excitement over their broccoli cheese soup in a bread bowl did almost have my fingers sparking with childlike glee. This shit is fucking good. I slurp it up and make a note to order a few bowls to go. Birdie would love this.

"Nothing to say for yourself?" my brother, Rom, cuts in.

I glare at him, still hunched over my food. Busting my balls, as usual.

"What's done is done." I shrug and dig back in.

"You exploded a statue in the middle of town. Someone could've been killed, Rex. The damage to the small businesses along the plaza has been all the Chamber of Commerce has talked about for weeks."

"Then they'd know there's a process for damage claims." I shrug. "The court's covering that with our fees. My friends have been racking up enough penalties with their antics to float repairs for all the cute latticework fences or whatever your business owner buddies need."

Rom glares. "That doesn't sit right with some of them."

Oh. Demons. I huff and take another bite before continuing, "Listen, if people want to keep the property damage off the books—lower insurance rate, avoid paperwork, whatever—have them text me. I'll fix it up, no cost. I've come into some free time lately," I grumble begrudgingly, imagining all the kisses I'm forgoing trying to follow the stupid fucking rules and be a good dude.

Noelle is smiling at me and I have no idea why.

"What're you grinning at, lunatic?"

She giggles. "You blew up Alaric Infernus! You have no idea. There are more locals that want to kiss you guys than harangue you. Rom is mostly annoyed because it was a little dangerous."

"A little?" He looks at her then glares at me. "Noelle likes to roller skate at night to clear her head. If she'd been down that way—"

"Just protective demon fiancé things." Noelle squeezes his arm and kisses his shoulder. His jaw juts out, but he leans over and gives her a peck on the forehead.

"Sap," I say.

"Goon."

"Dickwad."

"Bonehead."

"Stop it, you two!" Noelle says. "That statue was a public hazard with those old natural gas lines. I signed a petition a few months ago to have it removed. But really, it's an open secret that Alaric Infernus was a real piece of work back in his day. You know Judy, the bailiff, has been trying to track down video footage of the explosion."

My face falls. "Oh fuck, would that bring our sentence back into question?"

"No! Everyone just wants to see it. You really exploded it? I mean, you must have. People were picking pieces out of the bushes for days. It was like a treasure hunt. I heard someone got a thousand bucks for his severed hand in an online auction."

"I actually started it." I puff up. "Thought it would be funny to melt that old dirtbag's face off. Then, my buddy Vale threw a fireball at his chest. The gas lanterns caught fire and"—I smirk, making an explosion with my fist—"boom."

"So cool," she says, starry-eyed.

You know, Noelle isn't half bad. A real sweetheart, actually. I lean back, soaking in the appreciation for my clearly well-intentioned public service. I really am shaping up to be quite the role model.

"Dessert?" I toss the smaller menu toward them, riding the good guy high. "My treat."

"That's so generous, Rex." Noelle looks over the menu while my brother studies me.

Demons don't comp meals for nothing. He knows there's something on my mind, a favor at a minimum. Thanks to Birdie paying me for working the tree farm lately, I've got some money in my pocket, so I offered to pay for their dinner once they got here. They're honor bound to hear me out in exchange for a meal.

"Well, what is it?" As expected, Rom is tracking the situation just fine.

"What is what?" Noelle looks up, then turns to Rom. "Will you split a butter cake in huckleberry sauce with me?"

"Add some ice cream and you've got a deal, goddess."

She grins and gets the waitress's attention.

I order a fudge sundae with extra cherries and some soup to-go.

Rom's eyebrow quirks. "Well?"

"I need your help."

Noelle clasps Rom's arm tightly. "Finally!"

Rom smiles and shakes his head.

"You don't even know what it is." I stare at her.

"Rex! We've been worried sick about you for two months. You disappear. We hear you're living in a barn! Are you doing okay? Have you been getting enough to eat?" She passes me a cracker packet, which I tear open, pausing just before I bite.

"You guys have been worried?"

"We're family." Rom shrugs. "So you need help. How'd you get in trouble this time?"

I roll my eyes. Classic family fuckup is what he thinks. "It's actually about Birdie."

Noelle's face falls, moisture brimming on her bottom lashes. She looks stricken. "How is she? I shouldn't pry, I know I shouldn't, but is she okay? A few of her friends, me included, have tried to call her but she's so quiet these days. I'm sure she's been through the wringer emotionally. Let her know she can always call me. I can be an ear to listen in, a shoulder to cry on—"

I hold up a hand. My future sister-in-law is kind of a lot sometimes. Like, take a breath, girl. I hold my tongue and focus on what's important.

"Birdie's fine. Better than fine. She got me to build her some shit—a big ole tent for field trips and educational stuff. Nearby that, she's got a new outlook spot with one of those big viewing scopes like at national parks."

"Mom would love that," Rom says.

"The telescope thing?"

"You know how into bird-watching she is."

I nod. Last year, I built a little pond and put up some feeders so Mom could nerd out with her binoculars over morning coffee. When we were kids, she used to raise scarlet finches, a local cave-nesting bird. They didn't like me much but ate right out of her hand.

"I bet she'd go crazy for Sunny." I laugh, imagining Mom meeting Birdie's venomous death owl. I'd like to see that. It does something funny to my chest. Mom would love Birdie—a brainiac who built a thriving ranch from scratch while doing good at the same time. Birdie would wow her. But could she ever meet my mom in the context of being, well, mine?

"Sunny is the little green owl, right?" Noelle asks, pulling me out of my thoughts.

I nod. Am I just another stray she's taken in? An almost criminal begging for scraps of her attention?

"Sounds like you've really been helping out."

I shrug. It's true enough, but I'm nowhere near confident I deserve more from her besides being the best damn rebound she could ask for. I want more, but is it realistic?

"I figured you'd be the perfect volunteer for her on account of you both being animal lovers."

I shake my head with a chuckle. That's a generous assessment, hinging on the fact I mostly just don't like people. Animals don't talk. Animals' needs are simple. Animals are easy to understand.

"I can't believe she's finally doing it!" Noelle says with an excited wiggle.

"Doing what?" I've been too lost in my head. Thankfully, this lady can keep up a conversation with a fence post. Case in point, marrying my introverted brother.

"Her work with local wildlife! It's what she's *meant* to do. I was so excited when she renamed the ranch Wild Hearts. It's just *perfect*." Noelle beams. I notice she left off the *Retreat* part of the title, probably because it never quite fit. "We went on a hike once and it was the cutest thing. She's like some kind of magical princess, traipsing around whispering to birds and squirrels. She knows so many fun facts about them, it's crazy! And then last year, she donated some historic handwritten journals to the library that she picked up at a garage sale. It's an account of the first ornithologist to visit the area."

"Yeah. Birdie's fucking awesome." I nod, a little dumbstruck. Damn, Noelle really does know everything about everyone. "Anyway, the help I need is with this big holiday event she's planning for the ranch. It'll be a couple days before Christmas, on the winter solstice."

"Eeee!" Noelle squeals and reaches across the table, grabbing my hand. "Tell me all about it."

I give them both the rundown of what Birdie's got lined up for the Wild Hearts Holiday event, even though some of the activities sound kinda goofy to me. I mean, children sitting on the lap of a grown man in a costume? Noelle assures me they're very appropriate for Christmas and will draw a big crowd. She's fully on board and already making to-do lists about the fliers she can print out and how she'll pop into all three school campuses to distribute them before kids go on break.

Rom suggests Perkatory sponsor a hot chocolate stand since our family business is still relatively new in town and the marketing budget has wiggle room. Why didn't I think of that? When I tell Birdie, I'll have to make it sound like it was at least half my idea.

With a couple of hugs, my to-go order in hand, and a promise to call Mom soon, I leave the diner with a full belly and two enthusiastic volunteers. Birdie will be very pleased. Pleased enough to give me a thank-you kiss? A horny demon can dream.

I find my lovely Umbran steed in the Hellfyre Inn garden right where I left her, chomping on some chili peppers. Mimi has been a good girl all morning on the ride up and well-behaved now, as I untie her and hop back on.

We trot merrily through town, earning a few curious stares, before making our way out of town and back toward the ranch. I stay just off the main road since I don't know the side trails as well as Birdie. With the recent cold snap and snowfall covering the fields, it's the smarter choice.

As we pass an old abandoned mill, Mimi stops short. My heels dig in to stay stable, and I pat her neck, looking around. "What is it, sweetheart?"

She prances over to a bush and nudges her nose at the middle, then down toward the ground.

I hear a high-pitched chattery noise followed by a hiss, and then I see the source—a calico kitten, no bigger than my hand, and that's being generous. Its back is arched and they're dancing side to side, trying to look big when there's no hiding the fact they're mostly skin and bones. Likely lost or abandoned out in the snow, alone.

I hop down on the opposite side of the horse and keep her reins in one fist while edging around her other side.

"Here, kitty, kitty."

The little bean's attention switches on a dime, from the horse head snuffling up in its space to me. They scoot further back under the brush with a noticeable limp. More hissing and high-pitched yowling follows as Mimi tries to follow with her nose. There's some blood on the ground, not a lot, but enough to tell me the poor thing's probably injured.

"Sorry, little one. I can't leave you like this." I drop to the ground. My free hand shoots out, snatching them up in one fell swoop. They scratch and howl and shake, but I hold firm, switching my hold to the scruff of their neck. Standing back up, I assess. "A girl, then. Hmm. Skinny as a stick bug. Got a nasty cut on your foot too." I murmur an easy spell to heat up my hands, just a soft, warm glow, not fire exactly. When I place one hand flat for her feet, the change is instant. She stops fighting. Freezes. Then, one foot presses cautiously against my heated skin. Another soft step. When her claws retract, I loosen the hand holding her neck a tad and give a tentative scratch with two fingers, up and down near the top of her skull. She leans into the caress, paws at me twice more, and starts purring.

"Feels nice, huh?" I give her a second to relax and sniff around.

She's pretty small and I'm not sure the protocols on food, but I hold her up to the front pocket of my overalls to see if she—

"Yep. Found my last piece of beef jerky, didn't you?" She dives into my pocket and goes feral, head thrashing as she tries to tear into it. That should keep the little killer busy and, I hope, distracted. I cup my hand securely over her tiny body as I hop back in the saddle and get comfortable. I crane my face down to check in once more and her smell hits me like a slap in the face.

"Oof, you're a stinky little imp, huh? A real mess and a half." I grin and click my tongue to get the horse walking again. "Birdie's gonna love you."

Chapter Fifteen
Birdie

It's sunny and snowy and zero degrees. The Christmas tree farm is in full production mode, including almost every member of my demon side of the family staffing the parking lot, register, or tree lot.

And I'm completely distracted.

"I've got this." Aunt Ethel grabs the new roll of receipt paper from my hand as I watch Rex stride purposefully in the direction of the supply shed.

"Thanks," I mutter, then refocus on her while my feet are already backing away. "I'm going to, uh, I think there are some extra pruning shears in the shed."

She sucks in a deep breath from her vape and exhales twin plumes of smoke. One side of her mouth kicks up into a knowing smirk that makes me walk away faster.

"You better grab 'em before they're snatched up by someone else," she says, eyes flicking behind me. "I'll hold down the fort up here."

Ah, crap. She definitely suspects something, but I can't correct her. I've committed to the ruse. No time to dither now. With a nonverbal sound of thanks and a wave, I rush off.

Only to find the shed door closed.

Did he already—

"Oof." Like a snake waiting to strike, I'm snatched inside, and pushed against the rough-hewn cedar wall.

"Hey, boss." Rex towers over me, his voice like a drug, lighting me up from the inside out. His lower body presses into me as he takes me in, like he hasn't seen me in years.

"Hey." I breathe out. "Also, I'm not your boss."

That grin of his makes me weak. He's only been away a few days, but it feels like something has shifted. He got a ride in from town this morning to help work the tree farm, and this was the first chance I saw to sneak away. I just wanted to be near him again. Since we've started kissing, I've got it bad. Really, really bad.

Maybe it's true what they say—distance makes the heart grow hornier.

It's bright outside, but the shed is only lit by the ambient light filtering in through the wood slats and the demonic glow of his eyes. He grabs my hand and kisses my knuckles before placing it over his heart. Mine responds in double-time.

"Looking for something?" he asks, dragging his nose over my hairline, the backs of his fingers featherlight over my hair.

"You." My hand claws into the soft flannel of his button-down before rising to slide around his neck and squeeze. "Just you."

He groans, eyes shuttering closed, and his lips find mine. The make out starts slow but quickly turns hungry and hot. This is what I needed, to light up with the full-body sensation only he seems to elicit. The pace turns syrupy and slow even as I grow heady with want.

Since our little spat in the lake, this is all we've done. Kissing and kissing and kissing, endlessly. A little groping, but it never goes further, and I'm not sure why. One distraction or another. A hesitation. *He's not here for long* I tell myself. Our first time was too explosive. Too brain melting.

Maybe I'm a little scared.

"You missed me," he says as I chase his lips, then leave pecks along his chin and neck. It's not a question, but there's surprise in his tone. I don't say anything, but when I bite at his pulse, he groans. His hands capture my face. "I missed you too, honey."

And I melt, like the last inch of a candle, so relieved to bask in his warmth again.

I love being alone, especially out here on the ranch. Or, I used to. Now, the shelter of his arms is my sanctuary. The fireplace I want to curl up beside. The place I feel safest.

But Rex had to help with repairs to some of the shops that were damaged in the statue explosion and ended up staying in town for almost a week. I hung on every text message he sent. While he's not the best conversationalist, he sends regular photos of his projects. A newly installed window. A freshly-painted railing. A filigree fence he welded back into shape.

I ate it up. What can I say? I'm a practical woman. Home repair makes me hot.

And I'm glad to have him all to myself again. Not just because he does all the dirty chores I avoid. I *have* missed him.

"Ouch. Fuck!" Rex wrenches back, sucking on his thumb, three visible scratch marks turn pink on his forearm. They didn't break the skin, at least.

"Sorry. I forgot." I pull the kitten who'd been napping in my sports bra out of the front of my shirt. "No claws, missy!"

I've done my best not to give the adorable, if feisty, stray Rex brought home a name. She's almost cleared by the vet and a central part of my be-social-and-talk-to-people-again plan today. I want to find her a good home before the holidays, and families visiting the Christmas tree farm are the perfect audience.

"I thought we were pals, killer." Rex pouts, and bravely wiggles a finger back toward her. She bats at him, claws retracted this time, and allows a scratch along her cheek. He flicks the white pom-pom at the top of the little red hat she's wearing, only slightly crumpled from her nap. "What's up with this?"

Much to my surprise, she didn't have any qualms about wearing the festive costume, another point in favor of her being a better fit with a family than as a barn cat. "It's a Santa hat."

"Oh, that's right." Rex's lips tip up on one side with a smart-ass smile. I hate how much I adore it. "That old burglar who sneaks into people's houses every winter."

"Oh, come on," I chuckle. "Santa's sweet. He gives away toys all over the world. It's a cute story." Though the breaking and entering is a little weird now that I'm thinking about it.

"Santa's a troublemaker, just like this one." He grabs the kitten from me, cradling her to his chest as his hands glow. Her rumbling purr starts up like an engine. "You know what? I bet he's a demon."

"Santa? Let me guess, because he wears red."

"Not just that. He trades toys for cookies, right?"

I think back on the Santa lore I know, which isn't much. Most of what I've picked up about him is from pop culture. Christmas isn't really a thing for most Turkish families aside from the prettily decorated trees in malls I noticed on our trips to Istanbul over winter break. And the evergreen tree farm I basically inherited from my demon stepfamily, who started it to try and cash in on the holiday. "Kids leave out snacks, I think."

"Snacks for toys. Sounds like a deal to me!" He waggles his eyebrows, and the kitten meows as if in agreement. "Homeboy's a demon. I bet he lifts some jewelry here and there. Not every house, just one in a dozen, maybe. Who would notice amidst all the cheap toys left in old socks."

Old socks? I'm starting to think he knows more about Christmas than I do. "Oh, the stockings."

"And let me guess, the rich kids get better toys."

I roll my eyes. Goofball.

"Demon." He shoots a finger gun at me. "He rewards kids with toys equal to the food or stolen goods received."

"The parents buy the toys, though." I cross my arms and try to hide my smile. "I hate to break it to you, but Santa isn't real."

"*Santa isn't real,*" he mimics me in a mocking tone. "That's exactly what a demon running an international home invasion racket would want humans to think." He brings the kitten to his face and puckers up. "Isn't that right, troublemaker?"

I shake my head, but he's got me thinking. All stories come from somewhere. Is that where the first idea of Santa started? He could have been a demon.

"Final point of evidence for the court," he says. "Let's circle back to his clothing. Red's a stupid-ass color for someone who's secretly running around giving away presents with no wish for anything in return."

He has a point.

"Maybe *he's* red. Not his clothes. His whole body." He sweeps an arm down his tall, bulky frame. But he's wearing a green flannel and jeans. If Santa was all red, he'd be—

"Naked?" I burst out laughing.

Rex grins. "I can't imagine getting down a chimney is all that easy. Big chunky dude like that? He might even have to oil himself down if he's on a time crunch and needs to hit a few houses a night. No clothes also means no evidence left behind to tie him to the crime."

I chuckle. "Your mind must be a strange place to inhabit."

"Think about it." He raps his temple and holds the cat, one-handed, at his side as he leans down to capture my lips again, his free hand grasping my jaw.

I soften against him but can't help giggling every few seconds, imagining Santa as a naked demon thief sliding down a chimney thanks to copious amounts of baby oil.

"You know what?" I jerk back, keeping hold of his belt loops as his panting mouth passes over mine. "If this is based on some older story, maybe he got caught and tried to pass off the presents the parents wrapped as ones he was delivering."

"Probably helped hide his junk from innocent eyes too." He pulls me close by the nape and kisses me again.

I'm grinning so hard my cheeks hurt. "You're kind of a genius."

"You keep saying that, I might believe it one day." I feel his smile against my lips just as someone walks along the outside of the shed wall, casting a shadow over us.

We clear our throats and break apart.

"Back to work?" He cuddles the kitten up against his face.

I sigh. "The holidays wait for no capitalist."

"That's the demon way of thinking." He winks at me, pulling up his phone. "I'll let you head out first. I wanna look up more of this Santa lore. I think I'm onto something."

I root around the shed until I find a set of old pruning shears, so I have a whisper of a cover story if Ethel looks twice, which I have no doubt she will, then grab the kitten and open the door.

"Wait one fucking second," Rex booms. His eyes are wide as he waggles his phone at me. "Have you heard about Krampus? This bastard even has horns!"

After he gives me a quick, gleeful rundown of some alternate Santa figure that I knew nothing about, I can barely breathe from laughing as I head out. The Middle Ages were a bizarre time for Northern Europe.

I drop the kitten off in her cage alongside a few of the other adoptable bunnies and ferrets. The tent is surrounded by space heaters and printouts explaining a little about each animal.

My phone dings with a new text.

It's Chad, a local park ranger. Over the years, he's passed off a whole host of wild animals to me to rehab and rewild. Today, he's here for a Christmas tree.

I pause to take a breath, resisting the urge to sneak home and hide out. He's a friend, but not close enough that he was invited to the wedding, and that one comfort keeps me from retreating. My socialization has been minimal. I'm finally responding in group chats and taking calls again, but have avoided a large portion of my guest list like the plague. With the tree farm running on all cylinders, my family has been treating me with kid gloves. Aunt Ethel in particular has been much kinder and gentler than usual. Normally, she'd call me out for insisting on helping operations from the background. Instead, she lets me stay busy toting supplies, bringing the staff snacks, and keeping the register stocked with cash for change. Any excuse under the sun to stay away from customers? I've thought of it.

But today, knowing a pet shop pop-up could help the kitty, ferrets, and rabbits find forever homes, I resolved to put on my big girl panties. A little emotional support animal never hurt anyone, though, and there's no one better for the job than my favorite prairie dog.

"Hey, Lemmy. Wanna keep mama company?" Even though he's not open for adoption, I didn't want him to be lonely stuck in the garage without his buddies. So I snatch him up, tuck him into the front pocket of the red apron I throw on, and head to the parking lot.

I can do this. I'm going to be normal and talk to people like I wasn't just publicly humiliated a couple months ago. Courtesy smiles are my bread and butter. Or ... they used to be. I wipe my sweaty hands on my jeans and approach his familiar station wagon.

"You made it!" I greet Chad and his family. I've met his niece and her daughter before in town, and I compliment the baby's elf attire. Just adorable.

"Birdie." He tips his hat at me. "You're looking as lovely as a swarm of Gosta fireflies at dusk."

I grin, always amused by his wonderfully goofy compliments that tend to skew pastoral. I don't even notice his companion until she steps around his tall frame.

"You're Birdie?" a beautiful demoness asks. There's an overly curious gleam to her eyes.

"I am." I gulp. I don't know her, but has she heard about me in the rumor mill? Her smile slants into a teasing line. Right before I start to spiral, I notice the blinking horn monitor she's sporting. One I'm exceedingly familiar with, so I hazard a guess. "You must be Iggy."

"Guilty." She grins, thrusting out her hand. We shake. Her grip is firm. She smells great. Her attire is fashionable in an edgy way with sharp eyeliner and a sleek bob to match. *This* is Rex's friend? They couldn't be more different. "I'm so pleased to meet you, Birdie. You've got a lovely property. And look at that." She points at the viewing platform. "I bet building way up there was a massive pain in the ass. Tell me, just how big and dumb was the big dummy you tricked into lugging all that stuff up there?"

I burst out laughing. Okay, the friendship is making sense now. She's got some bite.

"Real cute, freak," Rex says, coming to stand opposite me. His thick forearms cross and eyes dance as he locks onto Iggy. The amusement in his gaze sends a dark emotion coiling around my solar plexus. I have the irrational urge to call off the friendly chitchat and pull him away with a hissed, *Mine.*

Rude. Illogical. Completely uncalled for.

I hide the burning sensation well. I've always been good at that. The urge will die down. Maybe. Just because I'm letting my emotions breathe lately doesn't mean I need to go off the deep end. Control is key.

And patience has its reward. As our conversation continues, I pick up on what's really going on. Iggy is obviously flirting with my favorite park ranger, and Rex couldn't care less.

As we walk through the Christmas tree farm, anytime I risk a glance at Rex, he's already watching me with a hungry stare. Oh my, could he sense that little jealousy moment? Maybe, because he seems to take every opportunity to touch me—a brush of his arm or a hand on my lower back. It makes me desperate to be alone with him again, wondering how soon we can sneak away.

Turns out, not soon at all.

For the next hour, we're swept up in showing Iggy, Chad, and his family around the property. The sharp demoness has a real head for marketing. While Rex is volunteering with me, she's been with the park rangers and immediately hones in on my vision for promoting local wildlife through community education.

"Why not cross-promote with the parks department? Mutual interests and a shared target audience are a good foundation for a partnership."

I gasp. "Why hadn't I thought of that before?" They could lead educational hikes or host wilderness classes in my new space. My brain bubbles with ideas, and when Chad offers his help to get my proposal into the right hands, the excitement fluttering in my chest makes me feel like I could float away.

"Would you also share info about my upcoming holiday event?" It's a big ask, but he agrees readily, and my hands shake as I realize I don't have anything to give him. I pull out my phone to text him the time and date with a promise to send him more information soon. Dang it, I wish I had something ready. I really need to update my website and get organized.

"It's all here." Rex produces a roll of blue paper from his pocket and hands it to me. A stack of fliers.

A Wild Hearts Holiday: Solstice at the Sanctuary.

My hand flies to my mouth as my eyes cloud with surprised tears. Seeing it in black and white makes it somehow real, but it's the last word that really snags me in the feels—sanctuary.

Wild Hearts Sanctuary. Not a tree farm or luxury retreat. A sanctuary is what I really want the ranch to be known for.

The flier has the date and time with cutesy cartoons of animals drinking hot chocolate and pulling sleighs and decorating a Christmas tree.

"I didn't have time to show you," Rex says bashfully. "Noelle worked these up and printed out a bunch. She was ready to start papering the whole damn town, but I talked her into waiting until you approve the design."

"They're perfect." I grasp his hand, almost lost for words that they worked together to do that for me. I shove several at Chad with giddy excitement.

"One's enough," Iggy grabs it. "I can make copies. We've needed something seasonal for our local attractions board in the visitor center. This is perfect. I'll make sure everyone takes one."

I clutch the rest to my chest before stuffing them in my lower apron pocket, knowing Lemmy's buckteeth would rip them to ribbons in seconds.

The whole crew heads to the barn, since Rex promised Chad he'd show him all the fancy tools. They set up some logs on a cutting block to try out the axes and chainsaws.

"This looks fun," Iggy says, reading over the bulleted list of activities for the holiday event. "One last hurrah before Rex has to leave, huh?"

Rex has to leave.

The words rattle through my mind, darker and more sinister each time they echo. I watch him set up a log to chop, and that damn horn clamp blinks at me like a ticking time bomb. On the worst day of my life he was there to save me, in more than one way, from going over a cliff. I really lucked out when he offered to volunteer here. He's so insanely skilled at so many things it blows my mind, all the tiny competencies others might miss.

Even now, he walks Chad through the proper technique to wield a massive double-headed ax. How each blade has a different purpose—one finely sharp, the other a fatter angle for rough chops. There's a precise way to stand. A safe way to swing.

He knows it all.

I imagine running this place without him. I've done it for years. It's only a few extra chores and would entail finding some trustworthy ranch hands or contractors to do some of the projects I can't. But he just . . . fits.

I shake my head. No. This place isn't his responsibility. We had a deal. Twelve weeks. He's already done so much for the new and improved Wild Hearts Sanctuary as it is. I can be thankful without getting all weepy about him leaving.

"Rex seems happy," Iggy says quietly, folding the flier and tucking it into her pocket. "He looks like a natural here. Right at home even with his stupid flame tattoos."

My chest warms. Tightens. *Right at home.* That's exactly what it feels like to me, too.

"Wait, were you the friend that gave him those tattoos?" I cover my mouth in surprise and Lemmy pops out. Iggy was the *goth friend* who tattooed Rex in high school.

"Technically that's the coverup to my hack job, which was just a bunch of curse words." She chuckles with an impish smile. I imagine her hands on his neck, and again a possessive hiss whispers at the back of my mind. *He's mine.* But when she feeds Lemmy some of the peanuts I gave them for treats, I shake the irrational thought away. That was years ago, and there's clearly nothing like that between them.

"You guys must've gotten in so much trouble," I say.

"He did, for sure. His parents had a Devout demon tattoo the flames—a ritual design, so it was allowed for a minor as a religious exemption—then grounded him for an entire semester, all the way up until he moved away." Iggy glances to where Rex is chopping wood and cracks a nostalgic smile. "My parents never even knew about it, because he refused to rat me out." Her gaze cuts to me, eyes darkening as she grabs my forearm. "Rex is one of the good ones."

"I know." I squeeze her back, understanding it's not a deal she wants to make, but a truth, as a demon, she needs to share.

"Do you?" she asks, eyes narrowing and flashing at me. She doesn't need to convince me of Rex's true nature, the one he keeps well hidden beneath all his grumbles and bluster. If I still held any bad opinions about him, they're dust in the wind these days.

"His heart is solid gold," I say, using a metaphor common to demonkind. She nods and steps back, tucking her hands in her pockets and fixing her face to an impassive, cool expression again.

It's a high compliment that a demon friend, even removed from each other for years, would be so willing to defend his character. Be so protective. I like to think I'd feel the same about him too. Even after he leaves. Even if we only see each other every few years when he visits his family in town.

Oh, how that eventual reality makes my heart twist.

Rex is only here with me for a few more weeks. The recurring mental reminder of the time ticking by makes me antsy. We're already kissing every chance we get, but I want more. And why am I resisting? Women have casual relationships all the time. When he leaves, we can still maintain some friendliness.

I hope.

Wintertime, full of holidays and celebration, is the perfect time to embrace hope again. I need that now more than ever as I chart a new direction for Wild Hearts too.

Sunset rolls around soon enough, and the last families leave the Christmas tree farm as we close down. Most of the fliers are gone and I have some adoption paperwork to look over. I'm worn out. At the same time, my heart is full. My stepmom and family give me hugs as they pack up to head back to town.

It was so worth it to put myself back out there today. I finally feel like I can show my face in public. I can start living my life again.

Together, Rex and I load up a pull wagon to cart the adoptable animals back to the house, as the sun fades to pinks and purples around us. Usually we part ways at the fork in the road leading to the barn, clean up, then have dinner on the porch outside. But even with the space heater, it's getting colder every day. Is he still comfortable in the barn? Seems kind of ruthless of me at this point.

Tonight I'm going to invite him in. We can watch a movie together with the fireplace on. Cuddle up as the snow falls outside. He could sleep on the couch if he wants.

Or . . . with me.

I have to make the first move though. Rex has been patient with me, never pushing the kisses too far. While I'm still sweating about how to suggest he move into the house, he stops me.

"Hey. I have something I want to show you, but you can't be mad." He holds both of my hands, letting the wagon handle drop to the ground. "I broke into your house."

"What?" I rear back. He's in my house all the time. "It's always unlocked. I don't understand."

"Fuck, of course not. I'm saying this all wrong." He rubs a hand down his face. "It's a present actually. That doesn't make sense either. Just, uh, can I show you?"

"Yes, please." I watch him curiously as we head back. He helps me feed and put away all the animals in the garage, and when we enter the house he tugs me past the kitchen. My face flushes as we walk through my bedroom and into the master bath.

"This." He opens the sliding glass door and turns on a sleek black showerhead.

"Oh, wow." I recognize it from a picture on the box. It's my gag wedding gift, the one he joked that I could mastur-bate with. A delighted shock lights me up like a firework from my cheeks to my fingertips. I barely restrain the desire to laugh, to smack his arm, to cover my face in something close to embarrassment.

I must look as confused as I feel, because he shuffles his feet and stammers, turning a dial and clicking some buttons. "It's high end. I installed a steam mister too so it kind of stays warm all the time, like when you're using the detachable head. It has over thirty settings or some shit. Oh, and I turned off the flow regulator so you can get some serious water pressure." He spins around as I take it all in. "Shit, you hate it."

With the hot water raining down in the shower, a mist clouds the room, drifting around him and sneaking toward me like fingers of warm, scented air. I really shouldn't have waited this long to put us both out of our misery.

"No, I really don't." I step closer. "Although, I have a question for you."

There's no time like the present to grab this demon by the horns.

Chapter Sixteen
Rex

"**I** have a question for you."

Fuck. Crap. Dumbass shithead. I shouldn't have done this. It's wildly inappropriate, as she is probably about to say. Wait, no, she has a question.

"What?" I ask, my throat closing up in horror. Mother Below, let her put me out of my misery. Send me on my way with an angry—*Are you serious? Thanks but no thanks, weirdo*—so I can lick my wounds in peace.

Instead, Birdie surprises me. She bites her lip, looking for all the world like a blinking, doe-eyed innocent.

"What would a girl like me do with thirty settings on a showerhead?" Her tone is candy sweet.

Holy darkness. Is she for real? Every worry evaporates.

She's into this.

I grin, getting into character. The deviant bent on her destruction.

"Whatever you want, little lady." I swallow and take a step forward, pointing at the booklet on the counter "I read the manual. You want me to walk you through it?"

She nods, twisting a curling lock of hair around her finger. "It's probably best if I experience it in the flesh."

"Fuck yeah," I groan, before correcting. "I mean, yes please."

"So polite." She unties her red tree-farm apron and wiggles out of the rest of her clothes, hopping from foot to foot, shimmying and jiggling in all the right places as she discards one item after another.

"Fuuuuuck." I commit the moment to memory as she twists to pull off the white undies that barely cover her round, delectable ass. Did I even see her fully nude before? If so, it was not long enough, because she's a fucking work of art. Golden, dimpled perfection. Deadly curves. Pointy nipples that make my tongue want to roll out of my mouth.

"Doesn't seem fair." She steps closer, one hand on my belt buckle, the other fiddling with a shirt button.

"What now?" I feel breathless, trapped by those round dark eyes of hers that always make my brain fuzz out.

"If I'm naked, you should be too, don't you think?"

"I don't do a lot of the thinking around here, Birdie Lynn. What you say goes." And with that, I'm tearing at my flannel. As the buttons fly off, a couple pinging against the mirror, she laughs while unlooping my belt and tugging my pants down.

"Didn't get a good look at this last time." She settles on her knees, and when she glances up, my cock kicks in her hand. The thick beast is already glowing for her. Blood rushes in my ears.

I choke out a sound as she fists me, her thumb playing along one raised vein, watching the damn thing grow brighter. My dick is a little unusual, but whatever. I've always just gone with it. A glowstick for a cock isn't the worst party trick in the world.

I whimper when her lips kiss the tip, then lick down to my ballsack.

"I love that you glow." She hums excitedly as she suckles soft and slow, popping off lightly just to have another go. "Almost like the Gosta fireflies." I pant, my cock pulsing with brighter light. She looks up, just as her tongue circles the head. "Demons have incredibly diverse gene expressions. This one must be very rare. Lucky me."

On a growl, I snatch her up and hustle through the shower door right into the spray.

"Such a beautiful fucking nerd. You learn that in science class?" My lower half presses into her soft belly as I crowd her against the tile wall.

"I was a straight A student," she laughs as I paw at her breasts. Both our chests heave with the energy zinging between us. Water pelts our sides in an intense, almost over-hot sensation. Her sweet, musky arousal permeates the steamy air. I lick my lips to gather up the taste, burning for her.

"These perfect nipples." I dive down to bite each tip with an animal sound. She grips a horn and scratches through my hairline. Every fucking second feels so good with her. But I'm not ready to get off course. "Too damn distracting how much I want you."

"You have me." She gasps when I tug a nipple between two fingers. Goddess, such sweet words after the last two months of taking it so fucking slow. I'm not about to question why now, but I do take credit for the showerhead move. Shoulda stopped pussyfooting around and installed it weeks ago.

Needing to kiss her again, I grip her jaw to hold her still and take my prize. Her mouth. Her gasps. Her every surprised look. It's what I work for day in and day out, taking care of this woman who's never known what that felt like. Who takes care of every living thing before herself. Even me. Even right this moment, as she writhes and kisses me back, trying to give me everything she has.

But right now, it's about what she gets.

"I have a fucking job to do." I tear myself away and rip the detachable showerhead off the holster, punching the button for the overhead mister. I wanted her to be able to always have enough warmth surrounding her, so her body doesn't get cold while that pussy gets blasted into next week.

"Hmm?" She blinks up at me in a daze. Droplets cling to her black curling lashes and her hair is a sleek, shiny curtain falling to her waist. Goddess, her beauty. It knocks me on my ass every time.

"I still need to show you your present, honey." I flip a dial on the handle and aim the pulsing stream of water at her nipples. "Not too hot?"

"O-okay," she stutters, her lips so plump and fucking kissable, but I have to focus. "But maybe a little cooler if you're going to, you know . . ."

"Oh, I'm gonna. I need to get you clean first, though." I find a pump dispenser of some fresh-scented soap and get my free hand nice and sudsy. This is the life, having full access to Birdie's wet, naked body. I'd pinch myself if I could.

"Arms up," I say, and then I get to work, cleaning every inch of her in record time. While I rinse her off with painstaking attention to detail, she cleans me, lingering last on my cock and balls in one hand while the other slides over my ass, teasing between my cheeks until her fingers meet in a dizzying jumble underneath.

"Mmmm, trying to distract me again, huh?" I capture her hands and clean them up before rinsing us both again thoroughly. "Now where the fuck were we?"

"We were having fun." She wrestles her hands free and bites at my chest, clawing at my back.

I pin her against the tile wall by her jaw so she doesn't take me off course again.

"No, I'm making you come with your new present that I worked very hard to install after breaking and entering."

"You were a very bad boy." She grips my ass. I love it when she teases me.

"Just how you like me." I rub my thumb along her jawbone, relishing in the feel of her smart mouth restrained. In my control. "Now show me how much you like my gift."

Her legs widen and the invitation in her half-lidded gaze is clear.

"How's the temperature?" I slide the water stream over both nipples again then down the line of her stomach.

"Good, I think."

"The pressure?" I tease it over the curls hiding her sex and she wiggles.

"A little softer, at least at first."

"Yes, ma'am." I let go of her chin to make the adjustment, then get distracted teasing the peaks of her tiny tits. Her nipples are so pert. I could never get tired of playing with them.

"How's this, then?" I move the spray up and down her pussy, ending right where her clit is hiding under the curls.

"Good." She reaches down, but I capture her wrist and place it on my chest. Her nails dig in with a pleasant sting.

"That's my job." I explore her folds with my free hand as the water pelts around my fingers. She braces against my pecs, thumbing over my nipples. Shit, that feels good. Her clit grows stiff and slippery, but I need her open for the showerhead to do its work. On a grunt, I drop to my knees and hitch one of her legs over my shoulder.

"Oh!" Her hands fall to my horns for stability. That feels fucking great, how solid her grip is. I yank my cock as my nose digs into her cunt, smelling and tasting and taking it all in. I lick a rough stripe up her center and nibble at her lips, even as I aim the showerhead just above where I'm eating her like she's my meal. I drop my cock and use my fingers to spread her lips wider.

My thick tongue slides home, inside her, in a slow exploration. Longer and bigger than a human's, demons have more control of ours too, so I roll and unroll it from inside. When it's doubled over and thick, it rubs the rough patch right at the front of her entrance, opposite her clit, so as the water pelts down, her unholy noises tell me she's in sensory overload.

I can't see her because of all the water, but she dances on my face to a steady rhythm as I tongue fuck her. My fingers hold her open to be eaten, and I work my whole face—jaw, lips, nose, and especially my tongue—to please her.

Who needs to breathe when you can be waterboarded by pussy?

If I die, I die a legend.

Soon enough, she's so pliant and lost, her cunt clenches erratically on my tongue. I pull back to breathe and sink two fingers inside. My thumb circles her clit as I aim the showerhead right at the glistening center.

"Good, honey?"

She nods and swallows with wide eyes, her gaze bouncing from my face to where I'm working. Her soft belly quivers, incoherent gasps breaking free.

"A little more, okay?" I click the water pressure up one and move the spray even closer, so it's focused and pounding steadily right over her clit. "Look at this perfect pussy."

Her fist slams into the wall and she regrips my horns with ferocity as she really lets loose, riding my fingers fast and furious.

"I'm—oh—what's happening?" I move the spray closer and bite at her lips. "I can't s-stand—" With a trembling cry, she seizes. Her whole body hunches forward as her standing leg shakes. Before it gives out, I catch her, angling my horns safely away so she can notch her face at my shoulder.

"There, there." I chuckle and stand, holding her ass as I put the showerhead back. I position her twitching, doll-like legs around my waist and drop to a seat on the tile bench further back. "What do we think of my home improvement surprise? Not too bad, huh?"

I lick the arousal-scented water from her shoulder and the dip at her clavicle. Delicious. Every inch.

"You're evil," she mumbles against my skin, slapping my back half-heartedly.

We're out of the spray but warm from the steam when she bites my neck, a little harder each time, like there's more pent-up energy shaking loose.

"I think when you bite me it really means you like me."

Love bite I think but don't say. She's not even close to ready for that. The straining heavy bar of my cock makes thinking difficult, but I've got a little sense left.

"I'm the only one you're mean to," I say as her nails dig into my back and she sucks so hard on my neck I know it'll leave a bruise. Everyone else gets polite, smiling Birdie. I get her nails and her teeth. "Don't think I don't notice."

"I'm only mean to you." She jolts up, big eyes full of surprise. "Oh, no. I'm sorry."

"Fuck that," I growl. It's exactly what I want. I grip her jaw and bite her bottom lip. "Don't be sorry for showing me everything. Anything. But especially that fucking fire that's had me dazed since you first snarled at me when we were sixteen years old."

"My fire." She's like a butterfly in the rain.

"Your passion." My chest heaves. "Your anger. Your joy. Let me see it all."

Her eyes grow wet when she smiles. "You make me feel safe. That's why."

Everything within me flushes with pride, honored to be that for her. I pull her body against mine in a tight hug until we're forehead to forehead, nose to nose, my lips speaking against hers.

"Be mean to me, Birdie. Give me all your fire."

And her eyes light up. Shining. Sparkling. If she was a demon, they'd change colors and blaze, I'm sure of it. But hers are dark and bottomless. Even better somehow, because there's mystery there. She'll always have an instinct to hold back. I'll never understand every piece of her, even if I see what no one else does. Who she really is.

She rises up on her knees, rubbing my cock against her pussy. The shower is humid and damp, but her slit weeps for me. Warm and ready. She's already well fucked, but her expression says she's not done.

"I need you," she says, moving the head of my cock right inside her tight entrance.

Fuck. It's everything I've wanted to hear for months now. I grit my teeth and pray for restraint. *Please Dark Mother, don't splooge in ten seconds flat.* Actually, it's probably best if I don't move much. Play it cool.

"Ride me," my gravelly voice grits out the command.

"So bossy." She exhales against my mouth on a fragrant sigh as she sinks down. Her eyes fall closed.

I grip her ass in both hands and worry it was a mistake because she's so fucking thick and soft, it's all I can do not to thrust up. And if I do, I'm definitely done for. I didn't know intimacy like this was possible, that someone could find *safety* in me. The loser. The fuckup. With her, I never feel like that.

My hands fight the urge to grasp her even tighter as she takes all of me. I watch every microexpression. The way her lashes tremble. The warm flush on her cheeks. The slight relief and arch of her back when she reaches bottom.

Then those huge brown eyes open on me again, and it's like the world comes back into focus. Full color. Every sense is alive.

She shows me her fire, just like I asked, her gaze clear and fierce.

I have no choice but to fall.

I want to bite, consume her. Never come up for air.

I need to be deeper, even though I'm not sure that's possible.

She rides me faster, clutches me close, takes me inside her again and again. We're so full of each other, gasping for the same breath at the same time. The edge is closer than ever. Pressure builds, buzzing deep inside me.

Gripping harder, my hips tilt to match her, seeking that last impossible inch. Her eyes roll back and tits shake through a full-body tremor as our skin slaps together. I swallow her moan with a kiss when she finally comes, clenching around me in a choking, chaotic rhythm.

No one could survive her ecstasy. Every soft part of her is made for me.

I fuck her like the monster I am, untethered and brutal. Ugly grunts follow each thrust up. A savage, almost violent, emotion rises. Everything I want feels just within reach and so impossible at the same time.

I let it all go and give her everything I am.

My fire.

She watches me as my cock unleashes inside her, her mouth falling open. I'm sure it feels warm. Strange.

Good, I hope.

"Perfect," is the only word she says, and I groan as an unexpected second wave of cum pulses out. Her fingers trace my tattoos up my neck so sweetly it makes goosebumps prickle down my arms despite the steamy heat. She follows the bow of my lip next. My nose. The point of my ears. Like I mean something to her.

"You're gonna kill me," I pant, wrung dry, like every drop of cum is determined to make a home inside her, still kicking, wringing me out. "Fuck."

The shower comes back into focus eventually. I pick her up, turn off the water, and step us both out. She settles on the counter as I slowly dry her off in the lingering sex-scented air I never want to leave. Her skin is dark, flushed with color from the heat, and everything about her expression and body language screams satisfied.

I fucking did that. A bonfire roars inside me, feeling purpose and focus and direction, maybe for the first time in my life. She's it. What I've been both afraid to hope for and been waiting my whole life for. The wild jumble of coincidences that brought us to this moment don't seem so chaotic anymore. The way I was drawn to her all those years ago. Placed in the same shop class. Our group project. Choosing her mom's B&B. The day she got jilted was the day I was meant to leave town. Chasing her on horseback.

Like fate won't let us go.

Like we're meant to be.

"Stay," she says, then presses her lips together like she's second-guessing the word.

The command hits me square in the heart like some mythical fucking arrow. I worry my voice will squeak like an overeager teen so I simply nod, pick her up, and tuck us both under the cool covers of her bed until we're on our sides, facing each other.

In the cutest, silliest move, she drags her fluffy comforter over our heads, like we're at a sleepover telling a secret.

"Thank you," she whispers.

I can't help but smile. Being soft with me is new for her, I think. I could crack a joke, tease her more, or say the exact wrong thing to kill the moment. But I'm a demon learning his manners, and there's only one right thing to say.

"You're welcome."

Chapter Seventeen
Birdie

There's nothing like stove-brewed Turkish coffee in the morning, especially the way I make it, the way my mother taught me. It sets the bar for deep richness. All others fall short.

Rex and I have a big day ahead of us, heading into town to drop the kitten off at her new furever home then having lunch with my mom. I haven't talked to her about whatever is going on between us, but I'm sure we can play it cool.

I grab the pitcher of filtered water from the fridge and put it on the counter near the oven, where the sugar and container of finely ground Turkish coffee sit. I pull the *cezve*, a traditional long-handled copper pot, from the drying rack and fill it with the proper measurements of each ingredient. When I turn on the gas stove, I hear a rustle behind me.

"I've got it." Rex's deep, sleepy voice sends a shiver down my spine as he crowds me from behind. With a hand on my waist and a snap of his fingers, the burner lights in dancing blue-orange flames.

"Show off," I tease, which earns me a kiss at the temple.

Rex takes his coffee extra-sweet while I prefer only a teaspoon, to make the most of the rich cardamom flavor. After the coffee's boiling and foamy, I pour mine first then add more sugar to finish preparing his portion.

"Oh! Cream." He turns to the fridge.

Sacrilegious. I shake my head. Every day I think he'll forget and just try it black. Who needs milk with a strong Turkish coffee?

While I set up the tray with our cups on the table, Rex rustles around in the fridge and lets out a huff of laughter, peeking around the door to waggle a jar of mayonnaise at me. An almost empty jar of mayonnaise.

"Whatcha been using this for, miss ma'am?"

"No comment." My lips pinch on a smile. His shit-eating grin tells me he knows exactly what I've been using it for. My favorite guilty pleasure—grilled cheese that's easier to cook and tastes just as good as using butter on the bread.

He shuts the door, placing the creamer by his coffee, and crowds me against the table, poking at my cheeks until I'm grinning.

"No hiding those smiles, Birdie Lynn."

I can't seem to hide anything from him anymore, and I don't mind one bit.

He sprinkles cream into his cup and takes a long, delighted sip. "I drank way too much of your mom's coffee my first morning at The Deviled Egg and nearly sent myself into cardiac arrest."

"That's why your limit is one cup." I laugh, imagining him sprawled on mom's sofa after drinking a thermos of extra-strong Turkish coffee. "It's so different from American-style drip brew, which is why we use such small cups." I think back to the night he was drunk on homemade brew and ended up wrestling my pregnant goat. "We need a rule for you with new beverages. If it doesn't have a nutritional label, only consume after consulting with someone around you."

His glare is belied by an amused smirk. "I haven't even wiped the sleep from my eyes and you're busting my balls."

"When it comes to mind-altering drinks, you have a habit of getting into trouble, like blowing up giant statues." I flick his horn clamp, which he recently had to duct tape back together. Both it and my tracker bracelet broke and fell off. He hasn't had a chance to get a replacement but assures me it's still working fine and he's doing good on his hours.

Rex captures my hand and bites my knuckles, eyes dancing with mirth. "Can't get into any more trouble with the law out here."

"Only trouble with me."

"My favorite kind." His lips tip up.

"Scoundrel." I grin back and pinch his nose until he swats me away. "Oh, hey, do you need me to log you in for our ride to drop off the cat? If you need the hours, it could count since the trip is adoption related."

He stirs his coffee with a tiny spoon, seemingly absorbed in the task. "Nah, I'm good for today."

A couple hours later, we're at the Winter Bliss town square handing off the kitten I only narrowly avoided naming to her new mom, Officer Gertie Dale. I assume she wanted to meet us here because it's Saturday, her office is closed and, for professional reasons, she's not about to let her clients know where she lives. Not that a tall, bulky orc woman like herself couldn't do some serious damage if anyone threatened her. Better safe than sorry, always.

While I had a few applicants willing to adopt my feisty, half-feral cat, Officer Dale seemed like the best fit all things considered. And if it helps Rex's case in the end, I'm not above trading cute baby animals for a little goodwill.

When I see Susan, Randy's sister, waving at me across the plaza, I step away to catch up. A jolt of embarrassment still courses through me to see her in person.

"Hey," she says, flushed from the cold.

"Hi." I stuff my hands in my pockets. While I blocked Randy's number, we've communicated professionally enough via email, often through his sister since she works for him. There is no longer any association between Wild Hearts Sanctuary and his travel agency beyond their assistance in correcting communications about the holiday event. My moms and his family run in similar social circles in town, so everyone's stayed cordial, if a little awkward, around each other.

"The country club newsletter emailed out the corrected graphic today," she says, mouth tight and eyes wide "Sorry about all that."

"Not your fault. I'm relieved to hear it. Thanks for all your help, seriously." His sister's been extremely professional. She stepped up to run the brick-and-mortar side of their business while Randy's off being a digital nomad, whatever the fuck that means.

"I think the fliers and posters have helped a lot." She smiles. "Christmas and New Year's are the big holidays, but a winter solstice event is new. It's all anyone's talked about lately."

"Really?" I watch the bundled up people around us, mostly out buying last-minute holiday gifts, and wonder how many plan to come out to the ranch.

"Yeah, I'm really happy for you, Birdie." She nods. "In fact, do you need any volunteers? I know Randy offered a sponsorship, which you had every right to decline, but this isn't that. I'd be happy to pitch in just to help, what with everything that . . . well."

"We're all staffed up." I say quickly. "That's really generous of you, though." I tag on to soften it. With the end of this event, Randy is completely behind me, exactly the way I want it. But who knows, if he stays gone for good and his sister takes over, maybe we could partner again someday.

I recognize Rex's raised voice booming behind me. "I've gotta go, Susan. Thanks again for everything."

When I turn back to join him, it's obvious he's arguing with his probation officer. That doesn't seem wise. She gestures to his horn clamp, but I'm too far away to make out what they're saying. I hope she's not upset that it's so damaged. The nature of his work on the ranch has been so physical, it's no wonder it broke. I'm gearing up to offer to pay for a replacement, when he turns to stalk away and reaches me first.

"Everything okay?" I halt to ask.

Officer Dale has the cat carrier tucked at her side, watching Rex with an annoyed shake of her head.

"Yeah. Peachy. Let's go." His hand presses at the small of my back as I wave over my shoulder at her. Would it kill him to try a little harder to make a good impression?

The stoic orc gives me a friendly, if stilted, wave and nod in return, lifting the cat carrier. Oh no, what if it wasn't the horn clamp?

"You think they'll be a good fit? I had other applicants if the kitten was acting up and Officer Dale had second th—"

"No, the little troublemaker's fine. It's not that. She . . ." He huffs and flicks his horn clamp. "She's just as frustrated as I am about all the red blinking errors with this fucking thing."

"Oh." I exhale, relieved. "I'm willing to pay for a replacement."

"Nah, it's just a dud." He avoids my gaze, but grabs my hand, squeezing it tight. We're a little ways down one of the main shopping district streets when he stops and pulls me aside, grabbing both my hands. Instantly, I feel them warm with his fire power. "You're cold."

"I'm fine. Let's enjoy the day. The holiday spirit and all that." I glance around at the array of colorful lights criss-crossing the street, a horse-drawn sleigh ambling around the square, and the carolers two doors down.

"Yeah." He nods, taking a breath. "Forget all about this probation bullshit."

"Maybe tone down the cursing when we get to my moms'?" I arch a brow. He knows we want to keep this *thing* between us hush-hush. I mean, my moms already adore him, and he's leaving soon.

"I'll be a very good boy, boss lady." His head cocks, grin full of mischief.

"Boss?!" I pinch his tummy. He dances away, still keeping hold of one hand as he walks backwards. I point at him. "And a good boy? I'll believe it when I see it."

We spend the next hour ogling the impressive holiday window displays of the local shops, from the bakery's intricate gingerbread house village to the wondrous model train setup of the toy store. My favorite is definitely the library though, with its lit up line of rainbow mini trees and the dozens of holiday-themed books strung on fishing line hanging like they're floating magically in the air.

We make a quick detour into Perkatory for some hot chocolate then find a pair of demon kids running their own competing stand a few doors down.

"Little capitalists," Rex hands them some money, a hefty discount off Perkatory's price, and we do a taste test. His family's recipe is better by far, but we give the young demons their kudos.

Giant snowflake and flame cutouts dangle across the street advertising the annual New Year's Eve festival. Like Susan said, I notice at least three posters advertising my *A Wild Hearts Holiday* event. Each one makes my heart want to burst.

We sneak into the cheese shop last. They sell a limited edition cranberry goat cheese that's to die for. And we can't leave without picking up a gluttonous assortment of other specials. What better time to treat ourselves than the holidays?

Finally, ready for some good home-cooked food, we make it to The Deviled Egg. Mom and Orla made sandwiches and a red lentil soup, and since it's Saturday, it's just the four of us.

A good time is had by all. When I get full on soup, Rex eats the other half of my sandwich.

Surprise of surprises, he and I don't even argue.

Well, that's not technically true.

We got into it briefly over which TV show was better, the original Quantum Renegade or the newer reboot. The original, obviously. It tackled controversial social issues the current series never quite addressed. Rex is just a die-hard fanboy of the actor who plays Thraxxius in the new version. Totally blindsided. I have to remember that *fan* is short for *fanatic*. There's really no reasoning with people like that.

"Need a hand?" Mom pops into the kitchen as I'm washing the dishes.

"Oh." I almost drop a water glass. "Sure."

"You really don't have to do the dishes, *kuşum*," she says, turning the faucet to the left to rinse the ones I finish washing. "Though I appreciate it."

"I like to help," I say. And when Aunt Ethel popped by five minutes ago, I was desperate to avoid the knowing gaze she darted between me and Rex. Orla asked Rex to help her unstick the attic ladder, so I figured the dishes were better than anxiously waiting for small talk that could turn awkward and innuendo filled in a moment.

I don't think Rex and I are being obvious about whatever is happening with us, but I don't need it to be a topic of family conversation. Which is kind of Ethel's *modus operandi.*

"You and Rex are getting along better."

My eyes bug out, hands scrubbing the tacky bottom of the pot a little faster.

"You're seeing him differently?" Mom adds, carefully. I can tell when she's being precise with her words, holding back in hopes I'll open up. And I want to. I want to be closer to her. She's always liked Rex, even when we bickered like crazy.

"We've grown closer." I breathe out, my sudsy hand sliding over the lip of a bowl. That wasn't so hard to admit, was it? "Actually, he's kind of the best," I add. Not looking at her makes it a little easier to share, to say what I'm really feeling. "I'm going to miss him when he leaves."

Mom takes the bowl from me, running it under the water. "I can understand that. We'll miss him too."

"It's not just because he's helpful around the ranch, either. It's more than that. I feel . . ." I gulp, handing her the last spoon and wiping my hands down, moving to her other side to dry the dishes. "I feel so unguarded around him. Safe to be me, even if it means we still bicker."

"Like cats and dogs." She laughs.

"He's helped me see myself, believe in myself, in a new way. A way I like, even when it scares me."

When I look up, Mom is grinning at the dishes. "Demons have a certain magic like that, the ones we are meant to connect with." She peers at me. "They can see a hidden fire others may miss. One we may not have known we had within us."

My fire, just like Rex said. Is that what it was like for her and Orla when they met after the divorce?

"You found your person," I say.

"I had to find myself first, though."

I nod, smiling even as tears brim hot behind my eyes. The bitterness I've always felt over her leaving Dad and chasing her own happiness feels like ash in my mouth now.

"I never really . . ." My thoughts clash and swirl. I've spent my whole life following paths presented to me—perfect grades in school, my first career in the big city, even buying the ranch only when it was in dire straits to keep it in the family.

"You're getting there."

Mom drops the dishes and folds me into a hug. I cry, really cry, working through my confused, nervous feelings about Rex, the unfair resentment I kept bottled up for too long, and the simple relief at being held by her.

Imagine my surprise when the world doesn't crumble at my feet, when a surge of relief joins the thunder in my heart. She pats my back and soothes me in a rocking hug.

My emotions aren't a burden. Maybe they never were.

Chapter Eighteen
Rex

"**R**ex?"

"I'm here," I shout over my shoulder, putting the curry comb and hoof pick away.

"You didn't have to do the morning chores." Birdie's voice draws closer.

I huff and close the tack closet door more roughly than necessary, because I hear what's unsaid. She wants to start up the chores again. Tomorrow is the big event, and a week later, I'm out of here.

I should have been gone weeks ago when my horn clamp blinked and fell off, but that's a technicality I'm trying hard to hide. My probation officer's tech team thought they found a work-around to the overtime hours by disabling my device early, before the end of my twelve weeks, but jokes on them. I know my way around a roll of duct tape. Thank the Mother Below, Officer Gertie Dale wasn't willing to wrestle me in public to get it back. I'm not leaving a day earlier than the end of my probation, and that's that.

Soon enough, Birdie will be all alone in the dead of winter. I hate it. What if she needs help or an animal gets hurt? They're all chaotic-ass goobers who injure themselves for no damn reason.

"Mimi fucked up her leg," I grumble.

"What? How bad?" She rushes into the young Umbran mare's paddock, looking pretty as a picture in a long-sleeve red shirt and leggings that leave nothing to the imagination. She tempts the horse closer with a treat to check out the injury.

This is what I'm worried about. Sure, she's lived out here alone for a while since her asshole ex never really gave a shit about helping out—fucking shitbag—but still. I imagine her doing all this alone, tending to her dumbass horse who messed up her leg being a giant dork.

"It's just a scrape. Looked clean," I explain. "I dressed and wrapped it with some antibiotic but you should give her a look over too."

"What happened?" She moves to Mimi's side and lifts the injured leg, peeking under the wrapping. For being a thousand pounds, horses are fragile as fuck.

"Mimi and Vince are best buds, so she thinks she can run full tilt into the corner of the fence racing that hay-for-brains kid."

On cue, my plump little goat son noses through a crack in the fence, one he created I might add, to bound over to Mimi. With a one-two jump against the trough, he hops on top of her back. The horse doesn't even flinch as he prances up and down her spine. Thick as thieves, these two idiots.

"Vince?" Birdie asks.

"Oh, yeah. Dewdrop doesn't really fit anymore. You were right. Too whimsical for his goofy ass." I smile, forgetting I'd renamed him in my head a couple days ago when he broke into the supply shed and chewed through three sample cans of paint—red, green, and white. He was a pain in the ass to clean up too, snorting fire and smoke the whole time. "After turning himself into abstract fucking Christmas drip art, I thought of a new name. Vincent van Goat."

She snorts out a laugh. "You sure this name's gonna stick?"

"Vince!" I bark. His head cocks sideways and he stamps his back legs. I wink at Birdie. "He seems to like it."

"I'm glad he's made a new friend." She scratches Mimi's forehead up to the sensitive space between her still-growing horns, and Vince butts in right overhead, so she laughs and scratches him too. "He's gonna miss you, though."

Will you miss me? I wish I had the courage to ask. Then again, it's probably just asking for heartache. I know where we stand. We're fucking like bunnies until she gets to kick my chaotic ass out and regain her peace of mind. I like to think I bring more good than trouble to her life, but who really knows. Facts are facts. She only just got jilted. She's got this new direction for the ranch to focus on. There's no way she's ready for all my heart-eyed, forever feelings.

"I wanted to show you the eastern fence line I fixed up," I say.

"Oh, the one the moose herd overruns every year?"

"Yeah, I rolled some new boulders along the natural path they take then cleared some old brush so they're more likely to migrate over the land bridge instead of fucking up your fences." Their annual migration through Birdie's ranch knocks down her fences, and every year she has to put them back up since they're the biggest deterrent for bears.

"Oh, the upper ridge of that valley can totally be a land bridge. Smart!" The grin she shoots me over her shoulder hits me straight in the chest. "We'll see if it works next fall."

I nod with a noisy exhale. *Will we?* Unless I commit another major crime requiring a year's worth of community service, why would I be here?

I can't lie. The thought has absolutely crossed my mind. But I'm not dumb enough to think old Judge Grimshaw isn't just as likely to throw me in some ancient dungeon a mile underground instead.

"Let's ride Gigi out there," I say.

"Together?" Satisfied with the horse's dressing, she comes back to the stall gate I'm leaning over.

"We've done it before." I cock an eyebrow. It was the day she nearly got herself killed at the skin-melting Sula Hot Springs.

"Sure. Yeah." She's smiling, a little bashful, and I can't wait to get my hands on her. Relive a little history, but on happier terms than her in a torn wedding dress, stiff as a board against me.

We separate Vince farther away from Mimi—supervised visitation only from now on—and saddle up the larger mare. Gigi neighs softly, her tail high and swishing, showing she's eager to go out. And while she's a lot more steady and mature than her daughter, she's still an Umbran by nature with a wanderlust to ride.

"You comfortable?" I adjust myself in my seat behind Birdie, pressing her thighs tighter back against mine. Oof. The cleft of her ass is a perfect fit for my cock to rest, and it takes the opportunity to squeeze out all the additional space by going half hard in an instant. I clear my throat. "Sorry."

"It's okay." She grins over her shoulder.

Fuck, she's pretty when she's happy. I kiss her cheek and sigh against her hair as we get moving. She's got the reins this time, unlike the only other time we shared a horse. My hands tighten on her legs, moving down to the knees and back up, like I need to soothe myself.

"I don't know if I ever thanked you for saving me that day," she says, remembering the same thing I am. "I was so embarrassed. So shaken up. But that ride home, the two of us on Gigi together, I felt so at ease with you. It almost unsettled me how good it felt to be in your arms."

I squeeze them around her, my cheek rubbing against her temple, wanting to hold her forever. "You're not used to feeling safe, honey?"

"I'm used to my needs being mostly ignored." Her short laugh lacks warmth. "And I'm coming to terms with that partly being my fault, for not asking, for never expecting anything from anyone. Over time, I got used to being the only one who could make myself feel safe."

"But you liked that I made you feel that way?" I ask. She nods. "Good. I like it too."

We ride on, watching the snowy hills pass and the early morning sun glow around the mountain peaks in the distance. Watching autumn blend into winter in real time, on the land, is different than simply marking the months on a digital calendar, or in my case, living in a hot climate where it's hard to tell. Out here, the seasons matter. Time is a colorful, living thing that makes me really wonder what the fuck I'm doing with mine.

"I could easily live like this every day. Work outside. Be a farmer or some shit. I'd be set."

"Yeah?" Birdie's voice squeaks out. Shit, did I make that weird? It almost sounded like an insinuation I want to stay, which I do, but what a fucking gross overstep. Better to explain where my mind was really at.

"I used to spend summers with my uncle on a ranch kind of like this. A lot fucking hotter in east Texas though, I'll say that." I chuckle. "But that was the only place my parents could drop me off when my brothers went to the enrichment camps I never got accepted into, what with my bad grades and discipline problems. I've never measured up to them. I do what I can to help the family business, odd jobs and shit, but I'm sure I've always just been a disappointment."

And I don't feel like that here, I want to say, *with you.* But I already let slip that I could stay here forever and didn't mean to come off like I was angling for something.

"There's no way that's true!" Birdie's hands shake enough that Gigi kicks from a walk into a slow trot.

"Feels like it." I grab her waist and the pommel to steady myself until she slows back down. "In a family full of business-minded demons, I work with my hands more than my head. When I build something, it feels like it's mine. I did a thing. I'm a fucking loser unless you put something in my hands and give me directions."

"That doesn't make you a fucking loser. I needed your help. The sanctuary projects wouldn't even exist without you."

"I can nail two boards together. Woo-hoo. I do the easy shit other people don't have time for."

"I've seen what you're capable of, Rex Perchaz, and it's not just the easy shit. Aside from the big projects you finished for me, think about the everyday things—the leaky faucet you fixed in the barn that's been dripping for months."

"Two minutes with plumber's tape." I scoff. "It's not rocket science."

"My Jeep's flat tire last week. I'd have waited hours until roadside assistance came."

"I told you, stubborn woman. All you have to do is read the instructions in the glove box. Anyone can change a fucking tire."

She growls and pokes me with her elbow. "The tire leash so the goats can free-range graze. A loser didn't do that. I could argue someone with a stroke of genius did."

"I'm a genius now?" I chuckle. "Poor girl. The cold must have frozen those pretty brain cells of yours. Maybe I got you dickmatized." That's a nice thought. I shift in my seat when it makes me kind of hard.

"I said, *stroke of.*" She throws a cutting look over her shoulder. "Let's not get ahead of ourselves."

"I'll give you something to stroke."

"Pig!" She laughs.

"Alright, fine. You win. I'm the next Einstein."

"No." She whips around to face me over her shoulder.

"Ouch," I say.

"You're you, Rex." Her nose scrunches with a determined glare. "The most capable, inventive, and hard-working person I've ever met. That's not nothing. That's *everything*. You can *do* anything. I've seen it." She's huffing and puffing now, each exhale an angry steam cloud in the winter air.

"Now don't go getting mad at me for being awesome." I grin. Fuck, I love to see her passion break out in new ways, like her defending me against shit talking myself. Feels good.

"Have you ever thought . . ." She shakes her head. "Nevermind. I'm projecting."

"Spit it out."

She glances over her shoulder. "Maybe it's not that you don't fit in with your family business, but that your family business isn't the right fit for you."

Something inside me jolts like a record scratch. "I, well . . ."

"Not to send you into the same spiral I was in a couple years ago," she clears her throat. "But I spent way too long in a job I hated before realizing that as much as I love my dad, I'd rather live my life for me than him. I can make billionaires more money on their investments just fine, but I'd rather be here. And you know what?" She peeks at me shrugs. "My dad and I are still good, as is his business."

"That's part of what I worry about," I say, making a connection I never have before. "What would my family do without me to fix shit for them?"

"How have they managed these last few months?" she asks.

"Well, they've been working with a vetted list of contractors I know are reliable."

"I hear demons are really finicky about contracts," she jokes, knowing all too well how demons operate in business. "I'm guessing Perkatory is doing just fine."

"My brothers are total hard asses, yeah," I say absent-mindedly, realizing they don't need me. Shit. Not really. And while normally that would feed the inner critic that says I'm not useful to the family, this time it doesn't.

I feel . . . free.

I could work for myself. Odd jobs and shit. A general contractor maybe. I need to talk to Rom. He's a whiz with paperwork and legal stuff.

"You're pretty fucking smart." I squeeze the tops of her thighs. "Anybody ever tell you that?"

"Someone, yeah. A time or two." There's a smile in her voice. I move her hair to one shoulder and kiss her neck to keep her warm. "But so are you. I hope you know what a difference you've made here at Wild Hearts. For me."

"I might've helped you some, but you do the same for me, Birdie Lynn. You showed me that life can be more than just a hard day's work. That a hard day's work can be meaningful. That maybe I can make things better like you, not just chaotic and fucked up."

"Chaos is nature's way. We see it every day out here." Her arm waves at the wild terrain around us. "You're perfect, Rex. Just as you are."

I hug her tighter from behind, the knowledge soaking into me. Changing me. My body feels overly hot, throat tight. What can a guy say to something like that?

Each motion as we walk jostles her body against me, the slow rock of the horse's gait both predictable and maddening. I squeeze the tops of her thick thighs, just wanting to feel her closer. Every perfect inch. Every last second we have.

And then there's something else in the air. I flick my tongue out to taste the air then sniff down her neck.

I look down the open valley of her neckline to her leggings and recognize the source. It's not the bumps of her pretty tits or the slope of her stomach. It's where her legs split over the saddle. The smell. The taste in the air.

Her arousal is blooming for me. She doesn't have a steel rod of a cock giving her away, but I'm a demon, and her scent is just as telling. Just as affecting. I huff against her neck and kiss a spot right behind her ear, letting my hands wander again, squeezing the hard muscle of her quads, the soft flesh of her thighs.

The scent of her unique wildflower sweetness grows stronger.

"Birdie Lynn." I nip at her ear. "Behave."

Her eyelashes flutter as she lets a hint of a smile loose.

"I can control my body as much as you can." She snorts and wiggles against my cock. My hands move up to clamp down on her hips which makes her movement slow to a grind. "Besides, there's no behaving around you."

"That's fucking right." I hum, squeezing the plump flesh of her inner thighs again then trace the seam of the thick leggings keeping her warm and protected from the saddle burn. My forearm brackets her sternum tight against me while my free hand slips into her waistband. She gasps but doesn't stop me.

I slide my fingers under the leggings but stay over her panties. All the way down. I squeeze her whole pussy lightly, then start to explore the dampness right over the gusset. My fingers wiggle and press, tracing just enough to feel where her lips would give way.

"So wet," I growl, teasing her over the fabric, holding back from making contact with her slick skin. "You're so fucking hot for me here. I bet I'd slide balls deep in one go with how needy this perfect pussy is, wouldn't I?" Her chest rises faster. "You'd feel so fucking good warming my cock on a long, slow ride. I'd keep you there, full of me, until you couldn't stand it anymore." She trembles, her scent like a mist around me as she soaks through the fabric barrier between us, like her body is preparing to make space and take me inside her. I slide up a little and circle over where her clit is hiding.

"It's better if we wait, honey." Like how long I've waited to have her this pliant and needy in my arms, to smile at me without hesitation, to invite me into her life. Her home.

Still, I want more. I want it all. The future, not just a few more stolen moments. And I have to prove, even in small ways, that I'm not just a wild fuck. I'm someone who can take care of her, who she can be soft around. Someone who deserves her.

"Have patience." I land three soft strikes right there, love pats that earn a squeak of surprise. My hand pulls free of her leggings, as I'm barely resisting the urge to finger fuck her into oblivion. It would be so easy, but the tease is half the fun. I go back to fondling her over her clothing—her thighs, her waist, her soft belly, her gentle bite-sized breasts—until she's leaning back, cheeks dark with color, hot pants turning to steam in the cooler air. I suck on her neck, bite her ear.

"We should take our time."

"You're evil." She turns back and nips at my chin with a teasing smile. Her fingernails dig into the meat of my thigh, making my blood sing.

"And you"—my free hand reaches up to wrench down her thin cotton bra—"make it so hard to be polite." Her nipples, tight from arousal and the cold temperature, poke against her top, and I just catch sight of them down the valley of her neckline as she pushes her chest out. I pluck at them, plumping the softness of one then the other, salivating to get my mouth on her. Anywhere. My ex-hales turn rough as I suck at her pulse, feeling the warm lifeblood pumping just under my teeth. Her ass moves against me, purposefully exaggerating the rocking motion of the horse's gait.

"Can't help it can you? Grinding this sexy body on me, knowing how bad I need you."

"Rex," she gasps, legs tightening slightly with a little pinch between her brows. "I need you too."

"Get off the horse, Birdie Lynn," I order darkly.

She huffs, leans forward, and urges Gigi to a faster walk. Even that move, lifting up out of the saddle lightly to sit back down, drags roughly against my cock. When we turn to move down a hill, I clasp her upper body tight against me again so we can lean back together, breathing in sync with every motion.

Fuck, this feels so right.

We veer off into a grove of mountain aspen. It's a beau-tiful spot, hidden off the normal animal trails. Hundreds of trees with smooth white bark stand taller than tall in a field of downy snow, sheltered by a glacial-gray rock wall. Snow covers the ground and limbs like powdered sugar. An artist with an eye for the crisp, bright nature of changing seasons could spend a whole day painting the scene, marveling at how even early into winter's reign, many of the trees' giant golden leaves refuse to fall. Clinging to those last few days when they were bright and alive.

I know the feeling too well.

The horse slows to a stop, and I hop off, then lift Birdie down. Gigi gives me a snort and a sidelong glance, eyes dancing with flame. With my hands full of delicious womanly curves, I'd forgotten about Umbrans' emotional connection to their riders. Whoops. My apologetic grimace turns to a chuckle as she lifts her head imperiously and trots a little ways off, tail swishing with irritation.

And then it's just Birdie and me. She leans against the white trunk of the closest tree, a vision of dark hair and sparkling eyes in her festive ruby-red top.

The way she looks at me lately—unguarded in her playfulness, sensuality, frustration, everything—takes my breath away. Right now, her emotions are close to the surface, the taste and feel of her still fresh on my mind.

She wants me.

How much, though? And for how long?

I stalk toward her in three long strides and fold over her, holding her face in both hands. I want to know, want to see in her eyes what she won't tell me in words, because I can't bear to ask.

Do you want more too?

Not now though, right at the end of my charity-case deal with her, when she's finally succumbed to my advances and we've reached a new normal.

Let me stay longer feels too selfish to say.

She's got everything—the smarts, the land, the hopes and dreams. Could she really want me for more than something physical? The closer I get to our end date, the farther I fall, the more afraid I am to truly hope and the more inevitable it feels.

"Kiss me." She nudges me with her nose, breaking the dark spiral of my thoughts.

My chest aches as her lips pluck at mine, warm and wet, before biting me lightly. I take off my thick canvas jacket to place it around her shoulders, protecting her from the chill. I love taking care of her, every way I can. The only fighting we do these days is pretend, a lead-in to laughter, jokes we both share. She's all spun sugar and sweetness for me now. The hearth fire I never want to leave. She tugs at my collar with both fists.

"Kiss me, Rex."

"Anytime. Always."

Fuck. I need to get it together before I propose marriage or, knowing me, threaten to lock her away just for me, damn the consequences. After our little talk, I'm already thinking crazy things. What if I just quit Perkatory and worked for myself?

I'm already falling for a woman who may not feel the same but taking every last press of her lips on mine all the same. Every time.

Why not go all in?

I angle my mouth to kiss her deeper and my worries collapse. Her tongue strokes against mine, bringing me a direct hit of her sweet, minty taste.

"Need you," she whispers against my lips, unbuckling and unzipping me in smooth movements.

I wrench her leggings and undies off and snatch her up until we're face-to-face. Her legs lock around my waist, knees tightening. It only takes the slightest of adjustments for the hot tip of my cock to find her entrance.

Gravity brings her down. One soft, tight slide and she's there, rooted on me. Her eyes flutter closed.

"No, ma'am." I slide my nose against hers to rouse her. "Eyes on me."

"I'm here." Her breath hitches.

"Right here. With me." I lift her up and down, testing my strength against the onslaught of pleasure that is being inside her. Her arms hitch tighter at my shoulders, and she rides me back, making my cock buck inside her.

"I was right, huh? This needy pussy needs to be fucked."

"Balls deep in one go." She smirks, eyes dancing.

"Smart-mouth." I bite at her lips, thrusting faster until we share a rhythm and eye contact that's soul deep.

"Evil demon." She huffs a laugh, contracting around me.

"Can't lie to me now, pinned on my cock like this. You can't lie to me with those eyes. Not with your anger, not with your pleasure, and not in a million years with your passion. You never have to pretend with me, honey."

"Rex," she sobs.

"Give me that fire. Burn me up." We move together. It's different, more feral than being in her bedroom or the shower. Deeper. "I want every bite. Every kiss." I bottom out and with an iron grip encourage her to grind over the hairy spot above my cock. With my hands occupied and hers dirty from the ride, she needs to stroke her clit on something. "Eyes on me, honey. Get yourself there. I've got all the time in the world."

Her eyes flash up as her tempo stutters. That seems to unlock something in her, and she rolls on me, trying different motions until her pussy is fluttering and I'm barely holding on. It's a staring contest—my favorite kind—as I watch the pleasure take over, feel her clench on me, an orgasm taking her by surprise in a flash of heat and wetness. She fights every flutter of her lashes to keep her eyes open. On me.

My jaw locks, muscles tense, as I stave off my release and let her work through it, unwilling to leave her body more than an inch or two as I thrust lightly, gripping her ass tight, warming her up with my hands. "Slow and deep now. Wild and rough later. Messy as fuck every damn time."

"Yes. Please." She kisses me, her gaze cataloging my face between each pass, like she'll never see me again. Maybe she's just as fucked up over me leaving. Is it too much to hope for? "I never want it to end."

I growl. She doesn't know how deep that hits, how much I wish it were true, so I bite back every bonehead thing I could say and fuck her instead, just like I said. This time for me. Deep and slow, watching her eyes shine in the dappled light of the woods as the clouds shift above us.

Every time I see her, I find something new, a slight change. Her nose is more regal, the shape of her lips more enticing, her hair even softer. Does she look at anyone else like this—so open, I can see her whole heart, every flash of wonder just on the surface?

"I need more," she says, tightening her hold. "Closer."

"Fuck." My legs shake as the release rockets through me, imminent and heavy. "You take whatever you need." I hide my face at her neck, kissing and biting and sucking in turn. If I want to stay standing, I can't look at her right now. Her aftershocks flutter around me, like she's squeezing the pleasure straight out of my soul. "Everything," I whisper. "You own me."

Chapter Nineteen
Birdie

"Birdie Lynn, be reasonable." Rex finishes tying off the last rope connecting the banner for the holiday event underneath the Wild Hearts entry sign. His round hairy belly and plumber's crack are visible in the ridiculous red and white costume he's wearing. It takes everything in me not to giggle.

The Santa I'd hoped to hire has an exclusivity contract with the mall, so Rex stepped in. I ordered the largest available costume online and still it's two sizes too small.

"You care about science and shit, but you're telling me you don't give a hoot about historical accuracy?" He's been going on about needing a whip as part of his outfit all morning, the one currently tucked into his belt as he climbs down off the ladder. The whip he insists his Santa portrayal is not complete without.

I ignore him.

"Don't give a hoot. You hear that, Sunny? Hoot. Hoot." I put an animal-safe piece of jerky between my teeth and face the owl on my shoulder. My little friend gives a warbling hoot in response and snatches the treat, shaking out a full coat of pretty white feathers in the process. They've finally molted from forest green to pure white and right on time for the winter solstice.

It's gorgeous out. Snow covers the land but it's sunny enough to be comfortable with a thick sweater and scarf. I rock the prairie dog in my apron pocket up and down. He's sleeping and likes to be jostled if I'm not actively walking around.

A wildly loud cracking sound makes me jump. Lemmy pops out and Sunny shrieks. I twist my shoulder away from Rex, who's brandishing his whip and pouting at me for ignoring him.

"Unless you want us both passed out from *Lampros Ascalaphus* toxin," I snap, glancing at the deadly avian on my shoulder. "I suggest taking it easy on the whip."

"Sorry," he grumbles, now at ground level and folding up the ladder. We start walking back to the house to finish the last of the event setup. "But seriously. Krampus had a whip. Santa probably did too if he's leading a working team of reindeer. Which means if I'm meant to faithfully represent the old goat, I need a whip too."

"You can't go around beating kids for historical accuracy." I roll my eyes.

"I can be nice Krampus," he says. "And stern Santa. I mean, a little intimidation never hurt anybody. Toughen 'em up early, I say."

"Absolutely not!" I try to snatch the whip away, but when I see that telltale smirk as he holds it tight, I know he's just trying to get a rise out of me.

"You're evil!"

"Right on character for Krampus, honey." He strides forward, looking both so ridiculous and so wildly monstrous with his massive horns, fuzzy red outfit, and spray-painted silver hair, I contemplate detouring to the house first for a fifteen-minute break to seduce him into just giving up the whip already.

We just don't have the time. Not today.

"Fine." I say as we reach the big stone patio where all my volunteers are already setting up tents and tables. "Keep the whip but you can't use it."

"What's the point then?" He stops and puts his fists at his hips defiantly. "I'm capable and can be very careful. No beating people with it. I'm sure I can manage that."

"But then there's the sound. Not only did it scare Sunny, it'll frighten the other animals and all our visitors, most importantly the impressionable young children in attendance."

"Kids like cool shit." He shrugs.

"The whip stays at your belt."

"Except for demonstrating its usefulness," he counters. "You see, I have this idea. I put some of those gold spray-painted pinecones on a fence and whip 'em off, one by one. Skill with a whip isn't just relevant to ranch life, it's also—"

"Historically accurate," I finish with a long-suffering sigh. He's thought about this enough to get stubborn. My only option to get him moving and the event started on time is to make a deal with this demon. "Fine. Put the whip away except during demonstrations which will take place once an hour, no longer than five minutes, in a location far from the animals. All children present must stay back twenty feet and be accompanied by an adult guardian."

I hold my hand out.

He clasps my arm in traditional demon fashion, trouble-making grin in full effect.

"A deal is a deal," we say.

"And I'm holding you to it." I give him an arched look. He loops the whip up and dramatically tucks it into his belt before slowly stepping back. "Now get to work. Photo op with the volunteers starts in five."

"Yes, boss." He winks and dances away before I can shove his shoulder.

A Wild Hearts Holiday: Solstice at the Sanctuary.

I stare at the banner hanging at the entrance to the patio, decorated on both sides by lit up Christmas trees covered in shiny snowflake ornaments. The sign matches the one we just hung up over the open entry gate.

Any minute now, people will come to the ranch not for a Christmas tree, but to learn about the sanctuary work. This is a soft launch to introduce phase one. I'm opening up the ranch to the public one weekend a month to give tours of the animals and the hikes up to the viewing platform. Aside from that, I'll continue developing connections with the local school district, community groups, and even universities around the state.

I've done everything I can to prepare, and I've had so much help. Since the moment Rex and I woke up for morning chores, it's been an absolute blur.

Mom and Orla showed up at dawn with a few of my demon cousins to make us breakfast and get started on food prep. They brought a lot of premade snacks—yule logs, cheeseballs, deviled eggs, and pumpkin pie bites—but they wanted to get some open fires going for s'mores, roasted chestnuts, fresh popcorn, and grilled meat kabobs. They even have a sugar cookie decoration station which should be a big hit. It's probably too much food, but with Rex, there's really never too much food. It'll get eaten no matter what.

Rom and Noelle got here early too to set up the hot chocolate station and reading circle. My moms insisted on putting Rom next to them, and Noelle got busy implementing her vision. With only string lights, giant pillows, and an outdoor rug, she transformed the space into a cozy, magical, reading haven and has a big stack of holiday books she'll be narrating throughout the day.

Coco arrived next. We'd met months ago when Rex's actor friend, Vale, held a press event on the ranch for his new holiday movie. She's his fake psychologist wife. Well, fake wife. Real doctor. She also has a soft spot for animals and was more than willing to run the petting zoo. I got a few of my best-behaved little critters, each in their own holiday garb—a chicken with a Santa hat, a ferret and rabbits with elf ears, and three goats with white furry collars—including chunky Vince, of course.

Sunny and Lemmy won't be a part of the petting zoo, but I wanted to have them with me to show off some of the work I do in rehabilitating the slightly-more-wild animals that come through the sanctuary.

I check on Coco in the fenced off, heated area with the animals and make sure she's comfortable before heading to the last volunteers to arrive, still setting up their tent.

Rom swats Rex's hand away from the snack table, but I catch my mom handing him a plate of goodies as he rounds to her side. Noelle stops him for a selfie before he gets to his Santa photo op station, a quickly-crafted wood sleigh front filled with fake presents against the background of snowy Mount Winter Bliss.

"We have these fliers for the goodie bags!" Iggy snaps me out of staring at my favorite demon with hearts in my eyes. Right. My last volunteers.

"Oh, great." I grab the fliers from her, highlighting the parks department programs, and tuck them in my apron's bottom pocket. "I'll get those sorted."

Chad and Iggy offered to man a Junior Ranger tent, running children through quick lessons and activities in exchange for button "badges" they can pin on their coats. If they collect all six badges, they also get a fake ranger hat, just like the kind Chad wears with a custom ribbon reading *Junior Ranger-Wild Hearts Sanctuary.*

"I need one of these." I pick one up, eyes misting with emotion. The badges and hats were all Chad and Iggy's idea, but I sponsored the supplies. My first official partnership. "It's just adorable."

"Don't forget a set of badges for your collection." Chad hands them over. *Tree Expert. Hot Springs. Migratory Animals. Fire Safety. Volcanologist. Water Conservation.* "Do you need help with the guided hikes up to the outlook? You're doing them every hour, right?"

"Every two hours," I answer, tucking away my goodies. "The trail is open for anyone from 10:00 a.m. to 4:00 p.m. but I'm only doing the guided tour three times. When I did a practice run with Rex the other day, there was just too much to say."

"And show off," he adds, eyes sparkling with warmth. Chad loves the outdoors and has been such a huge supporter. "You've got a lot to be proud of expanding your work and opening the sanctuary up to the public like this."

"Thanks so much, you guys." I give him and Iggy a quick hug, still a little overcome with how much we were all able to pull together in such a small amount of time.

There's still so much ahead of me. This fun, exciting, chaotically thrown together event is just the beginning.

And it's happening exactly when something else is ending. Rex is leaving at the end of next week. We don't talk about it. And every time the thought pops up in my head, I push it away. It's a conversation for another day. Not today. Not when everything feels bright and full of possibility.

"Showtime in twenty minutes, everyone!" I clap my hands. "The gates are open so guests could be arriving anytime! If you want a Santa photo op, do it now." I bite my lip and try not to laugh watching Rex tug at his fake Santa costume, surrounded by fake presents in his fake sleigh. Giving in and letting him use the whip is the least I could do.

For a moment, I worry that this whole event, everything I want to accomplish, could be a total flop. What if no one cares? What if no one shows up except my friends and family hastily putting the finishing touches on each activity center?

You know what?

Fuck it, I think, channeling Rex's nonchalant confidence.

Spending a day with my loved ones could never be a waste. And chasing my dreams for the first time in my life is exactly what I should be doing.

The holiday event, it turns out, is not a flop.

Despite the frigid temperature and light snow, I'm sweating under my messy apron as I drop Lemmy off in his enclosure and prep for my final guided hike up to the outlook.

This group is my biggest yet. At least fifty people, maybe more.

"Sorry, folks. Just one second and I'll be with you." I hastily put my hair up, take off the apron, and chug a bottle of water. Sunny has long since flown off. The crowd was a little too much for my wild friend.

I wish I'd done a better job counting, but there had to be hundreds of visitors. The turnout is a little mind-boggling, including several bigwigs with the school district who seemed very excited to discuss field trip options and even an events coordinator from the Emberlight Resort. She was interested in organizing private tours for guests on a set schedule and the amounts she tossed out, even before proper negotiation, made my head spin. That partnership alone could help fund so much of what I want to do.

We had so many people show up, Rom had to send for more hot chocolate. Mom brought enough food to feed an army, so the snack table is still going strong. Iggy and Chad ran out of ranger badges and hats an hour ago. I'm just grateful I made triple the goodie bags I thought I'd need, filled with educational fliers and holiday treats, planning to let Noelle distribute them at the library. Instead, I'm down to my last couple dozen.

"Okay!" I walk back up to the group near the trailhead. "Last hike up to the viewing platform starts now! It's a quarter mile uphill but not very challenging. We'll take our time, learning about local flora and fauna as we go, and can accommodate most ages and abilities. I'll be leading but I have a few helpers." I point to three of my demon stepcousins who wave at everyone. "They'll hang back with anyone who needs to go slower. Don't hesitate to ask questions as we go."

We make our way up the hill, pausing at each of the informational signs Rex installed for me. I designed them to highlight information about the terrain and wildlife visitors may see on the way up to the outlook or from the top.

"Fun fact." I point to the last sign as we pause at the top and everyone takes in the view from all sides. "The Rocky

Mountains are among the youngest in North America. One of the ranges formed just ten million years ago. That may not seem young, but consider that the Appalachian Mountains on the East Coast are over 400 million years old. As you take in what you see, remember that everything around you is in a constant state of change. It's our duty to treat not only people and animals, but the land beneath us, with great care and responsibly."

As the group oohs and aahs over the view, I manage the line queued up at the viewing scope. I found that giving them a thirty-second timer was the only way for everyone to get a shot at peeking at the otters swimming on the opposite side of the lake and the herd of moose moving through a nearby stretch of woods. There's just so much to see and I can't wait to have even more scopes up here to show off next year.

As a few people start meandering toward the path down, I know it's time to leave and make a quick announcement for the group. Just as I'm getting ready to lead, a familiar face intercepts me.

Familiar and wholly unwelcome.

"Hi, Birdie."

"Randy," I say evenly, completely detached which is more than what he deserves. "If you'll join the others, we really need to get going."

"Sure. I just wanted to let you know I'm back in town." He leans closer. "I think we should talk. Clear the air."

Crap. Back in town? For good? I want to know, but I don't want to ask. If it's only temporary, that's good news. If it's longer, I need to come to terms with it.

I crack my neck and take a fortifying breath, only to see my demon cousin Simon's panicked expression. Randy clearly wants to speak with me alone, otherwise he wouldn't have waited until right this moment to show himself. I blocked him on my phone and just this morning via my email as well, so he's had no way to contact me. I don't know why I didn't see this coming. It's the holidays. If anything could bring him home from his world travels, it'd be Christmas with his family.

This can go one of two ways. Randy and I talk now and *clear the air*, as he says. Or I brush him off and he follows me back down. I have no doubt that would lead to a scene in front of visitors as well as my family and friends. Imagining Rex's reaction to seeing Randy anywhere near me makes the decision easy.

"Will you take the group down?" I look to Simon and my other cousins. "Randy and I should talk."

"Are you s—"

"I'm fine. I insist," I cut him off and look at Randy. "Let's get this over with."

My cousins herd the group away and then it's just my ex-fiancé and I on a windy hilltop, standing on the cement foundation that was supposed to be cabins for a luxury retreat he'd envisioned.

My new reality is so much better, it still doesn't feel real. But looking at Randy doesn't make me want to dwell on how awesome my life is now. The sight of him, well-dressed and with a healthy vacation tan, brings up everything I've kept safely locked away since the day he left me at the altar—all the disappointment and confusion. The panic. The shame. And eventually, the anger.

I'm boiling over with rage just being in his presence.

"I forgot how incredible the view is up here," he says, hands on his hips, looking around. He'd only hiked up here once to take measurements, bitching and moaning the whole time. "Cabins could easily go for twice the nightly rate I guesstimated with the way the rental market's going in the area lately."

I snort. "I don't fucking care."

His face spins to me, mouth popped open, chin pulled back in shock, giving him a neckless appearance that's anything but cute. "I've never heard you curse."

"You never really knew me," I say.

He nods and kicks his shoe against the cement, looking down. "You never really knew me either."

My jaw falls open and I want to laugh. So I do.

Again, he looks at me in shock.

"You're going to try and make it sound like you jilting me on our wedding day without a fucking word is even partially my fault?"

His arms fly up. "I-I-I'll own that wasn't cool."

"Wasn't cool?!" I shout.

"I fucked up." He swallows. Still, I take note, no apology. "I'm not saying I made the right call, but you had me backed into a corner. Like you said, we didn't really know each other as well as we should have, you know? I tried to get you to go on a honeymoon, but I didn't tell you how important it was to me, not just that trip, traveling in general. It's what I've wanted for as long as I can remember, but you weren't interested. You shut me down every time."

The conversation turns back to me being at fault so easily. How did I miss this before?

"I told you no," I seethe. "Because I have animals that need me and day-to-day responsibilities. My place is here."

"I always imagined we'd hand this off to a property manager and see the world. Your family is from abroad. Your dad lives in New York. It just made sense we'd travel. But you were so stubborn, you wouldn't even agree to the honeymoon." He shrugs.

"You thought you could convince me to give up this place, my home?" My mind reels for a second. "Of course you did. Because you always could before, steamrolling me into whatever you wanted to do!"

"I heard that Rex Perchaz is living here. That you two are cozy," he says, eyes going steely. If it wasn't his sister, it could've been anyone in town. I realize now that I put no effort into hiding him when we were in town together or even today. "Is that a monitor I spotted on his horn? You're okay letting him stay here and work with children knowing he's a danger to society?"

"That's a crock of shit," I say dangerously. "He's the best person I know, and if you dare—"

"Are you and him . . ."

"Fucking?" I grin. "Yeah."

But not just that. My feelings for Rex are ten universes larger than anything I ever felt for this man. If I could just pluck up the courage to actually talk to him, to ask for more. I need to keep fighting for what I want in life, and there's no doubt in my mind that Rex is it for me.

"I never cheated on you, Birdie." Randy shakes his head, like I'm the asshole. I'm the disappointment. Before I can even muster a response, he continues, "It sounds like we both got a wild hair out of our system. My trip was great and it gave me some awesome life experiences to share with clients, but I have to be realistic. My business is here. My life is here."

With me? My eyes are bugging out of my head because I know him well enough to follow his train of thought. And I remember what I used to be like, how I'd respond.

That old instinct to be nice and agreeable is so dead, I can't believe I ever thought we were compatible.

I could let him down easy. That's what the old Birdie would've done.

He deserves to get to know the real me.

"*My* life is here." I smile. "Winter Bliss is *my* home. You can go wherever the fuck you want. But if you choose to stay, I want to make one thing absolutely clear—your life and mine are not a Venn diagram that intersect anymore. You're nothing to me."

He swallows then starts to open his mouth, but I put up my hand.

"No. Crazy thing. I don't even want to hear it anymore, because you know what? You're an asshole." I poke him in the chest, and he flinches. "You come here, to my property. You hide in a group of people until I'm isolated. You try to fucking manipulate me into feeling bad or seeing you as the good guy or taking you back. *You!* You're the bad guy, Randy. And you never even apologized for what you did. The only regret I have is that I wasted as much time as I did with you."

He rubs his sternum, looking like he's about to cry.

"I have one more thing to say, and then you can go." I step closer, a predator closing in, voice soft. "You jilting me felt like the worst day of my life, but it wasn't." I chuckle, bewildered by how differently I view that day now. I feel nothing but relief that I didn't walk out of the Hellfyre Inn that day with a ring on my finger. I lift my arms and raise my voice, so loud it's almost a shout. "You gave me the best day of my life, Randy! It was the best thing that could've happened to me. None of this would've been possible without you. So thank you!" While I can see it all sinking in, I lower my voice and say, "And fuck you, Randy."

A trash can tumbles over nearby. The wind is picking up out here with a soft flurry that sticks to my eyelashes. I'll need to clean up the mess before I head down.

I push past Randy with one last dig over my shoulder, "You're not welcome at Wild Hearts anymore, and if you're not gone by the time I'm done up here, I'm calling the police."

I pick up a couple pieces of trash and turn the can right side up when I see a dark figure stumbling through the trees. They're on two legs, so I know it's not an animal. No one should be up here right now.

"Hey!" I shout and follow the shadow through the woods. When I break through the treeline, I recognize the demon sprinting away from me.

"Rex?" I mutter to myself, before giving chase. "Rex! Hey, stop!"

Chapter Twenty
Rex

Half an hour earlier

Perchaz Family Group Chat

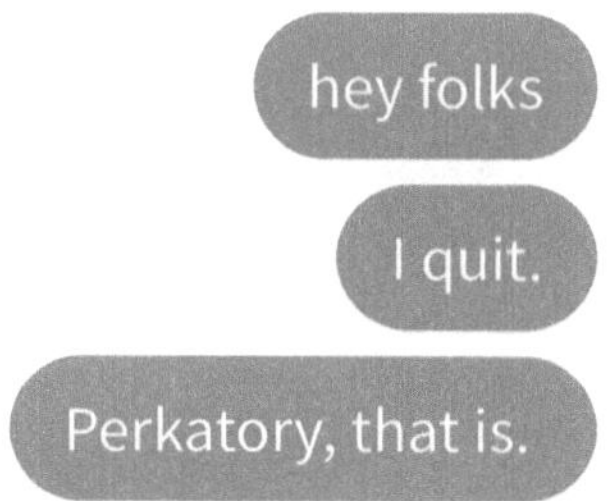

You're on your own for repairs and shit.

Good luck.

Also, my community service is done early. Yay me.

Also, also, I'm staying in Winter Bliss.

And hey, if you need me to wrap up anything from up here, I'm free. Otherwise, stick with the contractors I set you up with while I've been gone. All around good dudes.

and dudettes.

MOM

Rex, what's going on?

BOSSHOLE

You QUIT? Ever heard of giving two weeks' notice?

NERD

You said you were going to break the news gingerly.

BOSSHOLE

Rom knew before me?! Before Mom?

:/ sorry mom

And it's 10 days notice, dingbat. Close enough. I've been out for three months if you haven't noticed and y'all are doing just fine without me.

MOM

We have noticed, my emberling. Your work is very valuable. I'm just concerned. Why so sudden? Is everything okay?

BOSSHOLE

What did you do this time?

MOM

Holy Darkness, are you in trouble again?

MOM

Call your mother, please.

MOM

Jaromar?

NERD

> He's fine, Mom.

NERD

> He's in love.

BOSSHOLE

> Flame and ashes, what's in the water up there?

"You asshole!"

I was on my way to tear off this shitty Santa costume when I find my nerdy-ass brother hiding in a corner of the breezeway near Birdie's front door. I tear the phone out of his hand.

"That was personal," I growl.

I haven't told Birdie yet. I haven't even told *him* I'm in love, and he's announcing it like a textbook fact to our entire meddling family. This could all go horribly sideways. If Birdie doesn't want me, if she needs space after all the intensity and shit, I need to respect that.

Regardless, I'm staying in Winter Bliss no matter what happens.

If she's reluctant to give us a real try, I need to be ready to court her properly.

Woo her, respectfully.

I have no fucking clue how to do that, but I'll give it the old college, errr, high school try.

After having my brain scrambled with sex hormones during our ride around the property yesterday, the post-nut clarity felt like rainbows shining out of my eyeballs.

I could finally see straight.

Straight past all the stupid bullshit holding me back my whole life, every doubt and dark thought that kept me from taking a chance. Not just on her. On me too.

"I'm not staying just because of Birdie." I crowd him. "I have plans. Plans only you know about. Plans I told you in fucking confidence. You gonna announce all that without my permission too?"

I check over the family chat to make sure he didn't spill the rest of the beans. My slow-ass younger brothers are finally chiming in. But no, Rom kept his mouth shut on the other half of the reason why I quit.

"I thought we were cool." I push his chest until he staggers against the wall. He shoves me back but doesn't lean forward to lock horns. I'm pissed enough that I'd wrestle his ass to the ground, but nervous enough about what else I have to do today that I don't have it in me.

"Mom was gonna be on the first plane here as soon as you quit," he says, lifting his hands defensively. "If it saves her an aneurysm to know that you're staying for love, at least partly, you know it'd set her mind at ease. You should've called her first and talked all this over. *I quit. Good luck.* In the group chat? Come the fuck on!"

I growl. He's right. Mom's the level head in the family business, leading Perkatory to year-over-year growth with an iron fist, but she's also a romantic at heart. I saw it with my own eyes in how quickly she rearranged the entire corporate expansion strategy so Rom could live in Winter Bliss. Perkatory is still thriving and she's thrilled to welcome a daughter into the family.

I could've warned her about me quitting. I just wanted to talk to Birdie about all this feelings shit first. The old demoness, goddess love her, would've sniffed it out of me in two fucking minutes and got me all freaked out.

Birdie should know my feelings first. The rest are details.

I power down Rom's phone and shake it at him.

"You're getting this back after I talk to Birdie, asshole. Go makeout with your fiancée and stop poking your big nose in my life."

"Perkatory won't be the same without you." He punches me in the shoulder gently. "Ew. Why are you so sweaty?"

"This fucking Santa suit is a fucking nightmare! I was trying to change when you blew up the group chat."

"You blew it up first." He pouts.

I glare at him rather than admit he's right. Again. Sure, I could have done that *gingerly,* as he put it. Called Mom first then told everyone else. Sent in a formal notice or some shit. I shrug. Not really my style.

"Noelle is thrilled you're staying in Winter Bliss, even if the family is losing a lot with you stepping back from the business."

I harrumph.

"I'm thrilled too," he adds.

I punch his shoulder back, gently. Such a softie, this guy.

I'm really doing it. I'm striking out on my own. Turns out, Winter Bliss is hurting for skilled general contractors and handymen. I've made good connections in town. My orc buddy, Oatmeal, already offered to set me up with his overflow client work. And my week doing pro bono repairs for small businesses along the plaza proved just as fruitful. Turns out almost everyone has a list of easy-as-shit repairs and DIY projects they've just never gotten around to, and I'm the guy for the job.

"Promise we can still hire you on contract?" Rom's eyes swirl orange and red. "A preferred client relationship with a family discount of course?"

"Trying to sneak in a deal without a proper negotiation? When your brother is emotionally vulnerable?" I gasp in mock horror. "Let's talk business crap later, bro. It's a fucking holiday. Get your horns out of your ass."

"I know you don't love all the paperwork and data of the business side of things," he presses on. "But I do. How about I help you get on your feet with *Rex's Reliable Repairs*?"

I scoff and shake my head. He's really pushing alternate names, but I've made up my mind.

"It's *Rex Fixes Sh*t*. Get it through your thick skull." I can already see the name on the side of a heavy-duty work truck. It's gonna be totally badass.

"You'll put the asterisk in the curse word, at least?" He grimaces.

"That was good advice, yeah. Thanks for that," I grumble.

"And you won't entertain the other dozen suggestions I emailed yesterday? Once the paperwork is filed, it's hard to redo."

"Gotta lean into my brand," I say. Iggy gave me that advice. Real marketing whiz, that girl.

"You are good at fixing shit. Maybe even a little better than you are at breaking it." He cracks a smile.

"Thanks, I think." I walk backward into the house and waggle his phone at him before locking the dead-bolt on the other side of the door. "Fuckwad."

I hide his phone in Birdie's hoard of snacks and shelf-stable cheeses on the counter. Just one of the hundred reasons why I'm crazy about her.

In love, my brother said.

It made my stomach flip to see that in the group chat, to admit it to myself.

I'm in love.

I want to be the demon for her. The dream guy who deserves her. I have to give it a shot. My last shot.

Officer Dale threatened to stop by the ranch today to confiscate the court's tracker equipment that I stubbornly refuse to return. My time is running out, and I'm not about to let Birdie slip through my fingers.

I tear through the house, wrestling off the itchy red top first. With the last kids photo op behind me, I can take this damn costume off and breathe.

I should've gone with the bare-chested approach, wearing little white scrunchies at my wrists for Santa's furry cuffs or whatever. My skin is already red. Why did I have to suffer through this cheap-ass fabric in the same shade? Ugh. *The parents might not appreciate their kids sitting on the lap of a shirtless Santa*, Birdie insisted. I mean, the whip was a big hit. What does she really know about the appeal of a Santa photo op?

I'm just shoving the remnants of the fuzzy red suit in her bathroom's laundry basket when my phone buzzes. The family group chat, no doubt. I really need to set this shit on *Do Not Disturb*. They can live with a little mystery.

Instead, I see a message from my actor buddy.

VALE

> How is the event going?

> Any photos? Birdie hasn't posted anything on Nymphstagram yet.

I squint at the screen. Why the fuck is he asking me for—
Oh. That's right. Vale's new holiday romcom is releasing
soon so he just landed in Los Angeles for PR. And his lady
love is right here on the ranch.

> I'm not feeding you photos of your girl-
> friend like a creepo peeping Tom.

VALE

> She's not my girlfriend. She's my wife.

He's a demon obsessed and going through withdrawals.
What's the harm in needling him a little?

> Fake wife.

VALE

> (¬`_´¬)

> Is she okay? How does she look?

> Uhhh, brown hair. Skinny. I dont fuckin'
> know, man.

Vale

Mother Below, not what she physically looks like! Is she happy?

I'm not sniffing out your wife's emotions, bro. That's gross. Did you text Iggy?

Vale

Of course I did. She hasn't answered yet.

Second fiddle, I see. Listen, all I noticed is she was in charge of the petting zoo which is pretty much the coolest gig of all. Lots of smiling kids and animal snuggles. That tiny dog of hers was a big hit too.

Vale

Oh man, that sounds cute.

If only I had some photos to help me envision it.

You're a real piece of work, Hollywood.

Nut up and talk to the lady.

Why isn't she going to that fancy movie premiere with you, anyway?

Vale

Hmmm

That's a good question.

I chuckle. What a dumbass. The simplest solution hadn't even crossed his mind. On the Dark Mother's sacred panties, he's lucky I've got a head on my shoulders. If a woman's worth fighting for, she's worth having a single fucking conversation with. I give the poor guy a few more helpful pointers and right as we're wrapping up, another text comes in.

Unknown Number

Get out here now.

Huh?

Who is this?

Unknown Number

Ethel, you big idiot.

How does Old Ethel have my number? I blink at the screen.

UNKNOWN NUMBER

It's about Birdie.

Is she okay?

Shit. Why is Ethel texting me about Birdie? If that doesn't have me hopping into my jeans with hastiness. The closest shirt I snatch up is her favorite. A black pearl snap with subtle metallic threading in burnt orange and a pop of the same color at the pocket and sleeves. *Matches my eyes*, she says. My heart is racing by the time I get the buttons done and hear my phone chime.

UNKNOWN NUMBER

I guess we'll see.

WTF DOES THAT MEAN?

UNKNOWN NUMBER

Manners, my boy.

"Fuck manners," I grumble and hustle out of the house, shoving my feet into my work boots in the mudroom. What in the goddesses's holy name is that demoness on about?

Birdie's on the last hike of the day. She's been up and down those damn hills every couple hours, about three or four times total. Maybe she's dehydrated. It's easy to forget when it's cold outside. She could've gotten a cramp or twisted her ankle. I don't like that, but I can easily carry her down, just gotta get moving. If it's one of the visitors harassing her, I'll set them straight. Surely couldn't be that though. This is a free fucking event. What is there to complain about? She put her heart and soul into today and it all worked out beautifully.

I didn't have the time to talk to her for more than a couple minutes during the whirlwind of activities, but I saw her talking to a guy Noelle said was the superintendent of schools and then a coworker of Chad's who's high up in the parks department. A well-dressed demoness from the Emberlight Resort even asked me where to find her while I was wolfing down some kettle corn during a break between photo sessions. That's gotta be good news.

She must be thirsty or scraped up. It's the only thing that makes sense.

"Mr. Perchaz, we need to talk."

I turn to see Gertie Dale walking toward me. My probation officer.

"Fuck. Not now, ma'am. Sorry. Just . . . not now."

I sprint through the booths and trees until I find the demoness I'm looking for.

"Well?" I wave my arms. She's perched on a boulder, halfway through a long cigarette. Her gold eyes gleam, a steady, serpentine gaze locked onto the nearby hill. Always looked like a proper villainess, this lady. "What the fuck, Ethel?"

Finally she turns my way, exhaling out her nose as she studies me. I wave the twin curling plumes of perfumed smoke away. Hate the stuff.

"The almost husband is back."

"Huh?" Almost husband?

One silver eyebrow crooks in a dramatic peak.

"Randy."

The name sends an icy dread straight through my gut. It spiders out to every limb, freezing me on the spot. Only the words coming out of my mouth start to wake me back up.

"That shit-for-brains thundercunt." A firestorm follows, heating my blood in an instant, turning my vision a roiling red. What the fuck is that jabroni doing here? The rage builds in a physical desire to get destructive.

"The very one." She nods with a sneer.

"Fuck!" I look at my phone for the time. Birdie must've set off on her last hike maybe half an hour ago, which means she should be on her way down soon.

"Mr. Perchaz!" It's my probation officer. She just caught sight of me and is striding my way. "There's no running away this time."

"Gonna do something about it?" Old Ethel asks.

My decision is made. I tempt fate and one very fit orc lady.

I take off running.

The path up to the viewing platform is well-worn now, after weeks of clearing brush, laying gravel, and adding cute little markers for every tenth of a mile with a new *Fun Fact* about the surrounding ecology or wildlife. It's not far, but in my current state, feels like a fucking marathon.

At the first switchback, I find the group on their way down with one of Old Ethel's sons in the lead. My girl is nowhere to be seen. I grab him by the collar and shake, growling out, "Where's Birdie?"

"Up there! She's okay." Simon rears back, swallowing. "I offered to stay. She said no. Insisted she wanted to speak to him privately."

"FUCK!" I shove him off and keep running.

She's okay. How the fuck does he know that? *She insisted.* That might be a good sign. An okay sign? I don't know. This is her fucking property and he has a truckload of unearned audacity to dare speak to her after what he did, to sneak up on her like a snake in the grass. I'll lay him out where he stands.

My head is pounding as hard as my heart. Gods below, I'm not sure I'm cut out for this love shit. I'm gonna stroke out from the stress. It'd be great if she's really telling him off. I'd love to see that.

Maybe I'm freaking out for nothing.

Maybe I should respect her private conversation.

Naw, fuck that.

My mind spins. The worst case scenarios that float to the top feel the most likely, and I hate it. He's yelling at her, pushing her around. He's talking up the fucking cabins again. He's intimidating her into another business deal she hates.

What I hear instead, as their voices float toward me when I make it to the top, is somehow so much worse.

"You gave me the best day of my life, Randy," she almost sounds like she's shouting. "It was the best thing that could've happened to me. None of this would've been possible without you. So thank you."

I'm still hidden by the large trail map educational sign when it registers.

None of this would've been possible without you.

The best day of my life.

Thank you.

Something chokes out of me. Who knew the sound of a heart breaking was really just an ugly whining grunt? I stagger back and nearly fall on my ass, but knock over a trashcan instead which gives me a second to correct. It clatters to the side.

The best day. None of this would've been possible without you. She must have meant how well the event did today. The event was his idea originally. But she's thanking him for sending *one fucking email* months ago?

It's like the future unfolds at hyperspeed before my eyes.

I know where this is going. *The best day of my life.*

He's back in town with an apology. *None of this would've been possible without you.*

A few sweet words and she's already saying, *Thank you.*

It's only a matter of time before she takes him back.

I stalk off, blood roaring in my ears, vision so red and stormy I know fire is consuming the fists pumping at my sides. And I don't give a damn. My body remembers a path, so I take it. The same one I took months ago, when I was panicking for a completely different reason.

The stairs down to the lake.

Fuck it. Time for a swim. Anything to escape what I just heard. The unthinkable. That she's not mine, and she never will be. Maybe I'll swim across the lake and live in the woods. That sounds kinda nice. Peaceful.

Forget all about . . . everything.

Her. This beautiful place.

All the dreams I just started thinking could come true for me.

"Fuck!" My fingers card through my hair, wrenching my horns one way then the other, wishing I had a wall to butt up against.

"Rex! Stop!"

It's Birdie.

And I'm not ready to hear it. The letdown. The explanation. *It's not you, it's me. Randy is a better fit, always was. He just needed time to get himself together.* I work for months—blood, sweat, and tears—and he reaps the reward. Her thanks. Her attention.

"It doesn't make any fucking sense!" I hit my temple to try and stop the throbbing.

"Stop that!" she shouts. "Right now. Where are you going? Rex, stop!"

I turn down the stairs and almost bust my ass immediately. Fuck, these steps are too damn slippery. Need to fix that before visitors start actually using it. Wait, no. Not my problem anymore.

I shake my head. I mean, maybe I'll still fix it. I don't want anyone to get hurt. Especially Birdie. I just need to get away. Get some distance. I can come back later, incognito, and carve some divots into the smoothed out stone, maybe find a way to affix some rubber, drill it into the rock or something. There's got to be a way to make it safe.

My feet land on the wooden deck, a weathered but solid platform jutting straight out over the water. Just before I dive in, Birdie yells again.

"Stop! Right now." She's hustling down the steps and my stomach is in my throat.

"Be careful!" I shout back. "Fucking fates. Take it slow, woman!"

"Oh, now you've got something to say?" She's fuming. Goddess only knows why. I'm the one who deserves to be pissed!

"You had plenty to say to dickbag Raul back there."

"I did." She laughs. "And I didn't hold any of my feelings back. You would have been proud. I really gave him a piece of my mind."

Her solid grip on the handrail is the only thing keeping me from running up there and throwing her pretty ass over my shoulder. That, and the fact I have a worse track record falling off the damn staircase than she does.

"Piece of your heart, too, huh?" I grit out.

When she makes the final step onto the deck, I turn and dive in.

I can't hear anything right now. I'm too fucked up. Everything feels wrong, wrong, wrong. How can she look at me like she just was? Flushed and happy and relieved! While my heart is crumbling to ash in her tiny grip.

"What did you say to me?" she shouts over the distance when I surface. The water's warmer than people expect, comfortable. Not hot springs hot, but cozy enough there's always a light fog coming off the surface in the colder months.

"Go back to Rogan. He's to thank!" I shoot back as I keep swimming. "He's responsible for all this. The best day of your life!"

"Are you serious?!" she screeches. "That's what you heard?"

I wave her off, chest deep in water now as I start trudging forward on the lake bed. My flaming hands drawing a curtain of steam around me as my arms swish. Just around the bend is a shore. From higher ground I can plot the best route across the lake. Find a dry, dark place to go full caveman for a few days.

When I hear a splash behind me, I whip back. Through the water vapor, I can't see anything except a white circle of water near the deck.

Birdie's gone.

Then she pops up, sputtering to the surface and swimming toward me. That steely gaze of her is pure trouble.

"Just can't let me suffer in silence, huh?" I raise my arms. No sense running if she's determined to chase. "Stubborn as a mule."

"That's right." She's half wading, half walking so I keep backing up to a shallower depth until she can gain her footing.

"It's always a fight with you!" I splash the water at my sides as she gets closer. The steam swirls around us with a mind of its own.

"Yes, it is!" she says. "And always will be. I'm going to fight for you, Rex. Get used to it!"

For me? I scoff. "I can't. I don't have it in me." I start to back up.

"Oh yes you do, Ramonarex Cohl Perchaz." She dives forward and fists my belt buckle. The feral demon in me remembers every time she grabbed me just like that and had her wicked way with me. The boy in me remembers her learning my full name, how she never made fun of me for it. I pause to take her in, a spitfire full of heat and purpose. Just the sight of her makes my chest tight. She pokes me there, right on the heartache. "If you were going to eavesdrop," she says, "I'm pretty pissed you missed the full monologue. You think you can hear one out-of-context, completely sarcastic sentence and run off? I don't think so!"

Sarcastic. I narrow my eyes. *Out-of-context.*

"What's the context?"

"Well, I can't remember my exact words, but I said that I thought the day he left me was the worst day of my life, but it was the best."

"Huh? You said none of this would've been possible without him and then *thanked* him," I huff. "I remember that just fine."

"Without him *leaving*! And the *thank you* was sarcastic, goofball." She tugs at my belt. "You missed the part where I also said *fuck you, Randy.*"

Now that phrase brings back some pleasant memories.

"You did?" My mouth quirks.

"I also called him an asshole and a manipulator and said that he's nothing to me. Then I threatened to call the police if he doesn't leave right away." Her hands smooth up my wet shirt, picking at the buttons, loosening the last ones that were holding on for dear life until she's petting up my chest, eyes sweeping over me hungrily. "I didn't like how he was looking around the place, still saying how much money cabins would make."

Heat sweeps through my veins, imagining that slick motherfucker trying to weasel his way back into her life. "I'll cut his fucking nuts off. Light him up! Where is he?"

"Wait, hold on. What's gotten into you?"

"He's gonna try and win you back, especially if he's back in town for good. It's only a matter of time. Fuck!" I slap at the water and turn toward the shore, tracking the hills to try and get my eyes on him. I see something move and start trudging that direction. If I can just intimidate him a little, maybe he'll back off. Shit, I'll offer to pay for his plane ticket back to wherever-the-fuck.

"You make me so mad, Rex Perchaz!" She's splashing behind me, tugging at my shirt. When I stop to turn on her, she's furious again. "You think I'd just go back to him?"

I spread my arms. "When I'm your second-best option?"

"Second best?" she barks, blinking rapidly. "To Randy?" She cackles like a failed audition for a Hollywood witch. "I'm in love with you, you misguided doofus! You think I'm stupid enough to get back with someone who jilted me? Weak enough to settle for someone who strong-arms me into decisions I don't fucking want? Blind enough not to see my perfect fucking match is right in front of me!" She pushes me hard enough I actually stagger back a step.

"Wait." I press a hand to my forehead and retrace the conversation. "You love me?"

She laughs, this time less insane. More . . . bewildered.

"We're a perfect fucking match," I repeat slowly.

Her head cocks to the side, like I'm being purposefully obtuse. "I mean, if you disagree."

When she starts to slosh past me, I snatch her elbow and haul her up in my arms so I can get a good look at her face. Her knees hitch around my hips. A beat passes as we catch our breath. The wild beauty of the mountains surrounds us, but all I can see is her.

"I'm a mess with you," she says quietly.

"I know." I lean my forehead against hers. "I know I'm a disaster. I don't want to just make you angry and miserable all the time."

"What? No! I'm a *mess*." She laughs. "I can *be* a mess with you. I can shout and scream and cry." In the rosy fading light, her eyes shine with emotion. Maybe it's the tiniest hint of red in the brown, but nothing can turn me into a demon dazzled by firebliss quite like her eyes. A single tear falls, sparkling like a star. "I can cry. I never cried before you."

"I make you cry," I say, still stunned.

"You make me . . ." She sighs, dashing the tears away as more come, framed by wet curling lashes. "You make me *feel*. With you, it doesn't seem so scary anymore."

"Oh fuck, honey." I lean forward and kiss her wet cheeks, every salty trail. "Of course you can cry. Always. Gimme those tasty tears."

She giggles and squeezes my shoulder. Her sharp little nails sink five points of delicious pain. She makes me feel too. So much it does kind of scare me.

I pull back, heart full of hope. "You really love me?"

She softens, from her body language to the sweet shine of her eyes to the hand on my cheek. Her thumb traces my nose and my lips before pinching my chin with a little shake. "Who wouldn't fall in love with a demon as tender-hearted, protective, and smart as you?"

I shake my head and start laughing, leaning back to look at the clouds just to try and keep some of these hot tears from falling all over the damn place. You know what? Fuck that. She cries now. I can too.

"No one's ever said something that fucking crazy, honey."

"Crazy for you." She hugs my neck.

"You own my whole fucking heart." I jostle her in my arms. "But I'm not about to fuck off into the sunset for some long-distance sexting situationship. I need more than that. We're fucking dating."

"Good."

"I'm moving to Winter Bliss."

"Great." Her eyes widen, the only hint at surprise, but she doesn't say anything else.

"And when the weather's bad, I'm staying here." I push my luck.

"Fantastic." She grins.

"And not in the barn either." I give her a look.

She nods. "My bed."

I huff, pleased. Easiest negotiation of my life.

"Let's cut through the bullshit," she says.

Oh crap, here it comes. The hard bargain. "Listen here, Birdie Lynn. We're not putting timers and shit on sharing space. I'm just proposing we go by the weather, because I refuse to let you fuck around in the snow with these dum-bass animals always trying to kill themsel—"

"Move in with me," she says, unblinking. I stare back, waiting for the other shoe to drop. "Move in with me, Rex," she says, gentler.

"What?"

"Stay in Winter Bliss and move in with me. Why not? You've been here for months. We've already shared a house for a few weeks and haven't killed each other yet." She shrugs. "Fuck it."

A yellow firefly flickers to life behind her, followed by a flashing trio of pink.

"Fuck it?" I laugh. The sunset casts our little world in a warm, rose-tinted haze as more fireflies join in a slow-moving kaleidoscope.

"Yeah. Let's do it." She kisses me quick, right on the lips.

It's not enough. I crush her close, just to suck on her bottom lip. Tangle with her tongue. Taste her sigh. Urge her to bite back. Her nails dig into the back of my neck, and I groan. I'm the kindling and she's the ember, glowing brighter by the moment, holding nothing back. A fire unlike any other.

This kiss is different. Our first again. Pure magic. My body flashes hot, awakened to some primal memory—the first dance of flames.

A wildfire. That's us. Nature in chaos.

Breathless, I pull back. Her face is lit up like a swirling rainbow, turning brown skin and brown eyes and brown hair into . . . every color under the sun, a shifting canvas of blues and oranges, of purples, greens, and golds. Their pinpricks twinkle around her on all sides, a hive mind in concert.

"The fireflies. They're good luck," I whisper, glancing not at them but at their light reflected off her. Who could look away?

"Maybe they always were." Her smile is so sure. Fearless.

I think back to the quiet girl with the secret glare, to staring contests and fierce fights, to shared meals and long days of work.

She's really mine.

"You love me," I say.

"And we're living together." She gives me a humored, if impatient, look. "Is that a yes?"

It still doesn't seem real that I get everything I want and more. "Don't fuck with me, Birdie Lynn."

Her smirk turns teasing as she nips at my bottom lip. "What if I just fuck you instead?"

I growl, the only natural response, and haul her back to plunder.

Between pausing to whisper sweet nothings and dirty promises to each other, we stumble back to the lakeshore near her house, fully dressed and completely soaked.

"If I see that dickcheese Roscoe, he's getting a fireball to the face. I can promise you that."

"If he's still here, I'll allow it." She laughs. "He had fair warning."

From a distance, it looks like only the volunteers are left, helping clean up. Oh, and one more person, striding forward to intercept us.

"Officer Dale." I nod.

She extends her hand. "Give it."

Birdie looks from me to her. I kiss her nose and crane my face further down, "Can you pull off my horn clamp, honey? I'm a little overdue on turning it in."

Officer Dale huffs. "I wouldn't call three weeks a little overdue, Mr. Perchaz. You've been a real thorn in my side."

"Three weeks?" Birdie squeaks, smacking my chest. "You were done three weeks ago? Is that why my bracelet fell off?"

"I'm technically still on probation! They just wanted me to quit doing my job, and I wasn't about to leave you until the last possible second. Fuck the rules."

Officer Dale clears her throat.

"Sorry, ma'am. Just the truth." I shuffle closer so Birdie can hand over the device.

"Ms. Badem, your bracelet?"

"Of course." Birdie pulls out the necklace chain tucked under her sweater and slides off the "broken" bracelet she's been keeping safe there. "I'm so sorry. I would have absolutely returned it if this sneaky demon hadn't convinced me it was just normal wear and tear of an underfunded government office."

Officer Dale glares at me again as she drops both into the bag at her side.

Sorry not sorry I think but have sense enough not to say.

"You were supposed to wear that tracker until the end of your twelve weeks, but I had orders to get yours back early to stop the overtime." She points at me. "You've still got a final probation meeting the week after New Year's, though, so be on your best behavior. Maybe now I can finally take some time off." She turns to Birdie with a warmer expression. "And thank you for your service as a CSC Officer for the Winter Bliss Court, ma'am. I hope his volunteer hours were of good use to you and the community."

"He's the best." Birdie's teary-eyed, hands clasped under her chin. "Did you see the viewing platform and outdoor classroom? Is there an evaluation card I can fill out? His work is impeccable, beyond my wildest dreams. And he's so good with the rescue animals. You have no idea—"

She raises a hand with an indulgent smile. "Feel free to email me your comments. It'll go a long way to pacifying my leadership about all the hassle he's caused us with his overtime hours." She cuts a brief look at me, but it's lost a lot of its edge, before refocusing on Birdie. "Your sanctuary is really something special. I wasn't too pleased about tracking this guy down today, but I'm glad I came. It's nice to see Mr. Perchaz's probation service was a help."

"The biggest!" Birdie chirps.

"That's what she said," I whisper in her ear, earning me a good-natured smack on the chest.

"How's the kitty settling in?" she asks.

"Matilda Tortellini Dale is a real terror." Officer Dale's grin grows wide, her tusks pressing against her top lip with how happy she is. "I already love her to pieces."

Birdie bites back a laugh. "That's quite a name."

"Tilly Tortellini." I nod. "I like it. 'Lil TT for short."

Officer Dale studies me for a second in the way that shows her mind is working. I'd bet my bottom dollar she loves the nickname and won't admit it.

I grin back.

"Make sure you get a goodie bag on the way out," Birdie says. "Oh! And email me if you ever want to visit again. Maybe an offender education program? Animals can be very therapeutic."

"I'll keep that in mind." Officer Dale glances around, before nodding once more and walking off. When she picks up one of the last remaining goodie bags on the welcome table, Birdie pumps her fist in the air.

I set her down and she's back to work. We all clean up as a team. I take care of the animal chores, and by the time I get back, the last of the volunteers are headed out. As soon as that front door closes and our shoes are kicked off, I snatch her back in my arms and crowd her against the fridge. I just love looking at her face. So pretty it kills me.

And now we're right back where we started. That first time in the kitchen. Hot and fast. The chaos and chemistry that followed. As messy as it's been, I wouldn't change a thing.

Winter Bliss is my home now. The place I was always meant to come back to.

But first, we needed time to understand ourselves and find our place in the world before we found a way to each other.

Wild Hearts. Was there ever a more perfect name? Shit, I'm getting misty-eyed.

"Can't believe it." I chuckle and squeeze her tight until she's giggling. She's all mine. I live here now. Indefinitely. And we're in love. What the *actual fuck*! "A happy ending."

Her grin is lopsided and just this side of silly. "That's what she said."

Acknowledgements

First shout out to my husband, my favorite brainstorm (and life) partner! Between our two crazy kids, this never would have happened without your support as I hunkered down in the writing cave during crunch-time.

Huge thanks to my partners in mischief, Lark and Lucy. Lightning struck twice! Wow, these were some whoppers, and what an adventure we had this year. I'm so excited to discover what our next season will bring.

To my beta readers, you made all the difference. Hearing such varied, thoughtful, and constructive advice right when I needed it helped me polish Rex and Birdie to a shine. Extra special shout-out to my horse experts Chyanne, Emily, Jessica, and Britt'ny! And a thousand more thanks to Raluca, Luna, Anne-Marie, Barb, Selina, Raj, Mallory, Jenny, Amber, Melissa, Trisha, Sara, Ahren, Mallory, Holly, Andria, and Tia.

Special thanks to the Turkish readers who helped me add dimension, beauty, and a deeper understanding to the characterization of Birdie and her family. I hope I did y'all proud. Any screw ups are completely my own.

To the artists I partnered with on this book, I loved chatting and screaming (lovingly) at you through messages or email. Your creativity and unique styles always blow me away. H Holden, Emeline, Trisha, Lana, Lianne, Lucy, Daniel, Sali, Victor, and Serval – You're the real ones.

Okay, my brain trust! I'm NOT great at naming characters and this book had so many animals, I had to call in for help. Thanks to all the readers and friends who contributed names, including Chyanne, Sid, Selina, Barb, Caitlyn, Holly, Amber, Emma, Bailey, Jessica, Becky, Jen, Ash, Kate, Ahren, Poppy, and both Melissas.

Last, thanks to our incredible and enthusiastic ARC team. You all lift us up, make us laugh, and sometimes even cry. I'm so very grateful to each and every one of you.

Author's Note

I hope you fell in love with Rex and Birdie along with me. They are such a trip. Rex, in particular, is the easiest character I've ever written. I swear that foul-mouthed handyman jumped straight out of my imagination, cursing up a storm. Birdie, on the other hand, was a labor of love and a part of me in a different, deeper way. Her home, Wild Hearts, is based on my friend's ranch/animal rescue in central Texas.

It's not always intentional, but social causes tend to sneak into my narratives, even if only subtly. This story is for the animal rescuers. To the late nights and early mornings. To the lives you've saved along the way. Your mercy and compassion doesn't go unnoticed.

Sign up for my newsletter for extra scenes and regular updates on future stories.

Playlist

My top ten faves while writing this story...

1. Letting Go by Angie McMahon

2. floorboards Noah Henderson

3. She Calls Me Back by Noah Kahan

4. Something Blue by VOILÀ

5. For Cryin' Out Loud by FINNEAS

6. Hey Honey by Vision Arcade

7. Crush by FLETCHER

8. hotline by bby

9. Sweat by ALASKALASKA

10. Feel it All by Chance Peña

www.ingramcontent.com/pod-product-compliance
Lightning Source LLC
Chambersburg PA
CBHW030103310726

48970CB00004B/1125